Bury Me In Blood

A PREQUEL

LITTLE DEATHS
BOOK THREE

TYLOR PAIGE

To me, a child of the 90's, who wanted to grow up and write books.

Foreword

This book is the prequel novel to Seven Little Deaths. It is set in 1994.

Content notes

This book while not my darkest, still has subjects that I'd like to mention before you go into the story. Please be mindful of what you can read, and don't put this story above your mental health. This book contains blood, murder, self-harm, suicidal ideations, cheating, and racism and prejudice.

Preface

I have lovingly, not so lovingly dubbed this novel, 'my love letter to suicide'. I wrote this book while I was deep in my grief over the loss of my father. It was some of the darkest times mentally for me, and that came out on the page through Scout and Desi both. This book was one I'd wanted to write for a very long time, and while it was hard, I'm glad I am finally able to put it out into the world and say goodbye to that dark place I was stuck in while writing it.

While I have battled and pushed through my depression and suicidal ideations, I know others are still struggling. Please, if you need help, talk to someone and get help. The world is better with you in it.

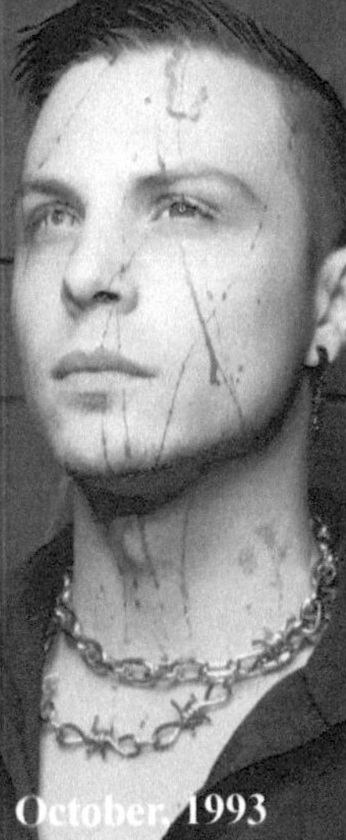

CHAPTER 1

Desi

October, 1993

"How long has it been now?"

I scowled at my friend, Eric. "A year to the day."

He shook his head. "Today, of all days? See, that's where you messed up. You don't do anything relationship-related on your birthday. Now, you're always going to remember it."

"That's the point." I slid a cigarette between my lips. "Otherwise, I'll have her on my ass every year about it."

"Your old woman." Randy added.

My lip curled up in distaste for the phrase. "Why has this come up again?"

"Because she's coming up behind you." Mick snickered.

I spun around to see the tall blonde throwing up her arms and tossing them over my shoulders.

"Desiderio! I've been looking all over for you!"

"How'd you find me?" I glanced around me, noting my

friend's looks of annoyance.

"Hmm, well, considering you weren't at your house, I figured it was a safe bet to try Frank's." Aleida gave me a forced, uncomfortable smile as she nodded to the convenience store behind us.

"It's a good wall." I pushed her away and stepped back to stand in line with Tommy, Mick, Eric, and Randy. "And we don't have to do beer runs."

"Yes, I have heard your speech before." She sighed. "I'm about to leave, and I wanted to say goodbye." She reached out for another hug, and I reluctantly moved to give her one. She pulled away after I stiffly patted her back and glanced at my friends, who were staring at us.

"I thought you already left." I took another drag of my cigarette and flicked the cherry on the asphalt.

"Tionne was thirsty so we had to wait until she could get something to drink." She slid her sunglasses down just enough so that I could see the red irises. She winked. I swallowed, knowing full well what she meant by thirsty. It wasn't water she wanted. It was blood. They needed to feed.

"Are you guys good now, then?"

"Absolutely. We're heading to the airport now. We'll be back next weekend. Are you sure you're okay with this? I know we celebrated last night, but still." She pouted.

I looked away. "You're good, babe. Go, have fun with your friends. I'll see you when you get back." She threw herself at me again, pressing her sticky lips against mine. I didn't kiss her back, but she didn't seem to notice. Or maybe she did notice, she just didn't care. Either way, it satisfied her enough to let me go.

"I'll bring you some new Tarot cards or something." She patted my front pocket, where my current deck was. I never went anywhere without it.

"See you lame-o's later." She flashed my friends the peace sign and sprinted back to Tionne's bright orange Porsche and hopped in. The pair sped off into the night.

Relief washed through me as the orange speck disappeared. I turned back to the guys,

"Where'd Tommy go?" I asked.

"Beer run," Randy said. The Smashing Pumpkins came on, and I closed my eyes to enjoy the music. "I still don't think you'll go through with it."

I looked up from the ground and eyed Randy. He shook his head at me. His long, blond hair covered his face.

"What other choice do I have?"

"You call it off and live your fucking life, man."

"Is that all I have to do?" I patted his shoulder hard. "Thanks, friend. I didn't realize it'd be that easy."

"Oh, boo hoo. Mr. Trust-fund would have to get a job." Tommy smirked as he came out with a case of Budweiser. He put it on the ground and opened it. Then, he handed us each a fresh can.

I gave him the middle finger and popped open my new beer.

"Among other things. I think I'd be completely disowned."

"Who cares? You have us, man. Womb to tomb." Eric offered me a high-five. I took it, and he continued, "We've been friends since the third fucking grade, man, and we're not going anywhere."

Mick chuckled. "We're gonna be old men in the nursing home, smacking nurses' asses and causing hell."

"As long as it's one of the places with the good drugs," Randy added.

"Yeah, us five and Desiderio's old woman." Mick nodded.

I gulped and looked off toward the empty parking lot. If only they knew how wrong they were. Maybe the four of them would be friends in their old age. I only had a year before I would never see them again. Before my heart stopped, I grew fangs, and was forced into the darkness as a new vampire.

"Why did she fly out at night?" Tommy asked.

"Because she's a creature of the night." Eric laughed. "Did you see what she was wearing?"

"Hey!" I warned him.

Eric put his hands up in innocence.

"Yeah, what's with the sexy goth look?" Mick asked.

I reflexively reached for another cigarette. Whenever Aleida Linotti came up in conversation, I had the urge to smoke.

"She's gone for a week. Will you guys just let me enjoy my vacation?"

"You're a fucking schmuck." Randy laughed.

"Must be good puss—" Eric started, but I punched his shoulder.

Memories of my relationship flashed through my mind. The sex was good then. Fucking phenomenal. But it was different than love, and it didn't make a good marriage. We knew why we were getting married, and it wasn't for love.

Honestly, the sex wasn't even that good anymore. Lately, it felt like she was trying to tear me in half. Which, I guess, wasn't her fault, considering she was a vampire now, and I was still a human.

For 365 more days. Then, we'd both be vampires, get married, and have all the little bat babies our parents wanted.

What a fucking life.

"Girls, Girls, Girls" came through the boombox, and I began to sing with Mötley Crüe while I finished my smoke.

"What time does the movie start?" I asked, kicking off the wall.

Mick brushed his long, dark hair off his shoulder and drained his beer. "Let me go call *Moviefone*." He walked over to the payphone.

"What are we going to see again?" Eric asked.

"*Return of the Living Dead III*."

"Hell yeah. All right." He wiped the liquid from his brown mustache and gave me a high five. "Happy birthday, man."

"Twenty-six. It's a good year." Randy lifted his beer. "Welcome to the club."

I was the youngest of our group, and they never let me forget it. Much like my biological family. Mick returned just as Tommy reached into the beer case to give us another round.

We popped the tabs and held our cans toward each other in a circle.

"Let's toast. To Desiderio Amato, may your last year as a free man be a good one. Happy birthday!" Randy cheered. We clanked our beers and then chugged them. I was the first one to finish, and I dropped the can to the ground and howled.

"Whoo! Fuck yeah!" The rest finished their drinks and did the same. Tommy grabbed his boombox. Mick picked up the case of remaining beer, and we started off on foot toward the movie theater. Randy put his arm around my shoulder as we walked unsteadily down the sidewalk.

"I love you, man, but you got to do something about her."

Indeed, I had to.

I had one year to figure out how to get out of marrying Aleida Linotti, a full fucking vampire, before I was stuck with her for eternity.

CHAPTER 2

Desi

"Got enough candy?" Randy smirked at my arms full of licorice and peanut butter cups.

"It's my birthday." I took a red strip of bendy goodness and popping it into my mouth. We scooted into the seats of our nearly empty theater.

"You look like you just went trick or treating," Mick chimed in.

"That's next weekend," I shot back.

"Take this," Eric whispered, handing down beer after beer to the row. We glanced around, and thankfully, there were only a couple of pairs of teens making out in the back.

I popped my tab, and it hissed.

"Drinking game?" Tommy suggested.

"Sure, every time we see a zombie, we drink." Mick laughed.

"Sounds good to me!"

The movie started and despite us trying to keep our voices low, a man in a red vest came down the steps toward us with a scowl on his face. "Excuse me, men, but we're gonna need you to keep it down."

I took a sip of my beer and stared straight ahead. "Get a life."

"Yeah!" the others added.

Scowling, the man slunk away. The movie ended.

"Where to next, Birthday Boy?" Eric asked.

"The night is young and you're a free man," Mick added.

"I'm hungry," I muttered. "Let's get some food."

"What's open this late?"

A cold gust of wind swept past us on the road, and I shivered. I pulled my leather jacket tighter over my shoulders, covering up my faded Van Halen shirt.

"What about that diner across town?" Randy suggested.

"What diner?" Tommy scoffed.

Mick said, "The one that makes bomb-ass burgers. It's a twenty-four-hour joint, right across the tracks."

"Since when do you hang out over there?" I asked.

Randy rolled his eyes and shoved my shoulder. "Not all of us have daddies with trust funds and suspicious ties to the mafia. Some of us…" He paused, waving his finger between the semi-circle we were standing in. "…have these things called jobs."

It was my turn to roll my eyes. I reached for my smokes and quickly lit another one. "All right. Let's go get a car and head over. I guess I can slum it with you guys tonight," I joked.

"Who's gonna DD?" Eric asked.

"Well, it is Tommy's VW."

"Fuck you!" Tommy slurred. We shared a look. He was not going to be sober by the time we got to the car.

"Well, it's my birthday," I said, putting my hands on my chest. We argued it all the way back to Tommy's and finally decided that Randy would drive us to the diner, as he was the one who had brought it up in the first place.

"I can have fun without alcohol," he tried to boast, but we all called him on the six-pack he'd had earlier that night. I rode up front with him so I could control the tape deck.

"Where's *Fear of the Dark*?" I asked, looking for my favorite Iron Maiden album.

"Should be in there," Tommy said from the back. I found it and shoved it into the tape deck. "Fear is the Key" blared from the speakers, and I relaxed into my seat, enjoying the view passing by me.

I didn't travel to this side of the city. This was more blue-collar, whereas I'd been raised in the upper-class part of town, and had moved to a house not far from my family. As we drove deeper into the city, I longed to be a part of this life, rather than the one I'd been given.

If I could only get pieces of both, the money and complete freedom, I'd be happy.

I shook the thoughts from my head as we pulled into a brightly lit diner. I forgot. I don't get to be happy. I just get to be rich and immortal.

"Come on, Birthday Boy, I need a milkshake!" Mick grabbed my shoulders from the back and shook me.

"Does this place have beer?" I asked. It was one of those old-school ones, like from *Grease*.

"Oh yeah. Don't let the bright colors fool you. We all come here after our shifts and have a few beers every Friday," Randy said.

I was the last to go in and blinked as I adjusted to the bright lights. Prince was playing from the speakers overhead. Everything was either pastel pink or mint green. I was still skeptical about all of my friends' positive reviews but joined them at a booth in the back anyways. I was hungry and my buzz was wearing off. I needed a beer.

I sat on the end and peered out. It was pretty busy for a

Saturday night at a diner. A shadow appeared and I looked up. For a moment, I stopped breathing.

"Hello, gentlemen. Do we need five menus?"

I couldn't take my eyes off of the beautiful woman. Large curls were pinned in a loose, messy ponytail on top of her head. Dark black eyes were hidden under thick lashes. Her lips were deep red and so perfectly shaped. What had she said?

"I've never seen you here before." Randy smiled at her. "You new, kitten?"

The stunning Hispanic woman almost rolled her eyes but caught herself. "I'm the night shift. I'm assuming you'll want a pitcher?" she asked tightly.

"Yes, ma'am." Randy sat up straighter and eyed us. "I'll take a Pepsi. But a pitcher for everyone else."

"I'll be back." She turned around. Her uniform was just a black skirt and tight top, nothing fancy, but she made it look sexy as hell.

"Damn, I should come here at night more often." Tommy whistled.

Disappointment flooded through me as a different waitress came to our table with glasses and two pitchers.

"You look like you're about to cry over there, Desiderio." Mick laughed. "You that deprived?"

"I knew you still had a dick." Randy grinned wickedly as he started to pour drinks for us.

"Did you guys get a chance to look at the menu?"

I was startled again, by the stone cold fox with the large gold hoops and slight Mexican accent.

"I got the chance to look at you," Randy quipped.

"Is that your best game?" She raised a thick eyebrow. "Because I can come back later."

Embarrassed, he dropped his head. I smirked.

She had a smart mouth. I liked that.

"I'll take an olive burger," Tommy blurted. "With cheese fries."

The waitress pulled out a pad of paper from her skirt and began to write down everyone's orders. Randy reluctantly looked up and opted for chili dogs. She got to me, and it was then that I realized I hadn't even looked at the menu. I'd been too busy watching her. She hadn't glanced at me once.

Her eyes fell upon me, and she took a deep breath. For a moment, we stared at each other, soaking in each other, as if caught in time, where it was just her and I. Then, she blinked and cleared her throat.

"And what do you want?"

My mind went blank, except for one single word.

You.

"What took you so long? You've got tables waiting for you," Deanna, my coworker, scolded.

I glanced back at the booth with the rowdy men. My heart sped up when I saw the one on the end with his head turned to look at me. He quickly turned back to his friends. His friend had to order for him apparently.

"Sorry, I've got a drunk table." I ripped the slip off the pad and hooked it to the string for the cooks. "What table first?" I searched for the irritated customers. Deanna pointed to a few, and I hurried over to take their plates and cash them out.

They were immediately replaced with new patrons, and I sighed. Tonight was going to be a busy one. The first half of my shift had been relatively quiet. I made my rounds before heading back to the table of guys. I forced a smile as I looked around the table, making eye contact with each one. I needed to good tip tonight.

The men were all in their mid-twenties and looking all right. The one who called me pretty had long blond hair that hung over his eyes. Then there was one with short brown curls, one with long brown curls, and one with short, clipped dirty blond hair. I'd forget them as soon as they left.

All except the one on the end. He was incredibly good-looking. He almost looked out of place with his friends. While they were all dressed the same, in ripped jeans and faded band tees, he stood out.

"How are you guys doing? Can I get you any refills?" I said as cheerily as I could, picking up the two empty pitchers.

"Just keep the beer coming," the short blond said. "We're celebrating tonight."

"Oh?" I raised my eyebrows as if I didn't hear this every night at a dozen tables.

"It's Desiderio's birthday!" He smacked the man on the end on the back. I took the excuse to look at him.

Desiderio. What an interesting name.

"It is? Happy birthday!"

He blushed and averted his gaze. I caught a hint of a grin as his blue eyes dipped to the table. "Thanks."

"He gets shy when he sees a pretty woman," his friend teased, shaking him some. Desiderio elbowed him.

"Do you like pie? I've got apple and cherry in the back."

"I wouldn't mind eating your cherry," the man who'd been harassing me said, getting a loud laugh from them. All but Desiderio. He glared at his friend…murderously.

I waved the empty pitchers in my hand. "I'll get a refill and check on your food. Is there anything else you need right now?"

"Your name."

The sound was so soft, I almost didn't hear it.

But I did.

Because it came from the man on the end.

Desiderio.

For the third time tonight, my heart went insane.

"Scout." Fleeing, I set the pitchers down in front of the beer tap and made another round for my other tables. I tried to distract myself from the thoughts of the handsome man, but I couldn't stop thinking about him. His voice echoed in my brain, over and over again as I worked.

"Your name."

I made it to the kitchen just in time as Donald, a line cook, put up that table's food.

"You forgot their beer, but that's okay. I brought it to them." Deanna said from behind me. "I get why you're all…" She waved at me and grinned. "Flustered."

"Me?"

"Oh, come on. They're all so cute. Especially the one on the end."

I gulped. Deanna was bold. If I didn't say anything, she'd take him for herself. I shook the thoughts from my head. It was crazy talk. He was just some guy who stopped in for a burger.

"Thanks. I appreciate the help. It's busy tonight!" I exclaimed.

"October always is." She nodded. She'd been working here for three years, while I was going on eight months. "All the way up to January. On the plus side, most holiday diners leave good tips. So, go, earn your tip, and give the hotties their food." She waved at the tray full of burgers and fries.

My hands were sweaty, and my chest was heaving as I walked to the back booth.

"Hello again!" I said cheerily. "I see you got your refills."

"Yes, the other girl got it for us. You're slacking, Scout." The blond with the long hair smirked.

I swallowed and ignored his comment. I handed each plate to their intended person.

"All right boys, enjoy." I put my hand on Desiderio's shoulder. He looked up at me with surprise. I grinned. "Just let me know when you want that pie. It's on me." I removed my hand quickly as if his leather jacket had burned me. My heart pounded as I walked back to the back room to get a drink of water and relax.

What's wrong with me? Why did I touch him?

"Are you ready for your check?" I asked politely after their food was cleared and another round of beer had been served.

The man in the middle stretched his arms out behind the booth and sunk down in his seat. "Actually, we'll take another round." He motioned to the empty pitchers.

I held back a deep sigh. Tables came and went. Tip after tip came, but still, those five stayed, ordering beer. The longer they stayed, the more my irritation grew. They were loud and obnoxious. Every time I went to check on them, I received another gross comment with no tip in sight.

Deanna commented on it when we had a slow moment. "You got some lingerers, huh?"

I nodded and glanced their way. "You know how many tables I could have turned?"

She gave me a sympathetic smile. "Sometimes, it's like that." She checked her watch. "Shift's almost over. In a bit, you'll be home, in a hot shower, forgetting all about those men."

I definitely hoped so. I was exhausted. With fifteen minutes left, I went to the booth with their check in hand and slammed it on the table.

"My shift is over. So, you can pay your check now, or I'm going to give you over to the next girl."

"What's she look like?" one of them said, getting a laugh from the table.

I folded my arms and waited for an answer. The blond with long hair sighed and took out his wallet. He looked at the bill and pulled out a small handful of fifties and tossed them on the table.

"Let's go, boys. We got a hangover to nurse tomorrow."

The men stood. I thanked them while collecting the money. I cashed out for the night and went to the back room to change and count my tips. They had actually tipped me pretty damn good. *Really good.* I crossed myself and looked up at the ceiling, thanking a god I didn't believe in for the tip.

I changed out of my skirt and back into my baggy jeans, then slipped my Chicago Cubs jersey on, leaving it unbuttoned. Grabbing my backpack, I waved to Deanna and the others still working and then stepped out into the cool air. I took a deep breath and smiled. *Finally free.*

At least until tomorrow.

I stepped off the curb to head to my car when a voice stopped me short.

"Scout, wait!"

I spun around and froze. There, leaning against the diner with his friends, with one hand holding a cigarette and the other outstretched toward me, was Desiderio.

CHAPTER 4

"Yeah?" I furrowed my tired brow at the men standing in front of the diner. Desiderio, the handsomest man in the line, took a step toward me. He flicked his cigarette out into the parking lot and smiled at me.

"Where you headed?"

I stared at him blankly. Was he serious? It was four in the morning.

"I just did a full shift. I'm going home." I turned away and started walking toward the sidewalk.

"Hold on, you need a ride?"

I glanced over my shoulder. He trying to catch up with me.

"I'm good."

"Where do you live? We can take you home."

"I said I'm good." I stopped and turned around to glare at him. Immediately, I softened.

Something about this man drew me in. Since puberty, I was used to men catcalling me or trying to get me to do stuff with them. Tonight should have been no different than the others, but this man… Desiderio.

He was different.

He put his hands up as his striking eyes widened. "Sorry, I was just trying to be nice. I, uh…" He looked down and then back up at me. He gave me an almost painful smile, but I felt like he was telling the truth. "Do you, uh, have a last name, Scout?"

Despite wanting to take the ride and tell him all about myself in hopes that he'd do the same, instinct took over, and I lied.

"Ruiz."

He grinned, and my stomach fluttered. He was so strangely handsome.

"Scout Ruiz," he said my name and it was like whispering a prayer in my ear. He nodded and took a step away from me. "Well, it was nice to meet you, Scout Ruiz."

"Happy birthday, Desi." I smiled and started to turn but then I paused when he blinked and went expressionless.

"What?" I asked.

"No one's ever called me that before."

"No?"

He smiled again. "No."

"Well, goodbye, Desi." With every step, I wondered and hoped that he was watching me.

"It's stupid! ¡Stupido!" I shouted.

"Why? You said he was cute, right?" Brenda, my roommate, insisted.

"Yeah, but cute only goes so far. And his friends were loud drunks."

"And your past choices in men weren't?"

"Yeah, but they were—"

"Mexican?" She snickered.

"Not all of them. But they weren't like him," I defended. "He spoke differently than the others."

It was true, his friends spoke louder and were more foul-mouthed. Desi's way of speaking was more formal, despite his appearance.

His blue eyes filled my mind while I showered, and his odd smile was the last thing I thought of as I fell asleep. I woke up after noon, and still, all I could think about was the handsome stranger to whom I wished happy birthday last night.

"You didn't get his number?" Brenda leaned across the couch and swatted me gently on the shoulder. "Fool!"

"I know, I know." I pulled my feet up and stared sadly at the TV. *The Fresh Prince of Bel-Air* just wasn't doing it for me today. How could I lust after Will Smith when I couldn't get Desiderio out of my head?

Desi.

Even if I never saw him again, he'd always be Desi to me. Brenda was right; I should have gotten his phone number.

"What are your plans for tonight?" I asked. It was my night off, and we usually had friends over for drinks.

Brenda sighed, but I could hear the happiness in her voice. "I have to pack. I've been putting it off but Alexander is coming in a week and he said we'll need to leave as soon as possible. Work didn't give him much time off."

"This is our last weekend together." I whined.

"Yes, but you'll see me at the wedding."

"Wedding? Alexander proposed?"

"No, but with me moving across the country for him, he better be picking up a ring on the way." She put her arm around me, pulling me toward her. "And when that happens, I want you as a bridesmaid."

"Thanks," I muttered. Already, I was imagining the price of a dress. I'd have to save for weeks.

"Or who knows? Maybe I'll be coming to yours first?"

"Mine?" I pulled away, laughing at the thought. "Sadly, my magazines don't talk back."

"I still think you should try to find this guy. What did you say his name was?" She went to the kitchen.

"Desiderio." I stood and followed her. For some reason, I was protective of the shortened version of his name. He had told me that I was the first to call him that. I wanted to be the only one. She pointed at me as she opened the fridge and pulled out a bottle of vodka and a carton of orange juice.

"Desiderio. What do you think that is, Italian?"

"Maybe. But it doesn't matter. Relationships have never been my thing."

"I think you just never met a good match."

"How do you know he is?" I countered.

"Because you light up whenever he's mentioned. I never saw you smile like that for Hank Derris."

My last real boyfriend was embarrassing to even think about. We lasted two months when I should have called it after the first date.

"Or—"

"Okay, I get the point." I put my hands up to stop her.

She poured us two drinks, and I took one.

"If I see him again, I'll ask for his number," I lied. I knew I'd chicken out.

"Good. Now, let's go get some boxes from behind the dollar store." She looked at her wristwatch. "It's shift change so they'll be clean ones by the dumpster."

Hopping into her car, we drove to grab boxes and pick up tape and markers to get her packed up. When we got home, I turned on my stereo system and we listened to *Open House*

Party while we got drunk off screwdrivers and folded her clothes into boxes.

"Are you gonna be okay? You know, with the rent and stuff?" Brenda asked me during a small break. I brushed back my hair and rolled my eyes. We'd had this talk over and over since she told me she was leaving last month.

"I always land on my feet. Don't worry about me." Everything in the house was hers. Except for my stereo and bed.

"You can keep the couch. Alexander doesn't have room for it."

"Thanks." I'd need to pull a lot of doubles at the diner until I found a new roommate. I was grateful for anything she left here.

"Has anyone called from the flyer?"

"Nope. Which is fine, I guess. I don't feel like painting the walls yet." We walked into her room and stared at the mural I had made for her two years ago when we first moved in. I had used permanent markers to create the cityscape of Seattle for her, where Alexander lived, so that they could always see the same view. She hugged me tightly.

"You're gonna do something with this someday. Promise me," Brenda urged.

"You know I'm saving for school."

We left the room and had more drinks, forgetting about all of our worries. I pretended for just a night I wasn't in dire financial stress, and she pretended to not notice. It was a great last Friday night. When I finally went to my room to sleep, my mind drifted back to the night before at the diner.

Would I ever see Desi again? Was it stupid to hope so when I had more important things to worry about?

Still drunk, I stumbled over to the tall pickle jar I had under my bedside table. I pulled it out and stared at it.

Art School.

I rolled my eyes and reached for a marker on the table. I crossed out the words and added a new one above it.

Rent.

Sighing, I lay in bed, and really, really hoped that I'd see Desi again. Even if in just my dreams. After all, that's all I had anymore. And what a surprise, to find him there, when I closed my eyes again.

W hat are you doing?" Randy asked me the next evening. He was swinging by to get some weed and caught me going through the phonebook.

"I'm looking for a number, duh."

"The pizza places are on the fridge."

I ignored him and continued searching through pages and pages of phone numbers and addresses. I found the R's and put my finger on the page to start scrolling.

Ramirez

Reed

Reyes

Reynolds

Rhodes

Roberts

Rodrigues

Rogers

Russell

Ruiz

There it was! I let out a small groan as there were a half dozen Ruizes. But only one with an S. I went to my kitchen.

"If you're ordering pizza, get me a sausage and pepperoni!" Randy shouted from the couch.

"I ain't ordering you shit. Especially if you're gonna smoke and not pay me 'til next week."

He flipped me off. "I just took your sorry ass out to dinner last night. You know how much that fucking cost me? Along with that fat tip you made us give that bitchy waitress."

"What are you talking about? She was fine."

"Fine for you. You were drooling every time she came by. 'Cherry Pie is on me,'" he mocked, raising his voice. "If it wasn't your birthday, I would have told you to fuck off and left your ass there. I don't know why you wanted to stay so long just to stare at the girl."

I didn't know either why I wanted to see her so badly. She was a total stranger who didn't seem all that interested in me.

"Happy birthday, Desi."

Her smile, albeit tired and a little forced looking, was still stuck in my head. I dreamed about her last night, for Christ's sake. I had to call her. I reached for my phone and took it off the hook, tugging on the spiral cord. With a deep breath, I typed in the seven-digit number and waited. My heart pounded as the phone rang and then chimed.

"Please dial the area code before making your call." I listened to the monotone woman's voice three times as my heart settled, and I cradled the phone.

"Are we gonna burn or what?" Randy asked.

"Just smoke without me." I stared hard at the number. "I'm doing something."

"Jerking off?"

Round two. Ignoring him, I dialed the area code and the phone number from the phone book. It rang once, and my heart felt like it was going to explode, waiting for that second ring, and then it did. And then a third time. Finally, there was a click, and a gruff male voice came through the line.

"Hello?"

I slammed the phone back onto the wall and closed my eyes. What the fuck. Was I a kid again? Making prank calls? I pressed my back against the wall. I blew my breath up and my hair flew everywhere as I went through what just happened. I tried to call a girl up and hung up on her dad!

I'd just have to try again.

Randy called for me, and I went back to the living room just in time for him to pass me the joint. I inhaled and handed it back to him, slowly breathing back out.

"So, who'd you call?"

"Aleida," I lied. "I wanted to make sure she got to her hotel all right."

"Makes sense. I can't believe you just let her go like that."

"What do you mean? She's fine." I eyed him suspiciously.

"You're not worried about her cheating?"

"No, not really. You were right. We're not a good fit."

He took another hit off the joint. "So, does that mean you're finally gonna break it off? Man, don't make me buy a tux for a marriage that isn't going to last more than a year," he groaned and handed it back to me.

"I've told you a million times. It isn't as easy as just calling shit off. Our parents—"

"Yeah, yeah. I've met them. I'm still not entirely sure he ain't part of *Goodfellas*."

He wasn't far off. Add a little blood-drinking into the mix and he'd be spot on.

"Is her family the same?" he asked.

"You got it. That's how my parents got together, and hers, and a lot of couples in our… circle. It's pretty common."

"Yeah, but I've met your mom. She's a peach. Aleida is not. Bangable, yes. But she's a bitch. You can't marry someone you can't stand." He took one last hit and then smushed the joint into the ashtray on my coffee table.

"That's most marriages, isn't it?" I chuckled. I'd been so used to defending my engagement to Aleida Linotti, it was reflex now. There was little I could do. Our parents were vampires. They lived forever, it would shame our name if I disobeyed them. I couldn't go against their code. Despite feeling relaxed and lightheaded from the weed, I was bummed. I didn't want Aleida, I wanted the beautiful brunette waitress from last night.

My interactions with the woman had been brief, but there had definitely been something there. She was incredibly attractive, but also intimidating, despite her size. She was short, but it felt like she could stand toe to toe with the toughest of them.

"I'm hungry." Randy scratched his stomach and yawned. "You really didn't order a pizza?"

"Nope. Feel free to." I motioned to the kitchen where my phone sat on the hook.

"I want cheese fries. From the diner. Did you have any?"

"I don't remember."

"That's right. I forgot your eyes were glued to the waitress's ass."

"You want to get more fries?" I started to stand "I'll drive and pay."

"Nah." He waved me off. "Let's just order from them. They deliver." He took account of my irritated expression and laughed. "You just want to see that girl again, don't you? Seems kind of pointless since you're engaged."

"I don't ask about your love life," I snapped, starting toward the kitchen. "What do you want to eat?" Randy shouted his order, and I called the restaurant. I was slightly disappointed when an older woman's voice come across the line, but I rattled off our order along with my address and hung up. With my hand still on the phone, I squeezed the teal plastic. Should I try to call her again?

Taking a deep breath and steadying myself, I dialed a second time. It rang three times before someone picked up.

"Hello?" a woman answered.

"Hello."

"Who is this?" Her Hispanic accent was thicker than Scout's had been.

"Uh, Desiderio, I mean Des—"

"Who?" she demanded again, and I panicked and hung up. Again. I leaned against the wall, hanging my head. What a fucking idiot. A moment later, the phone rang. I stared at it for a moment as it continued to go off before I reached out with shaky hands and answered.

"Hello?"

"Desiderio?"

CHAPTER 6

Desi

"This is."

"This is who?" the woman on the other line asked. I was speechless. Who was I? I was a nobody, calling up a woman like we were kids. I couldn't talk to her parents. I hung up again.

Fuck.

"How long did they say the food was gonna be?" Randy called from the other room.

"Thirty minutes."

"Did you get the bubblegum ice cream?"

"Yes!" I shouted. I closed my eyes and ground my palms into them. Why was I acting like this? I was almost fucking thirty, and I was acting like a kid. Was it because of her, though, or just because I was sick of Aleida? I went to my fridge and grabbed a pair of Budweisers before returning to the living room.

Randy was watching some new show.

"Have you seen this yet? It's pretty good."

"What is it?"

"*The X-files*. I missed this week's episode last night, but you have satellite TV and they're already replaying it on another channel."

"Start paying my bills, man." I laughed and put my legs up on my table. I popped open my beer. "You watch more TV than I do."

"I'll start helping when you pay your own bills." He snickered. "Your pop helps your brother and sister as much as he does you?"

"My brother and sister are married. But yes, until they were married, he did."

Randy clicked his tongue. "I'd kill to be in your shoes, man."

I do have to kill to be in my shoes, man.

"It's not as fun as you'd think."

"Right. The whole arranged marriage thing. It does feel a little outdated. People a hundred years ago did that stuff. We're in the age of technology. Your family needs to grow with the times."

"I don't disagree." I reached into my flannel pocket and removed my cigarettes. I lit one and took a quick puff. "But it is what it is."

"What happens after you get married?"

"I go to work for my dad."

"And that is…"

I smirked. "Nice try."

"One of these days, I'm going to figure out the Amato secret."

"Then I'll have to kill you." I smiled while saying it, but I wasn't lying. He'd be lucky if it's me that finds him first. At least I'd do it as quickly and painless as possible. Gianni or Caterina however…

I'd witnessed all of my family feed throughout my entire lifetime. It was always messy and slightly jarring. I didn't want to be like them, but somewhere deep down, I knew I would be. In less than a year, I'd be ripping out throats and tossing dead bodies into the river as if they were nothing. With one year left, I was stuck right in the middle of my two worlds. The vampires and the humans. Right now, I'd give anything to be simply human.

Randy had been begging me to watch this show with him since it started a month ago, and finally, I decided to give in and relax. I was getting sucked into the story of Scully and Mulder when my doorbell rang.

"Oh, hell yeah, food's here." Randy slammed his beer and stood. "You get the door; I'll get us more drinks."

I went to the door nervously. What were the odds that it'd be her delivering tonight? I opened the door and… it was not Scout but the other waitress that had brought us our drinks.

"Oh, it's you." She blinked as she handed me the brown bags of food.

"Me?" I pointed to my chest.

"Yeah, the guy from last night. Scout had your table all night."

"We were celebrating."

"I noticed. You have a fun group." She stood on her tiptoes, and I turned my head to see Randy passing from the kitchen back to the living room. "Are they all here tonight?" She eyed the food.

I probably over-ordered. The bags were a result of the munchies.

"No, just Randy."

"Oh, well." The girl smiled and looked at the steps she was standing on. "Is he dating anyone?"

"No, actually. I don't think he is. You want me to get him?"

"Maybe just his number. Consider it my tip." She winked at me.

I scrambled to grab my wallet from my back pocket. "What's the total?"

"Thirty-four seventy."

I gave her two twenty-dollar bills, and she gave me a pen. I looked at it for a moment before realizing she really did want Randy's phone number. I tore a piece of the bag off and scribbled the digits, then handed it to her.

"Thanks." She stepped off my steps. "Maybe I'll be seeing you around some." She turned and started toward her car.

"Wait!" I set the bags down on the floor and ran after her. "You know Scout, right?"

"I do."

"Is she… is she single?"

She grinned. "She is."

"How do I—" I wasn't quite sure how to word my request.

The delivery woman laughed. "Why don't you come in tomorrow night? She's working the rest of the week. I'll make sure she gets your table." I looked to the car she was driving. She saw and waved off my concerns. "I'm just covering delivery tonight. You come in, and I promise you'll get to shoot your shot."

"Is there anything you can tell me about her?" I was desperate. I had already screwed up the phone call. I couldn't mess this up.

"She likes to draw." She turned back and hurried to her car. "I gotta go. I'll see you tomorrow."

She wasn't asking, it was more of an order. I nodded and went back inside, grabbing the food.

"What took so long?" Randy complained as I set the bags

on the coffee table. "Commercial's over."

"I just got you a date," I smirked and grabbed a container. I opened it to find cheese fries. My stomach rumbled, and I plucked one out and popped it into my mouth. "Chick digs you."

"It's the hair." He flipped his blond locks out of his face. "You should grow yours out."

"I'm good. I need to stand out somehow." I was the only one out of our group who shaved regularly and had my hair cut every few weeks.

"Stand out for who? You were given a smoking piece of ass. Aleida isn't going anywhere, even if you were ugly."

He had a point. There was no way I'd be able to get rid of her. "Who knows, maybe I might stop caring."

My mind drifted back to Scout. Out in the parking lot, with her oversized jersey open, revealing her belly shirt…

I was going to that diner tomorrow night.

Randy froze with his burger in the air to look at me. "Are you saying you're going to give all this up?"

"Maybe, if I had good enough reason to."

"Leaving Aleida is a good enough reason, trust me. She's a bitch." He took a bite of his burger. The rest of the night, I sat with him and watched TV, drank beer, and smoked weed. Later, Mick and Tommy picked him up while heading to a party.

"You coming?" Mick shouted to me from his car.

"I'm tired. I'll see you guys later!" I shut the door and started shutting off the lights in the house.

I stripped off my clothes and put my wallet and tarot deck on my nightstand. I climbed into my bed and ran through the conversation I'd had with the delivery girl. I'd bring my deck tomorrow and order some cheese fries and a beer. But… what was I going to say?

"I hate that you're gonna miss Halloween." I sat down on a box and sighed.

Brenda packed up her last box and set it against the wall before turning to me.

"Yeah, but now, you won't have to worry about people sneaking into your room to fuck," she pointed out.

"You got me there. I don't even have a costume."

"You should have said something! I just threw out the *Flash Dance* outfit I wore last year. You would have looked great in it."

"I don't need a costume. I just want to get drunk." I pointed out.

"At least you still get to party. We'll still be driving probably."

My watch beeped, and I took another deep breath. "That's my cue."

"Another double?" She raised her eyebrows as she followed me into the living room.

"No, just a twelve."

"You should go to day shift."

"I want to. I just have to wait for a spot to open up. Those tips are good." I rubbed my thumb and pointer finger together.

"Well, have a good day, I guess." Brenda pouted. "I hate that we can't hang out the entire week before I leave."

I grabbed my backpack and shoved my feet in my Nikes.

"You want a ride?" she asked.

"Nah, I like the walk." I pulled out my Walkman from the bag. "I just got Xscape's new album."

Brenda's mouth parted, and her brown eyes lit up. "You did not! How have we not listened to it yet!" She tried to snatch the tape cassette from my hand, but I pulled away. "No. That's it. I'm giving you a ride because I need to hear both sides." She grabbed her keys and started out the door. In her car, I popped my tape in and turned the dial-up.

"How'd you end up with this?" She demanded.

"Nalida sent it to me for my birthday. It just came in this morning."

"Nalida, your friend from home?" I nodded. Nalida and I had grown up in the foster care system. We were never adopted, so we grew up together in a group home, and eventually aged out.

"I love her," Brenda gushed in between songs. She drove me to work and then popped the tape out, handing it to me. I climbed out of the car and thanked her.

"When I get home tonight, we'll listen to it all," I promised.

"Absolutely. Have a good day at work!" She waved, backed out of the lot, and disappeared. I had set my watch for walking time, not a drive. Entering the restaurant, I was surprised to find the tables full.

Phyllis, the hostess, hurried over to where I was trying to

slink in undetected. "Can you clock in early? We're slammed!"

"Yeah, just let me change and I'll be out." I hurried to the back and slipped on my skirt and the tight shirt. I grabbed my apron and tied it around my waist. Then, I went back to Phyllis.

"Tables sixteen and five were just seated."

It was four full hours before it settled down enough for me to take a moment to breathe. The sun had gone down, making the air even colder when I went outside. It felt good on my warm skin.

"Scout, right?"

I looked up at the sound of a man's voice.

Desi.

"Desi!"

He smiled wide, and I admired his face. He was so incredibly handsome. "You're working tonight?"

"I am." I kicked off the building. "You and your friends coming in for a bite?" I walked over to him and motioned to the restaurant. We started up the stairs together.

"Just me tonight. I wanted that cherry pie you offered me the other night."

"What?" I stopped at the door. His face paled, and his smile fell. He cleared his throat.

"It was my birthday, and you offered me pie. I was just —" He swallowed hard, blushing bright red.

"Oh, right! Yeah, let's get you in there and I'll bring you a slice. Cool Whip or ice cream?" I laughed and opened the door for him.

"Uh, Cool Whip sounds good." He hurried inside. I went to the back and poured myself some coffee. My regular eight-hour shift was about to start soon. I put some creamer in and was stirring my cup when Phylis burst into the back, causing me to jump.

"Did you see that guy just walk in? He's so fine!" She sighed and her blue eyes went to the ceiling, and she pouted. "And my shift is over. You guys are so lucky." She looked around the kitchen to the night shift waitresses wandering around.

"Who?" Deanna went to the kitchen doors and peeked her head out. "What table?"

"He's over at twenty-seven."

"Oh, that's Scout's table," Deanna said quickly, popping her head back in.

"He's all alone?" Jennifer, another waitress, asked after she took her turn in peeking out. "Oh wow. Scout, I'll trade you tables."

"Fat chance," Deanna said before I could answer her. "Let me guess, you'll trade her the family booth?"

"It's a bigger tip," Jennifer protested.

"Let her have an easy one," Deanna argued.

I rolled my eyes. Those two were always fighting. I pulled out my notepad and pen and clicked it.

"While you two argue, I'm going to go see what he wants."

They glanced at me and continued bickering as I shoved through the swing door. Despite my heart hammering, I walked as confidently as I could and forced a smile.

"Hey, stranger."

Desi leaned against the wall with an open book in his hand. He grinned. "Hey."

"You thirsty?" I lifted my pad to write his order.

"Uh, yeah. A Budweiser will work."

"And food?"

"Uh, what do you have?"

"Oh, let me get you a menu. I'll be back with your drink in a moment." I spun around, silently scolding Phyllis for being too dumbstruck by his ridiculously charming smile to give him a damn menu. I grabbed his drink and returned, then placed the menu on the table. "I can come back in a bit and take your order."

He nodded but didn't reach for it. Instead, he picked his book back up.

"Are you not hungry?" I asked. "Or maybe waiting for someone?" My gut fluttered, praying it wasn't the latter.

"No, it's just me. I kind of wanted to relax here a bit tonight, if that's okay?"

"Yeah, of course." I grinned; thankful he hadn't come here for a date. "I'll come back in a little bit." On my way to the kitchen, I was fighting back the urge to squeal, but it came out the moment the kitchen door swung closed.

"Oh my God!" Jennifer plowed through me from behind. "Scout, that guy was staring at you the entire time you were walking back here." She sighed. "Why do all the good ones want everyone but me?"

"What makes you think he's a good one?" I crossed my arms, trying not to smile wide. He was staring at me? Is it possible he came back just to talk to me?

"Did you see his car outside?"

I shook my head.

"He's got a brand-spanking-new black Mustang."

"That doesn't make him good. Just rich." I reached for the coffee cup I had set aside earlier and brought it to my lips.

"Isn't that the same thing? Anyways, he asked me if you were seeing someone the other night."

I choked on my drink, and coffee spilled all over my shirt and chin. "What did you say?"

CHAPTER 8

Scout

"Are you awake?" I called out the moment I closed the door of my place. "Brenda?"

"You're early." She popped her head out of the kitchen and gave me a finger to hold on. She had the phone to her ear. I dropped my bag and kicked my shoes off, then I plopped down on the couch and waited for my friend.

"All right, I'll talk to you later, Papi. I love you too." She put the phone back on the hook and came into the living room, crossing her arms. "Why do you look so happy to have had your shift cut by, like, three hours?"

"I know, normally I'd be stressing out but… he came back," I gushed.

"Who?" She cocked her head and then her eyes widened. "The guy from the other night?" She hurried over and sat, crossing her legs on the couch. "Forget my story, tell me yours."

"What's your story?" I laughed.

"My dad. He's getting prank called. It's so dumb but he was going off." She waved it off. "This is more interesting. Tell me what happened."

I told her about Desi showing up at dinner and staying until ten. "He was reading a book and just sitting there smiling and watching me."

"That's it?" She frowned. "He just watched you?"

"No. We chatted some. Every time I passed by, he had something stupid to say." I grinned, recalling how cute his smirk was. "And then we got slow and they were sending people home. I'd fight to stay, but then someone offered me a ride home…" I raised an eyebrow. "In his 1992 Ford Mustang."

"A Mustang? What color?"

"Black." I bit my lip, recalling the smell of the leather. It was the cleanest car I'd ever been in.

Brenda swore. "Fucking lucky." She pouted. "Alexander just has a rusty truck. Wait." She paused. "So that's it? He took you home and said good night?"

"Yeah, he was really nice. Didn't even try touching me or anything."

"And what's his name again?" She squinted.

"Desi. Or Desiderio, but I call him Desi."

Her hands shot to her mouth to hold in a gasp.

"What?" I frowned.

"That's the guy that's been prank-calling my dad!"

I was nervous all day, waiting for my shift. I had never been excited to get to work before. But today, I wanted to get there as soon as I could to see if Desi would be there again.

I had to fight my nerves to sit around at home. Our friends came over to decorate for Halloween.

"All these boxes are gonna be gone?" Teresa asked while trying to step over them to hang up orange streamers.

"Yeah. All of this will be empty space."

"Perfect. We'll put the keg here," Maria said, pointing to a spot in the living room with a pile of boxes.

We danced and hung out, listening to SWV, Xscape, and TLC, while sipping on beers. Finally, I was able to put my backpack on and grab my Walkman.

"I'll see you guys this weekend." I waved goodbye and hurried outside before I was offered a ride. I needed this time to prepare. I was either going to have another night with Desi, or I was going to be disappointed. I needed to be ready for both. I'd been let down so many times in my life, so what was one more?

He never said he'd be back. I had just kind of… hoped.

And there it was. I got to the parking lot and was flooded with sadness so hard my eyes watered. His car wasn't there. I blinked away the tears and hurried inside. I changed quickly and went to find Kiki, the hostess. She was grinning when she listed off my tables.

"What?" I forced a smile.

"Nothing. Have a good night!"

I gave her an odd look but started my tables. The first three were tables and last was a booth. I got the drink orders and started toward the fourth, only to freeze.

Desi.

He looked up from his menu and grinned.

Oh, the butterflies were back.

"Hey, stranger."

I had never smiled so wide.

"You must really like the burgers here," I joked, walking to his table.

"Food's not bad." He smirked. Damn, I adored it.

"How about I bring you a beer?"

"Beer sounds good. You know, I'm still waiting on that pie."

"Is that why you keep coming back?"

"Something like that."

"I'll see what we have in the back." I couldn't let him see how excited I was that he had come back, but the moment I broke through the kitchen doors, I screamed. I was so excited to know that I'd get to talk to him at least a little bit tonight, but then fifteen minutes later we were slammed and I was given six more tables. Every time I stopped by his table, he tried to talk to me but I couldn't spare much time, which I think disappointed us both.

I came back with his check eventually as he was laying out a deck of cards.

"What's that?"

"Tarot. Do you use them?"

"No. I was raised Catholic." I fought the urge to cross myself. "I don't practice now though."

"Well, you should practice this, then. When you get a break, come, and let me show you the cards."

"A break?" I motioned around us. "I'm not getting a break tonight. I'll be busy 'til two am."

"Okay then, I'll be here until two."

"You already paid."

"Can I have some coffee, please?" He grinned.

Despite his annoying insistence, I wanted him to stay. My stomach tightened and my chest hammered every time I passed him. He stayed, ordering cup after cup of coffee, and playing with his cards while I worked.

The clock struck two, and I sunk into exhaustion. I hurried to the back to change and grab my bag. When I returned to the front of the restaurant, Desi was gone. I went to his table, only to find his bill paid with a hefty tip. I took the cash and waved goodbye to the crew. I went outside, confused, only to find him leaning against his car, shuffling his cards and grinning at me.

"I thought you left." I laughed, going over to him.

"Why would I leave now? Plus, you haven't drawn a card." He extended the deck to me. I was hesitant but took it. They felt heavy and almost evil in my hand. My days in mass listening to father after father tell me things like Tarot cards and fortune telling were witchcraft and would send me to hell formed a pit in my stomach. I swallowed and cut the deck a few times.

"Just one?"

"One card and show me."

I pulled a card and turned it toward him. The blood drained from his face, as did the smile and glint of mischief I had begun to enjoy in his blue eyes. I looked at the card.

"The Hanged Man. What's that mean?"

"It means you're gonna meet someone who's going to change your life."

"Oh, like you?" I rolled my eyes. The grin I'd grown attached to returned.

"Maybe. Can I give you a ride home?"

I smiled and decided this was the moment I'd been waiting for all night. The words slid from my tongue with ease. "Sure, if you stop calling my roommate's dad late at night and call me instead."

Desi

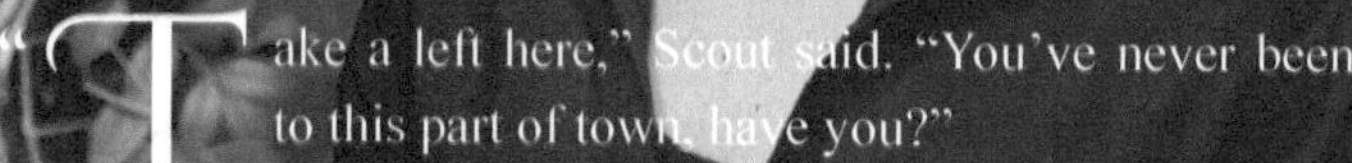

"Take a left here," Scout said. "You've never been to this part of town, have you?"

"Why do you ask?" I gripped the wheel tighter. My hands were damp with sweat, and I was sure she could tell I was nervous.

"You look lost. A little scared."

I gulped. I had somehow managed to get this beautiful woman to agree to let me take her home. But what now? I wasn't familiar with this anymore. My stomach muscles were tight with nerves. It was like my entire being could feel her presence just feet away calling to me. My fingers twitched at the wheel, begging for me to make a move.

"I didn't realize that wasn't your house I was calling." My cheeks flared, recalling just moments ago when she asked me to stop calling a stranger's house looking for her. "It was the only name in the phone book that fit."

Her hands quickly covered a gasp, followed by a fit of giggles. "You did not!"

"I did," I admitted.

"What would you have said if I had answered?" Her

accent, while hardly there, was pleasant and almost warm as she asked.

"I have no fucking clue." I drove on, the tension now gone, and eventually, much to my dismay, we pulled into the driveway of a small, white house. I put the car in park and shut it off. We stared at each other and then back at the house.

It was a stark difference from the homes in my neighborhood. Would she invite me in?

"You left a light on." I pointed to the window.

"That's my roommate. She stays up late."

"The roommate whose dad I was calling?" The tension grew as she didn't move for the handle to get out. My tongue tingled, and I panicked when she shifted in her seat. "Do you want to sit and talk somewhere?"

She smiled wide, and my chest expanded in such a way I'd never felt before. I lived for that beautiful grin. She nodded, and I pulled back out of the driveway.

"Where to?"

"There's a park a few miles that way," she suggested. I followed her directions and pulled into the park. I took in a deep breath of the cold, crisp October air, and then looked around after stepping out of the car.

"This is a nice little place," I admired.

"We used to come here every day after school."

"You grew up around here?"

"I did. Did you?"

"Yeah, my family has been here for a long time."

"What year did you graduate? I don't remember you." She furrowed her brows as she stared at my face.

"Eighty-five, but I didn't go to public school."

"Oh, homeschooled?"

"No, uh, Catalina."

"Catalina, the private school?" She whistled. "Damn boy, you really do have money."

"My family has money. Not me. It's not something I'm proud of," I admitted, shoving my hands in my pockets.

"Why not?" She scoffed, then turned and pointed to my car. "If I had something like that, I'd be driving it past my homies every single day!"

"It is pretty slick, isn't it?"

"You're into cars then?" I followed her until we reached a picnic table. She climbed on top of the bench and plopped down on the table, folding her legs in, she turned to me. I joined her.

"Not really. I needed a new one and the dealer convinced me I needed this one." She was making me so… aware of myself. My friends had always called me names and teased me about my family's money, but I'd never really cared until now.

"What are you into then?" she asked.

"Movies. Music. I like Iron Maiden, do you like them?"

She made a sour face. "No! I listen to a lot of hip hop and R&B. My roommate is obsessed with Selena right now."

"Selena?"

"You don't know who Selena is?" She slapped my shoulder. Her chocolate eyes lit up. "Selena is the biggest Tejano singer out there right now!"

"I don't know what that means."

Her accent had come on thicker when she got excited. It was adorable. She rolled her eyes and laughed.

"Spanish music. It's so good! Hold up. If you listen to one of my tapes, I'll listen to one of yours."

"Right now?" I looked around. It was nearly three a.m. "I mean, I probably have my Walkman somewhere in the car."

"No, silly." She rolled her eyes again. "Later. Look, I'll

make you a mix of all my favorite songs and you can come get it next time you're at the diner."

God, how gorgeous she looked with her eyes to the sky and a smirk on her lips.

"I'm invited back, then?"

"I can't really say no. I don't own the place." She laughed again. "But sure. You come in and we'll trade tapes. Put whatever you want on it."

"What about you?" I asked. "What do you do for fun?"

"Fun? I can't afford fun. Especially now that my room-mate is leaving."

I didn't know what to say. I'd never had to worry about money.

"Sorry, I shouldn't have said that. It's nothing. I like art," she said.

"What kind of art?"

"All kinds. I like to draw, paint, and play with clay. Anything that gets my mind stirred. But I mostly draw."

"Like fruit or animals?"

"People, I like drawing people."

We sat and shot the shit for hours until the sun poked out of the trees.

"I didn't realize it was so late. Or early." She yawned.

"Yeah, sorry about that. We should get you home."

"What about you? Don't you have a job? Aren't you tired?" She uncrossed her legs and began to scoot off the table. I panicked. Despite her acting like she didn't judge me for my family's wealth, I didn't want to make it worse.

"I work nights. I took some time off for my birthday," I lied.

"Where do you work?" My mind ran through a list of places that would make sense. Night shift, but she couldn't come visit. Ever.

"The Pleasure Den!" I blurted. She stopped in her tracks. Why did I say that of all places?

"The dirty movie theater?" I nodded.

"I don't partake." There was a moment where we stared at each other before she began to laugh, which turned into a full-belly laughter as she bent over and held her stomach.

I slid off the table and chuckled. "See, this is why I didn't want to tell you!" The lie rolled so easily off my tongue. She put up her hand to get me to stop talking.

"Well, I hope you have this weekend off."

"Why?"

"So you can come to my Halloween party."

"I'll figure something out. What day is Halloween?"

"Friday. You better be there," she urged, and together, we started back to my car.

"I'll be there." I swallowed the lump in my throat, only for it to knot in my stomach. Aleida would return on Friday.

CHAPTER 10

The rest of the week was torture. I had to lie to Scout again to buy me time to figure out what to do about the little thing that could end this. My engagement to Aleida Linotti.

"I was supposed to return to work on Friday, but I bet if I go in a few days early, my boss will let me have it off." I'd never had a job before. Did that sound realistic? She didn't seem sure herself but finally shrugged, thanked me for a fun night, and gave me the details for the party.

"Halloween starts at about seven. There'll be music and beer."

"Cool. I'll be there." The words were meant as truth, but the lump in my throat after saying them made it feel like a lie. Would I be able to escape Aleida's grasp long enough to visit Scout? Caught in my lies, I couldn't visit the diner for the rest of the week, despite having nothing else to do. That was all I wanted to do. I sat at the house, drinking beer and getting high with Mick and the others when they'd pop in after their shifts.

"I don't get how you stay so built," Tommy commented

after the third day of finding me lying on the couch, feeling miserable. "All you do is sit around and smoke."

Vampire genes.

I wanted to protest, but I was too exhausted. I felt like I was withdrawing.

From Scout.

I couldn't eat, I couldn't sleep. I didn't want to do anything other than stare ahead. I wanted desperately to see her again.

"Is being away from her that hard for you?" Eric asked as he came from my kitchen.

"Who?" I sat up to allow them to sit. Both men let out groans and retreated.

"Woah, man, go shower."

"She'll be back tonight, relax, Desiderio."

I lifted my arms and grimaced. I may have skipped a shower or two.

"Yeah, I'm thinking about ending it," I confessed. It felt so good to say out loud. Their eyes widened. I took off toward the bathroom. When I returned, they had all sorts of questions.

"When are you planning on doing it?" Tommy asked.

"No clue. Aleida comes back tomorrow."

"It's Halloween, dude," Eric argued. "I already bought my costume."

"Don't do this to us, bro." Tommy groaned. "Aleida's friends are total babes. Can't you wait 'til Monday?"

They'd been begging me to do this for a year and now they wanted to wait? "Fine. But I'm probably not going to the party. You might want to look for somewhere else to go."

They stared at each other, silently communicating. "Whatever, dude. Randy told us about a party he's going to with some babe. If we can't get into Aleida's party, we'll crash that one."

I picked up Aleida at the airport that evening. I had no desire to, but she called me and whined until I agreed and drove over there.

"Hey, baby! I missed you so much! Did you have a good birthday?" She threw her arms around me and planted kisses all over my face. I kept turning every time she leaned toward my lips, causing her to kiss everything else.

"Yeah. Did you enjoy celebrating *my* birthday in Vegas?"

"Yes!" She ignored my snark. "This mini vacation was needed. We had so much fun!"

"What about Tionne?" I looked around for her friend but didn't see her. Aleida frowned and forced me to take her hand. She began tugging me through the airport and into the night.

"We were hanging out with these really fun humans and then one of them confessed that he knew about us."

I stopped walking. "Is Tionne okay?"

Aleida nodded and gave me a tight smile. "Yeah, but uh, Leo swallowed some tacks."

"Okay?" I started walking again and stepped right past her.

"On purpose."

I still wasn't understanding, but then it hit me all at once. The guy had killed himself.

"Desiderio, he turned. He's a Bloodshed."

"What?"

"Tionne is staying with the Bloodshed until he gets the help he needs."

"What does that even mean? How can you help someone who would do that to themselves?" I took her suitcase from her and shoved it in the backseat. Bloodsheds were vampires turned when a human killed themselves. Their creation was frowned upon in the vampire society. I pulled out of the parking lot quickly.

"They have no clans. I don't know of any covens for them. Bloodsheds are unheard of, Desiderio, he's not safe."

"Tionne shouldn't have stayed with him. No one knows what goes on in their heads."

"They're sad human beings." Bloodshed vampires were not something we came across often. No one understood why some humans turned and others didn't, and the unknown was scary.

"Anyways, let's stop at my apartment so I can get some sleep before tonight. I got the cutest matching costumes in Vegas."

I didn't go in with her, and instead left her at her apartment and tried to sleep during the day, but all I could think about was how I was going to attend both parties. Eventually, I got up, showered, and drove over to Aleida's. I was going to figure out how to tell her we were over, and then together, we'd figure out how to tell our families.

I couldn't be the only eligible bachelor in the vampire community.

"Put this on." Aleida thrust a hanger at me the moment I stepped through the door. I took it and looked it over curiously. It was just a black muscle shirt and dress pants. She disappeared, and I followed her into her bedroom. She was curling her hair in front of her vanity.

"What is this exactly?" She rolled her eyes and pointed behind her in the mirror. I looked at the bed and saw a pink tutu dress. I shook my head, not getting it.

"We're Johnny and Baby from *Dirty Dancing*!" She huffed. "Hurry up and get dressed. You're late."

The words to end this were on the tip of my tongue, but I

didn't say them. I was a fucking coward. I knew if I said them that we'd spend the entire night fighting and I'd miss Scout's party. Instead, I went to the bathroom and changed into the clothes. I looked nothing like Patrick Swayze, but whatever shut Aleida up, I guessed.

I returned to find her slipping her dress on. "Just a few more touches," she said, as she picked up her aqua net and sprayed it all over her blonde curls. She turned and flashed me a smile with her fangs. "Let's go."

We were heading to a popular vampire club. It was invite-only, but I got my friend's tickets tonight for the floor. The VIP sections were for vampires and their specific guests.

That's where they fed.

Aleida wanted to dance, so I attempted to, all the while looking at my watch. Seven passed, then eight and then nine. Aleida's stamina didn't waver. Her vampire body was more equipped for a full night of dancing. I finally accepted that I was going to miss Scout's party. Aleida wouldn't let me leave her side.

"I want a drink!" I shouted to her through the crowd.

"Me too!" She grabbed my hand and led me through the crowd to the stairs leading upward. "I need a bite!"

"Now?"

"You'll understand in a year. It's better when they are happy. There's a bar upstairs you can sit at while I find someone."

Her words disgusted me. When *they* were happy? *They?*

"I'm not going to sit while you grope some innocent guy."

"Desiderio, it's not like that." She stomped her feet. "You don't get it."

"You're right." I threw up my hands. "You go have fun

with all of the others. Suck someone dry or whatever. I'm leaving."

"Where are you going?" Her lips trembled, and her eyes grew red with vampire tears. Blood tears.

"Don't worry about it." I turned and stormed through the crowd. I kept my angry scowl all the way to my car, and as soon as I was inside and peeling out of the parking lot like a madman, I smiled.

I was going to see Scout.

It was ten-thirty. I sat on my steps, drinking my jungle juice, kicking my legs, waiting for Desi to show up. If he would at all.

The party was both inside and out, but mostly everyone was in the back. I sat alone in the front, looking like a fool. I bobbed my head to SWV and stared out into the darkness, trying to not feel so deflated. I should have known he was too good to be true. An attractive man with a job, a car, and interest in me? That didn't happen.

"You're too pretty to be looking so sad." I turned to see a man with dark long hair smiling down at me. "Care for a drinking, buddy?"

I motioned to the spot beside me. "Go for it." I took a large gulp of my drink. No one else was going to sit there.

"You're the waitress from that diner." He pointed play-fully at me as he sat beside me. There was plenty of room on the step, but he sat so close our thighs and legs touched. I flinched but then looked up at him. He wasn't unattractive.

And Desi wasn't coming.

"I'm Mick." He extended his hand to me. I shook it and quickly let go.

"Scout."

"Scout. I like it. Why are you sitting out here all alone, Scout?"

"My friend was supposed to come, so I was waiting for him."

"Ah, you got stood up. What an idiot." He smirked and brought his beer to his lips. "Well, I hope you'll take my company as a replacement of that loser."

"He is a loser." I wasn't particularly in the mood to socialize. I thought I might get sick now that I had accepted the truth. It was so stupid. I barely knew Desi. Why was I so attached to a stranger?

Because Desi wasn't a stranger. Not to my heart.

"I saw your drawings in there. You're pretty good."

"Thanks. I get bored and I'm poor."

Mick laughed too hard. "Same here. I work at the foundry seven days a week. Me and my buddies go to the diner sometimes on Fridays after our shift."

I nodded, not really listening.

"Is this friend something serious?" Mick asked.

"It doesn't matter, it's dumb. What about you, Mick, what made you come out here? You're missing the party." I turned to point to my front door.

"I came out for a smoke." He reached into the pocket of his flannel. "Do you mind?"

"Go ahead."

"You smoke?"

"I tried once when I was sixteen. I was trying to impress a boy." I recalled that day with Nalida. She wanted to hang with all the other cholas and we had to prove we were chingonas just like them. "I ended up throwing up on his feet."

"Probably for the better. Cigarettes are a nasty habit," he said as he put one between his lips and lit it. He took a long drag and blew out smoke. "But damn if it's not nice to have one with a beer."

I sipped my juice and bobbed my head to the music. While I wasn't enthused by Mick himself, the company was oddly welcomed.

"This is your place, right? How long have you been here?"

"Two years. I rented it with Brenda, but she just moved out."

"Do you have someone lined up to move in?"

"I'm gonna try living solo for a while."

"I get it. I'm ready for Eric, my roommate, to move out, too."

"Eric? Is he here too?" I furrowed my eyebrows. "Who invited you?"

"My friend Tommy wants to get in a waitress from the diner's pants. We got kicked out of this club on the other side of town so we all came here. Well, everyone but Desiderio. Lucky bastard got to stay."

A lump caught in my throat.

"You know Desi?"

"Who? Desiderio Amato? Yeah, he's been my friend since we were kids. He's—" Just then, the sound of an engine roaring came from down the road. My heart soared as Desi's car pulled up next to the others. I started to get up, but I forced myself not to be too eager, and instead, raised my glass to him.

But he wasn't looking at me. His eyes were little slits, and his face was stone cold as he glared at the person sitting too close to me. I was suddenly hyperaware of the fact that Mick had been moving his hand over to mine, and our fingers were touching. I pulled my hand away quickly, but Desi had seen it.

He stepped out of his car and slammed the door, causing me to jump at the sharp sound. He stormed across the yard, and I fell backward as he ripped Mick from beside me and threw him over his shoulder, tossing him onto the grass.

"Care to explain what the hell is going on here?" he demanded of his friend. I caught myself on my hands and struggled to right myself back up. Desi circled Mick, his fists clenched and ready to hit.

"What are you talking about?" Mick yelled, rolling over. "What are you even doing here?" Mick sat up and tried to stand on his own but Desi grabbed him by his shirt and pulled him up. He lifted him off the ground.

"I could kill you right now," Desi said through clenched teeth.

"What the hell, man?" Mick was as confused as me. "Let me go." He kicked his feet in Desi's direction, but it didn't land.

"What are you doing?" I stepped forward. "We were just talking."

"Just talking isn't something Mick does," Desi snarled at his friend and let go of his shirt, dropping him hard to the ground.

"Well, that's something I do. And I was doing it because you weren't here. I didn't think you were coming," I snapped and crossed my arms.

"I said I would." Desi turned to me and threw his arms up. "I didn't think my best friend would try to—" He looked at his friend, who was gawking at us. "Mick, go inside."

Mick brushed off his acid-washed jeans and shook his head. He pointed to Desi. "This isn't over."

"Fine. We'll talk later." Desi twitched his head to my front door. "Go."

Mick gave him one last glare and shoved past him, heading back into the party.

"We were just talking." I said once we were alone.

"It didn't look like just talking."

"I thought you stood me up."

"Why would I do that?" His eyes looked almost pained at the thought. "I would never."

"Then why were you so late?" I cocked my hip and doubled down. He couldn't be mad at me for his mistake.

His Adam's apple bobbed and his blue eyes flickered behind me for just a second before returning to mine. It felt like time had stopped as I waited for his response. Was he going to drop a bomb on me? Had I been too hopeful? Was it all too good to be true? Was he here simply to tell me he couldn't see me ever again and that this was all a mistake?

"I was at work."

CHAPTER 12

Scout

"It was a full house of pervs. They needed all hands on deck," Desi said, his head hung low.

I grimaced at the picture in my head and softened. "Oh."

"I came as soon as I could but you gotta mop after each viewing. Did you decide to blow me off that quickly? For Mick?"

"He came out here while I was waiting for you."

"I know Mick. He wasn't just talking."

"Well, I was." I looked him over and raised a brow. "Is that a costume?" He was wearing all black, and everything was tight. He looked good, but it wasn't the Desi I was used to seeing. He raised his arms and looked down at himself.

"I'm Danny from *Grease*, you know, without the jacket."

"Do you have a Sandy?"

"No Sandy. Do I get to see your place?" He nodded to the house.

I turned back to my house. I had been nervous about this all week. I cleaned the baseboards and scrubbed the carpet even. Just based on what Desi had told me about his life, I knew he was slumming by coming here. My nerves fluttered, but I nodded.

"Sure. It's a little crowded right now, but I'll walk you through. The keg is in the backyard." I extended my hand, and he took it, squeezing. His warmth seeped into mine as I tugged him forward.

"You look good, by the way!" he shouted as we walked into my house with the loud music and even louder guests. I glanced down at myself. I was wearing jeans and a belly shirt, like normal, with a flannel over it. I had, however, taken time to curl my hair and do my makeup.

"Thanks! You hungry? We have pizza!" I pulled him through the living room to the kitchen. I took him to the flimsy card table. There were only a few pieces left and they looked depressing at best.

"I'm not hungry." Desi offered a polite smile, but I saw the look of distaste on his face, which made me cringe. I felt like I was watching him piece by piece, realizing he had made a mistake. He looked at the blankets covering my windows, the yellow, smoke-stained walls, and the old pizza. He was out of my league, and we both knew it.

I tried to let go of his hand, but he squeezed it tighter. His smile relaxed me. Was this all in my head?

"Let's get you a beer!" I called over the music. We rushed through the rest of the house, which wasn't much, and went out into the backyard.

"Woah. I didn't realize the party was this big." He blinked when he saw the full yard with people, more speakers, a bonfire in the back, and alcohol everywhere.

"My ex-roommate used to use this as my birthday party and Halloween. She invited everyone she ever came into contact with and now it's just a thing everyone knows about."

"It's your birthday?"

"No, it was last week."

"When?" he demanded.

"The day before yours. The twenty-second."

"Why didn't you tell me?" He looked almost… hurt.

"Because you were celebrating yours? Plus, why would you care? We just met."

"I do care." His lips tightened. "I know I shouldn't, but I do." His voice came out as barely above a whisper. "How old are you?"

"Twenty-six."

"Scout! Is this the cabrón you were waiting for in the front?" I turned to Chino, one of my friends, calling to us. He waved us over. "Come, get a drink!"

I turned to Desi and said, "We can talk about our birthdays later. Let's have fun tonight."

He snapped out of it and followed me to the keg where a group of my friends stood.

"¿Nuevo novio es blanco, eh?" Chino smirked as soon as Desi and I stepped into the circle. The others chuckled. I glared at him, and he looked up at the night sky. I glanced at Desi, and it was clear by the look on his face that he understood at least some of that. *Blanco.*

"Ignore them. They're just jealous that I didn't wait out front for them." I motioned for Chino to pour us drinks. While Chino did so, Julio extended his hand to Desi and introduced himself.

"I'm Julio, this is Birdie, Catrine, Chino," Julio said.

"I'm Desiderio," Desi replied politely.

"It's nice to meet you, Desiderio." Catrine grinned at Desi over her cup. She was eyeing him up and down with a look that made me want to snatch her by her ponytail. She swayed and looked at her best friend, Birdie.

"Birdie and Catrine are my homegirls," I said to Desi but

looked directly at Catrine. "They go with Julio and Creeper." I pointed to a guy across the lawn playing hacky-sack.

Catrine glanced nervously at Julio and then nodded. "You got that right. Where did you two meet?"

"We met at the restaurant." I reached for Desi's arm protectively.

"Blanco—" Chino began but was cut off.

"Don't be jealous, Chino," Birdie scolded.

"Jealous of what?" he mocked.

"Jealous that you invited her to the car show and what did she say?" Catrine teased Chino.

"I have to work!" Catrine and Birdie said in unison and proceeded to laugh in Chino's face.

He threw down the hose to the keg and stormed off.

"I'm not sure what to do here," Desi said, bringing us all back to the small circle.

"Nothing, he's just stupid," I said. "I'm glad you came."

"That's all that matters, then," Desi replied. We shared a look, and it felt like everyone had disappeared. It was just him and I, suspended in the moment. Julio coughed, and we broke our stare.

"I'm glad you came, Julio. I wasn't sure who would show up now that Brenda's gone."

Julio cackled and threw his arm around me, pulling him into a hug.

"Like we'd forget you just because you don't live that cholo life anymore. You'll always be one of us, homegirl."

"Cha Cha is always welcome back whenever." Birdie raised her hands in the air and began to dance.

"Cha Cha?" Desi snickered.

"Long story." I rolled my eyes.

"I'd love to hear it."

"Oh, well then." Catrine pointed her long fingernails at

Desi and smirked. "Let me tell you—" Quickly, I pulled Desi away from my old friends and back toward the house.

"Wait." Desi laughed. "I want to hear about Cha Cha."

I stopped once we were away from all the partygoers and reached for his hand. I laced my fingers in his and pushed them against his hard muscular chest. I leaned in and stood on my tiptoes to whisper, "Oh? I thought you'd rather see my room."

"Well, I suppose the story can wait."

I laughed and took a step back to direct us back inside when I heard my name.

"Scout!" I turned and squinted. Way in the far back part of my yard, someone was waving to me. It took a moment, but finally, I recognized that it was one of my foster sisters, Gigi. "Can we use this for the fire?"

"Wait here," I told Desi. "I'll be right back. I don't know what they are trying to burn."

"You want me to just stand here?"

"Go, socialize, have fun." I waved around the yard and hurried off before my friends tried to burn my garage down.

Desi would be fine for five minutes.

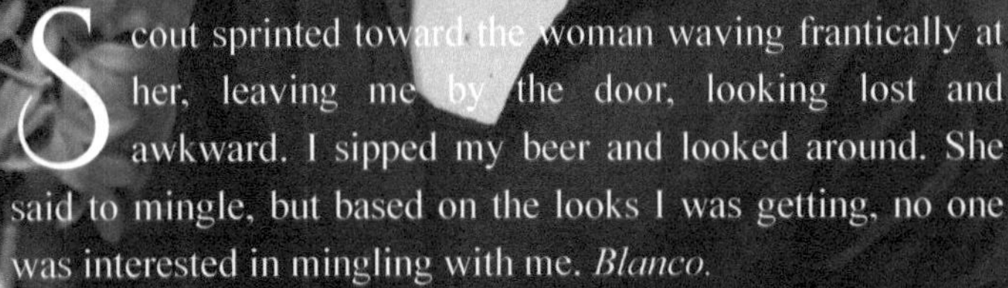

Desi

Scout sprinted toward the woman waving frantically at her, leaving me by the door, looking lost and awkward. I sipped my beer and looked around. She said to mingle, but based on the looks I was getting, no one was interested in mingling with me. *Blanco.*

Suddenly, the door behind me screeched open. "Oh, sorry!" I ducked out of the way. "Randy?" I blinked in confusion as my friend stepped out of the house.

"Desiderio? What are you doing here? Aren't you supposed to be—"

I slammed my hand over his mouth. "Shut the fuck up."

He batted me away. "Whatever, I get it. The party across town was a dud. Aleida didn't tell us it was a sex club."

"Don't say her name here," I pleaded. "I don't want to think about her. What are you doing here?"

"Tommy invited us after we got kicked out of Ale—" He cleared his throat when I glared. "The other party. It's pretty good. Did you get some pizza?"

I grimaced. "You ate that?"

Randy shrugged. "So why are you here, then? If you came here alone."

I took a sip of my drink. I could feel the heat rising in my face. "A friend invited me."

"A friend? Who? We're your friends." He pointed to his chest. "And we were already here."

I tightened my jaw. Already, the few lies I had created were coming back to bite me. I wasn't sure how to get myself out of this.

"Look," I started, but was interrupted by a tall redheaded woman coming up to us.

"You're the guy with the good weed, right?"

I thought she was talking to me, but she was looking at Randy. Randy glanced nervously at me and then nodded.

"You wanna smoke?" He reached into the top pocket of his jacket.

"Yes, please." She took his hand and pulled him away. "You can come too." She glanced at me with little interest. My lips twitched, and the strong need for a cigarette burned my throat. I grabbed the pack from my jacket pocket and shook my head.

Would Scout approve of my habit? I had never cared before if a chick hated my smoking. Aleida hated it. If Scout didn't like it, I'd quit.

Smoking relaxed me. It loosened me up enough to stop standing by the door and walk around a bit. Which helped the other guests relax in turn. I understood, though. I was different than them, and that made them uncomfortable.

It was obvious that we came from different worlds. I heard many people speaking in full Spanish as I walked by. While I wasn't fluent in the language, I remembered some of my high school Spanish. *Blanco* wasn't being used as a compliment.

Five minutes came and went. I wasn't sure what to do. I didn't want to be a sick puppy trailing after her. She told me to mingle. I could do that. I finished my cup and opted for another. I returned to the keg to find Chino and the girls from before still standing around it, along with a few others I didn't know.

"This is Scout's friend, Desiderio." Catrine smirked. I wasn't entirely sure what side she was on. Every time I caught her glance, she looked… hungry. But then every time she opened her mouth, she was mocking me.

"Friend?" One of the new men raised his eyebrows. "Since when?"

"We met a week ago," I explained.

"At the diner," Birdie added.

"You work there too?" He pointed.

"No, I was just eating there."

"Be nice, Chester," Catrine scolded, then looked at me. "Any friend of Scout's is a friend of mine."

"Wouldn't be the first time." Chino smirked.

I turned away, silently pleading for Scout to show up. "I'm going to go get some pizza," I lied and hurried away. It felt odd walking through her house without her, but I figured I'd go back up front and wait. As I walked through the hall, I paused to stare at the markings over the wall. It was… a mural.

The entire wall was a story. Two faceless lovers, entangled in each other. They were running from shadows. In between city buildings and cars, but the shadows kept chasing them. They ran until the woman collapsed, and then the man turned and decided to fight. But there was nothing there. The drawings promptly stopped.

"She's good, isn't she?" A man's voice startled me, causing me to come out of my hypnotic stare and turn.

"Who?"

"Scout. She draws all this shit."

"Scout drew this?" The razor-bald man with the dark goatee and long shirt nodded.

"She's an artist."

"Do you know her well?" I asked. My own insecurities were suddenly flaring. The way this man spoke so highly of her, as well as his good looks and Hispanic heritage, gave him a leg up on me. I was a stranger in her world. Why would she want me when she had all these guys fawning over her?

"We go way back." He licked his lips. "We all grew up in the same neighborhood. You?"

"We just met."

"I saw you outside, talking to Chino and Julio. They give you shit for being white?" This guy was blunter than the others, but I appreciated it.

"Some," I admitted. Not wanting to come off as a dick, I shrugged it off. "It's nothing I can't handle. So, Scout likes art." I tilted my head to the wall. "She go to school for it?"

"You mean like college? Only rich people do that." He patted my shoulder and smiled. "All good, homie, you don't gotta worry about me. I ain't your competition. Scout's like my little sister. They call me Mota." He licked his lips and eyed me up and down so quickly it made my muscles tighten. "And you don't gotta introduce yourself, because I know who you are."

I gulped. A million thoughts ran through my mind all at once. What was he going to say?

"Yeah?" I reached up and rubbed my neck.

"It took me a bit to figure out why you looked so familiar. And when I remembered, I knew I had to come and talk to you. I know your secret."

CHAPTER 14

Desi

"My secret?" I chuckled lightly, and Mota did the same.

"How you have the best weed on that side of town." He pinched his fingers and brought it to his lips, simulating a joint.

"Is that what they're saying now?" Relief washed over me. I stood up straight and dusted off my shoulder.

"That's what I'm saying. Desiderio Amato, you need a nickname. You can't keep going by all that," he chastised.

I do have one.

Desi.

But only Scout called me that.

"Maybe." I patted his shoulder. "You get to thinking, and I'll be back later to hear what you came up with."

"Names from Mota come at a price." He laughed again and brought his imaginary joint to his lips again.

"Sure. Find me later. I was in the middle of something. Probably don't mention this to Scout," I told him.

"You got it. Your secret's safe with me."

Worry settled into my gut. What would Scout say when

she found out I sold weed? I mean, out of all the things me and my family were involved in, marijuana was the tamest thing. Still, did I really need the extra cash? Not really. I did it out of pure boredom. I could stop selling if I had to.

I found more and more drawings all over that I hadn't noticed on the first walk-through. Scout drew faces so realistically it was hard to pull my eyes away. She was able to catch the emotion so vividly, it drew me in.

"When I said mingle, I didn't mean with my walls."

I turned to see Scout with a sly grin that made everything around us disappear.

"*Blanco* kept coming up every group I passed by outside. I thought I'd have better luck inside, where my skin wasn't as reflective of the moon."

Her beautiful brown eyes widened. "Desi, I'm so sorry. They just—"

I put my hands up and laughed. "No, I get it. I'd rather be made fun of for being pale than for my money," I answered honestly.

"Oh, Desi." She sighed. "I'm sorry I had to ditch you right when you got here. They were trying to burn stuff they shouldn't and then Gigi started throwing up so I had to hold her hair and—"

"Scout, it's fine. Seriously, this is your party. I get it. I'm just a guest tonight. I'm not going anywhere."

"Promise?"

"Promise. Now, you're an artist?" I motioned to the wall behind her, where a rather impressive portrait of Will Smith was drawn with pencil. She looked back and frowned. She brought her hand to it and rubbed his ear.

"People are smudging it."

"Scout, you're really good at this stuff." I pointed to the other walls. "You should be doing something with it."

"Ha, like what?" She scoffed. "I thought I invited you to a party. Not to talk about stuff that'll never happen. Come on, do you like this song?"

I raised my eyes to the ceiling to focus, trying to pinpoint the song. "Candy Rain."

"Is that your way of asking me to dance?"

She bit her lower lip, and I melted. I could dance all night with her. As I held Scout's hips, I thought back to an hour ago, where I was exhausted and hated the idea of dancing. Now, I didn't want to stop moving.

Most of the music I recognized, but every few minutes, a Spanish song came on and I was lost. Scout turned around during one and threw her arms over my shoulders. She began to sing along with the woman vocalist. I swallowed thickly. She was rubbing her body against mine, and it was sexy as hell.

"I didn't know you could speak Spanish," I shouted.

"I can't. It's easy to memorize the lyrics."

"Is this the girl you were telling me about the other night?"

"Selena!" she shouted, and the rest of the room followed in unison.

It startled me, which made her laugh.

We continued to dance, and I was surprised at how relaxed I became and started to enjoy myself. As the night went on, it grew hot, and Scout took off her flannel, leaving her in a shirt that barely covered her chest. A slow song came on, and I put my hands on her lower hips, and we swayed. She stepped closer, bridging the gap between us. She pressed her body against mine, and instantly, my cock stirred. My face flushed, and I tightened my lips.

Eventually, it went down, but she stayed close to me as another slower song played. The party began to die down.

People kept interrupting our dancing to hug and tell Scout goodbye. We gave up dancing, and I helped her clean her place. Bottles, cups, and trash items were scattered everywhere.

"You can go. I took tomorrow off so I could clean up."

"I've got no plans."

"I thought you had to work." She paused while holding a black trash bag. "Because you took tonight off."

I blinked.

Fuck.

"Oh, right. I guess I should go." I rubbed the back of my neck reflexively. "Maybe I'm more tired than I thought."

"All right, let me walk you out."

I wasn't tired in the slightest, but I slumped my shoulders some and lowered my gaze to appear as much. She took my hand and led me out of her home and to my car.

"Everyone was asking about your car." She chuckled. "I told them you charge for rides."

"Is that so? Do you think I could make a decent buck?"

"Absolutely. Off Chino the most, I bet." We reached my car. I stared down at her and wished I didn't have to go.

"I'm glad you were able to make it," she said.

"Of course. If you'll keep asking me around, I'll figure it out."

"At least our schedules are the same. Maybe we can start hanging out during the day."

My lips curved upward and hope swelled in my chest. "I'd like that. I feel like I've been creeping around. I'd like to just be… normal."

"Normal? What's that?"

A smile curved my lips. Oh, she had no idea.

"I like you, Scout," I confessed.

"But?" She raised an eyebrow and stepped back.

"No but. I like you. I… want you to like me…" I swallowed.

What was this teenage bullshit? Since when did I get nervous like this? She laughed and shoved my shoulder.

"Hey, cabron, I like you too. That's why I want to hang out."

"Well, ideally, I'd like to do more than just hang out," I blurted. Scout's face turned red as she gasped. I cringed and started to apologize but she popped on her tiptoes and caught my mouth in mid-conversation with her own. And my brain chemistry was altered forever. My life was altered forever.

Because she kissed me.

CHAPTER 15

Scout

Our lips locked, and my brain exploded. All of my nerves were on fire. Red and yellow stars sparkled behind my eyelids as I took in the taste of him. He tasted of beer and cigarettes. It was paired with something else I couldn't pinpoint, even later that night, but it was Desi.

That next day, I sat cross-legged in my living room. Cassettes were scattered all around me, while I held a notebook on my lap. On one side of me was my stereo, and on the other was my boombox with a blank tape loaded into it. I had just pushed play on my stereo and record on the boombox when there was a knock on the door. Before I could welcome them in, it opened and Catrine entered.

"I came to see if you needed help cleaning—what are you doing?"

"You messed it up!" I scolded and stopped the boombox, rewinding it to record again. "I'm making a mixed tape."

She came to sit with me, crossing her legs and picking up my Mariah Carey tape. "I love her voice."

I nodded and reached over to turn the volume on my

stereo down and push play. Mary J. Blige came through the speakers. It wasn't the right song anyway, I decided.

"It looks good in here. You cleaned all this already?"

"I had some help last night," I muttered, not looking at her.

"Oh? By that guy you brought around?"

"Don't start," I warned.

She put her hands up in innocence. "I'm not saying anything. Just that… he was interesting. It made Chino jealous. Me too a little," she confessed with a small giggle.

"Chino is only jealous because I'm the only girl who didn't jump in his truck the first time he looked at me."

"You could do worse than Chino. He has a big d—"

I interrupted her by covering my ears and singing loudly. "La La La, I can't hear you!"

She laughed, rocking and holding her stomach. "Fine. I'm just saying, don't knock all the other girls. But your new man must have something Chino doesn't, no?"

I grinned, recalling the kiss last night. I had wanted more than just a kiss, but still, this was all new and fresh. "He's really funny."

"Funny? I didn't see funny last night." She smirked.

I rolled my eyes. "And what exactly did you see?"

"Muy guapo." She grinned, causing me to blush. Then she added, "Pero un poco blanco." She pinched her fingers together.

He was white, and that was a problem. Maybe to her.

"Stop," I scolded. "You act like you've never seen a white boy in your life."

"Not with people like us," she said. "Don't try to deny it. We're both from the same neighborhood. I'm not saying there's anything wrong with—What's his name?"

"Desiderio," I reminded her.

"Desiderio." She nodded. "Just that it's different. People are…"

"People like Chino and Julio?" I accused. "Men who are simple-minded."

"Yeah, and men like yours that hate our community."

"Is this what you came over for?" I snapped. "To tell me that I can't go with a man that looks different?" I stood and pointed to the door. "Just go."

"That's not why I came. I was just trying to be a good friend and warn you."

"Warn me about what? That I might meet someone that likes me for who I really am? I'm sorry that you decided to sleep around and ended up with Julio, but that's not my problem."

"Please, we all know why you're interested in him. You looking for a rich daddy now, little orphan Annie?"

I fought the urge to rip the scrunchie from her head and smash her face into the wall. Tears stung my eyes as I pointed again to the door. "Get out. Don't come back. Any of you. I don't need you."

Catrine glanced around my nearly empty house and laughed. She reached for the door and opened it. "Ha! Sure. Get your rich white boyfriend to save your ass. I hope you don't end up on the news." She stormed out, slamming the door so hard it rattled the brittle windows of the house.

I screamed and dropped into my pile of cassettes. What was I doing? Was she right? Was I just interested in Desi because he had money?

No.

Of course not.

I recalled that first night I met him. On his birthday. I didn't know he had money. I'd never seen his car, or known about what schools he went to, and yet, I was crushing hard for him. The phone ringing in the kitchen pulled my attention back from everything that had happened in just a week. I got up and hurried to it, taking it off the wall. "Hello?"

"Scout?" Desi's voice came through the line, and my heart stuttered. "I, uh, I don't know why I called."

"Oh."

"No! Not in that way! Let me start over." He sighed. "I'm not good with this stuff."

I grinned. I could almost picture him, running his hands through his hair, looking erratic, his blue eyes shining with worry.

"I just called to say I had a fun time last night. I'm sorry for getting there so late."

"It's fine. I'm glad you came."

"You are?"

"Yeah. It meant a lot to me. I hope my friends didn't scare you off."

Former friends.

"No, not at all. I should probably learn some Spanish though."

"Don't worry about it. I barely know it myself. Just the dirty words."

"I wouldn't mind hearing them from your mouth," he said in a low murmur that sent a warm feeling to my belly. Silence flooded the line for a moment before he cleared his throat. I could almost see the blush in his cheeks from across town.

"I've got to work tonight, but I was hoping to see you soon. If that's okay?"

"I'd like that." I began to twirl the curly cord around my finger.

"When's your next night off?" he asked.

"Wednesday and Thursday this week. I usually work weekends. Better tips."

"Same here," he said quickly. "Busy time for movie perverts."

I still couldn't believe he worked at the dirty movie theater.

"How about Wednesday during the day?" he continued.

"Sure, what are we doing?"

"You like art, right? I know this guy…" he trailed off. "I wanna surprise you. You're gonna love it."

"What should I wear?" I asked.

"Just be yourself. I like you that way."

I couldn't believe that Catrine would come and try to say he was anything but perfect.

"Sounds great. See you then." I hung up and fell against the wall. I cradled the phone when it started to beep, and then squealed. We had a date.

Wednesday couldn't come fast enough. I worked my ass off at work. I took two extra shifts, not just to cover Brenda's side of the rent, but to have a little extra cash in case Desi wanted to go eat or something. I wasn't sure where he was taking me, but I wanted to be prepared. When I wasn't working at the diner, I was at home, trying to figure out what to wear and what else to put on the mixtape I was making for him.

I had filled one side and was working on the B-side, but nothing felt… right. I was worried I was overthinking what was between us. I had never felt this strongly about someone. The only person I could think about was Desiderio Amato.

Desi.

He had told me to dress normal, but this was our first date. I couldn't wear just anything. Was it even a date if it was during the day? We both worked the night shift, so it only made sense for us to see each other when we could, which was in the daytime. And, who knew, maybe our date would go into the night…

I wore a pleated black skirt and my favorite white baby doll shirt. The skirt went just under my belly button.

I put my hair up in the highest ponytail, letting my curls cascade down my back. Then, I spent an hour on my makeup, making sure I looked perfect. I had never put this much effort into a date before.

I was on pins and needles, waiting for him to come. He was late. I glanced at my watch. He said two. It was past three. Was he always late to things, or had I been stood up?

And then, a knock.

I flew to the door and opened it. Desi stood, wearing a leather jacket over his Iron Maiden shirt. His hair was styled and was freshly cut. He looked like he'd been sweating, but still, he was perfect.

"I'm sorry I'm late. I went and got a haircut and then there was an accident as I tried to get here. I was stuck in traffic for an hour." He let out a long breath and smiled. He looked me up and down. "You look great."

"Thanks." I slid a curl behind my ear. "Are we still going to… wherever?"

"Yes! Come on." He reached for my hand.

"Hold on, let me grab my keys. I'll meet you in the car." I locked up and turned to start down the path. Desi was standing behind his car with his hands on the trunk. He was leaning on it, looking down at the black paint. "Everything okay?" I asked.

"Yeah, of course. Ready?" He hurried to open my door. I climbed in, and he joined me a moment later. As soon as the car was on, he turned the music up and pulled out of my driveway, speeding off toward an unknown location.

"Do I get to know where you're taking me now?" I shouted over Whitesnake.

"No. Not until we get there. I promise it'll be worth it. Just tell me, red or white?"

"Red or white what?"

"Just pick one," he insisted.

"Red." I crossed my arms.

"Good. Me too."

He pressed on the gas and we went faster. REO Speedwagon's "Keep on Loving You" came on and Desi reached for my hand. My heart fluttered as he glanced over and began to sing the words. Soon, we pulled into the parking lot of a large white building.

"Greco's?" I read the sign on the front.

"It's a gallery," he told me as we climbed out of his car. He went around the back of his car and banged his fist on the trunk as he passed. Then he came over to me and put his arms around my waist. As if this was our movie moment, he pulled me to him and bent his neck. Our lips collided.

I hoped every kiss we had was like an explosion like the first two had been. So far, it was two for two.

He pulled away first and laughed. He wiped his lips, and a small trace of my red lipstick smeared across his hand. I pressed my lips together. Whoops.

"Worth it. You ready?"

"Can I fix my lipstick?" I asked, pulling the tube out of my purse quickly. I hurried to his side mirror and reapplied it. We made our way inside the building. Club music was pouring loudly from speakers all around us. The room was brightly lit, and we were met by a woman in all black, with a beret on her head.

"Hello, are you Desiderio Amato?" she asked him, barely sparing me a glance.

"I am. Philippe told you to expect us, I see."

"Yes. We are a night-only gallery, but Philippe makes exceptions for those he sees fit."

"I did him a favor." Desi's eyes grew dark. The lady was giving off a stuck-up air, and I understood his annoyance.

"Yes. Well, whatever it was, Philippe invites you to peruse and enjoy the exhibits. Would you like red or white?"

Desi and I exchanged a look, and he smiled at the woman. He put up a hand with two fingers. "Two red, please."

She nodded and walked away. Desi took my hand and began to lead me around the room, looking at all the art.

"I know nothing about this stuff," he admitted, rubbing his neck. "Is it any good?"

We stood in front of a collage, where the artist had taken clips of housewives from old magazines and graffitied words over her face.

"It must be to be featured in an exhibit." We walked, hand in hand, through the sculptures, paintings, and photographs. Everything had a general theme of vintage, with graffiti over it. I could do that.

"I wonder how much money people get for this stuff," I wondered aloud.

"Philippe's gallery does pretty well, I hear. So probably a lot."

The woman reappeared with a tray of cheese and crackers and two glasses of red wine. Desi took the glasses and gave one to me. He pointed to the blood-red liquid, and I under-stood now why he'd asked red or white in the car.

"Toast?" he suggested.

"To what?"

"I don't know. To our first date?" His eyes bored into mine. He was as nervous as I was, I realized. I clanked my glass against his.

"To our first date."

A young man in a gray suit came out of nowhere. "Desiderio! How are you enjoying your visit?"

"It's great. Thank you, Philippe, for allowing me to come visit during the day."

"Well, the sun's gone down now, we'll be opening soon to the public." Philippe gave him a look.

"You're the owner of this place?" I blurted. "You're so young."

"Twenty-seven." Philippe laughed. "Do you have a favorite piece?"

I nodded, and we began to discuss art. Eventually, when that conversation began to dwindle, the man turned to Desi.

"Were you able to do that favor for me?" he asked, digging his hands in his pockets. Desi paled. He cleared his throat and looked at the ground. "Yeah, I picked it up. I'll finish it tonight."

Philippe patted his friend on the back. "Good. Tell your parents I said hello." He reached out and hugged me, kissing me on the cheek. "Beautiful pair." He winked at me and walked away.

"What favor was it?" I pried.

"Nothing. He just made me pick up a package. I have to take it to the dump later." He reached for my hand. "You ready to get out of here? Maybe get some dinner?"

I nodded eagerly and finished my wine. "I'd like that. This cheese is too fancy for me. I need a burger. Do you want to stop at the dump first? We're gonna pass it," I said as we left the gallery.

He snickered. "On a date? Nah, I'll handle it later. I want to focus on you."

CHAPTER 17

Desi

Lies.

Lie after lie. I couldn't stop it. What other option did I have?

Hey, Scout, I have a fiancé that I'm supposed to marry once I turn into a vampire, but before I do that, I need to take care of the body in my trunk.

I couldn't tell her the truth. I'd lose her forever.

"Burgers and fries, you said?" I asked once we were back in the car. "You sure you don't want to do something more… datey?" I turned the car on.

"Like what?"

"I don't know. I know a guy who owns this nice Italian place. I can get a good table. They have live music and nice wine and—"

She cut me off with her hand in the air. "Actually, I'm not that hungry."

A flash of panic went through me. Was she reconsidering? Was she figuring it out? Of course not. It'd be insane for her to think that I was a member of a vampire family. I was still just a normal guy. That she knew, anyway.

"What? Why? I thought we—" I paused, looking for the right words. "Did I do something wrong?" I took my hands off the wheel and turned to her.

"I don't know how much money I have for a fancy place."

I sighed with relief.

"Scout, I—" Guilt creeped in. Money had never been an issue in any part of my life. "I don't want you to pay."

"I always pay my share," she protested. "I worked extra shifts at work just so I could."

"Yeah, but—" I gulped, trying to figure out what to say without hurting her feelings. Or pride. "I want to pay. Let me do this." We stared at each other for a long moment. Her face was hard and her mind made up, but finally, it softened.

"Okay."

I turned back to the wheel and put the car into reverse. "You're gonna love it. The food is amazing. My friend revamped the place when he took it over."

"You have a lot of friends," she remarked.

If only she knew.

"My family knows a lot of people," I said.

"Do you take all of your dates to fancy galleries and fancy dinners?"

"Tell me about your dating history," I said, changing the topic. "Is there anyone I should worry about?" I teased.

"What do you mean? You met them all at the party."

"All?" Faces flashed in my mind. All cold eyes and unfriendly greetings. "Oh. I didn't realize…"

She burst into laughter. I scowled and flipped her off. That only made her laugh harder.

"You're so easy. I wouldn't ask questions you're not prepared for."

"Come on." I rolled my eyes. "Tell me. What kind of guys have you dated in the past that have made you so…"

"So what?"

"Cautious?"

"I don't date often, but the ones I have were… from our neighborhood."

"You mean Mexican?" I decided to just say what she was trying to avoid.

"No! I mean, yes, some, most."

"I get it. I'll admit I don't get out much. I hardly ever came to your side of town before last week. But I'm glad I get to now."

"Really?"

"I am. Most of the girls I've dated were all the same."

"Which means?"

"The name means more than the person." My face darkened, despite my desire to stay upbeat and enjoy the day with Scout, anger was creeping its way in. I reached for the stereo and turned it up. Soon, we pulled up to the restaurant, and I helped her out of the car. We went inside and were greeted by a hostess in a cocktail dress. She looked at us and frowned.

"I'm sorry, but we don't have any tables."

"I have a standing reservation with Andre."

"He's not here right now, Desiderio." Her voice was cold as she looked from me to Scout. "And there's a dress code."

"I don't give a fuck about a dress code. I've come in before like this."

"Yes, but she hasn't. You know, now that I think about it." She paused to tap her chin. "I have seen you in here, haven't I?" The look in her eyes was like a douse of water on me. I didn't know her, but she knew me.

And she knew Aleida.

"Let's go, Desi. This is embarrassing." Scout tugged on my jacket.

"Yeah, let's go." I made a mental note of the hostess's appearance so I could call Andre later and ask that his hostess shut her fucking mouth. "Actually, a burger sounds good."

"And a beer?" Scout perked up. She was almost bouncing with happiness as we walked to the car.

"Beer sounds even better." I peeled out of the lot.

"I used to work at this place when I was a teenager. I used to get in trouble all the time for eating pickles out of the bin." She giggled.

"I can't wait to try it." The place was one where you parked and people on skates came to take your order. We got our food fairly quickly.

"Okay, now, beer run," she directed.

I drove us to a liquor store, and she insisted on going in. "You paid for the food. I'll get this." She came out with two six-packs and then we ended up at the park by her house, eating burgers and drinking beer while sitting on the table. We talked, laughed, ate and drank. Eventually, we were pretty buzzed, and stumbling out of the park.

"By the time I get you home and then walk back to my car, I'll be good to drive," I assured her. She paused by the car and suddenly we were kissing. One kiss turned into a second one, and our tongues entwined. We found ourselves in the backseat of my car. She straddled my lap, our mouths pressed together, while I explored her skin. She was so soft…

My hands roamed over her body, and I slipped under her bra and pinched her nipples. The groan that escaped her lips caused my cock to twitch, begging to be let out. All that stood between us was my jeans and her thin panties.

"Oh Desi," she groaned as I began to kiss and suck on her neck, moving down.

"Yeah?" I answered, as one of my hands abandoned her tit to slide under her skirt again. I pet her panties and found them damp.

Jesus Christ.

I slid them to the side and found her pussy smooth and freshly shaved. I was going to come without even being inside her. My fingers spread her lips apart, and I swirled her arousal around. She was drenched.

I had done that to her.

She wanted me.

"Oh god," she gasped as I slid over her clit and rubbed my thumb over it in small circles.

"You like that?" I asked.

She whimpered. I took it as a good sign and slid a finger inside her. Instantly, her body reacted. I began to thrust in and out, slowly, coaxing pleasure out of her. And then one finger turned into two, and I hooked them to find the spot I knew would send her over the edge. I bent down and nudged her shirt and bra away to take a nipple into my mouth. She gasped and I moved my fingers faster, needing to feel her release.

"Desi, Desi," she chanted my name in such a way that I realized this was all I needed. For the rest of eternity, just her gasping my name as she came.

"Come for me now," I demanded, nipping at the hardened bud in my mouth. A cry came from her body as she stiffened, and I dove my hand deeper, pressing on the soft button, dragging her orgasm out.

She was the most beautiful being I had ever seen. So surprised, so glowing, so completely undone. She fell against me, and I could feel our hearts banging against each other as if trying to get to the other. I closed my eyes and reveled in what we had just done. I didn't need to come. I could watch her do it forever.

Her breathing steadied, but neither of us moved for a long time. "I'm okay to drive. We should get you home."

She sighed and moved off me. "Yeah, you're right." We adjusted our clothes and climbed into the front seat. As I put the car into reverse, a loud thump came from the trunk.

"What was that?" Scout jumped.

"Nothing, just the dead body I have in there."

That was the first truth I told all night.

CHAPTER 18

Desi

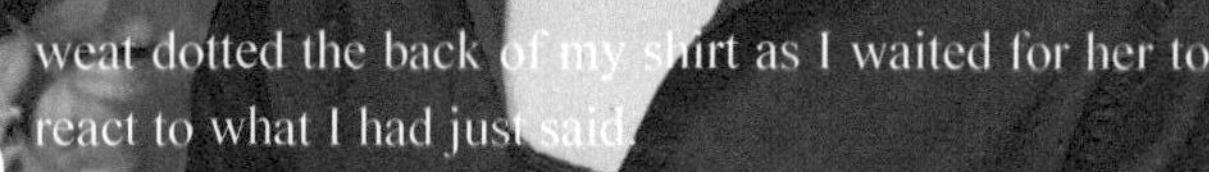

Sweat dotted the back of my shirt as I waited for her to react to what I had just said.

"A dead body?" Scout smirked. "Real tough guy, huh?"

Relief washed over me in such a way I almost dropped my hands from the wheel. I laughed and kept driving.

"Are you sure you don't want…" She placed her hand on my thigh and ran it along the inside of my jeans. The erection I had from finger fucking her in the backseat was gone after telling her about my trunk, but it began to stir from her quick touch.

"Watching you come all over my lap is fine for now." I reached down and strung my fingers through hers. "You make the sexiest faces, by the way."

"Stop." She blushed and pushed her hair behind her ear.

"Oh, now you're shy?"

"Stop!" The mood relaxed, and when I dropped her off, she offered to let me come in, but I refused.

"I would, but I want to take this slow," I said and shook my head. "I know, what happened in the car isn't exactly slow, but still, slower. I don't want you to run once you get to know me."

"Why would I run? Because you've got money? Or because of the dead body in your trunk?" She rolled her beautiful brown eyes. I never knew how much I loved that color of eyes before seeing them on her. Would she look just as good in the icy blue of a Bloodshed? No. That was blasphemous just to think. But they'd look absolutely stunning in Blood-born red.

"Yes."

"Well." She put her hands on my chest, and I savored the warmth before she pushed me off the stairs playfully. "Then let's take it slow. Good night, Desi. Thank you for today."

I stared at her for a long moment, praying that this wouldn't be the last time I saw her, but just in case, I still tried to memorize everything about her.

"I had a lot of fun. I'll call you soon." I turned and walked to my car. She stood on the porch and waited until I was out of the driveway before she went inside. I drove down her road and the few blocks after, and then raced to my parents' house. I turned my stereo up as loud as I went, blocking out all thoughts of before and now after, my date with Scout. Focus on the good.

She. Was good.

I drove through the gates of my parent's estate and followed the drive. The house was lit up, and I noticed my brother's car. *Good.* I'd need his help. I climbed out of my car and looked up at the house I had been raised in.

Until now, it had been rather unimpressive to me. It was just a house. Three stories, nine bedrooms, wings on both the second and third floors. Each of us kids having our own living area. We never had to share space, clothes, toys, or anything else. Everything we ever owned was new and the latest trend. We were privileged.

How had Scout grown up? Certainly not like this. She would make fun of me if she saw this. She would resent me. I couldn't ever let her see this part of my life. She'd never see me the same. I sighed, kicked off my car, and hurried up the tall stairs to go inside.

My sister, Caterina, was the first one I found. She was dancing all alone in the gallery. Judging by her movements, she was very drunk. I stuffed my hands in my pockets and waited for her to see me. It took longer than I would have liked. Her record player finally stopped, and she opened her eyes. She jumped when she saw me.

"Desiderio, what are you doing here?"

"I'm looking for Gianni. I saw his car out front."

"Why would I know where he is?" She scoffed. "Where's Aleida?" She looked around me as if she was behind me. "I haven't seen her since she turned."

"She's with her friends. She's become just as obnoxious as you, dear sister."

"You'll think differently once you've gone through the change." She shrugged. "He's probably with Daddy, in his study." It was my turn to roll my eyes. My sister was almost thirty, and still, she called our father *Daddy*. She was definitely more spoiled than I was. That thought made me happy, and I left her to dance to her Madonna records and drink more wine.

Our dad's office door was closed, so I knocked and waited for the invite.

A moment later, I heard my brother's sharp voice.

"Yeah?"

I opened the door and found him and both of our parents

sitting in chairs and sipping glasses of what looked like bourbon.

"Desiderio," my mother greeted me. "How are you?"

"I'm fine. Lounging in the office?" I questioned.

"Your brother had some good news he had come to share with us." Our father nodded to him, and the pair stood. I looked between the two. They looked so alike, both men of the same gene pool, frozen in time. In time, I too, would have my heart stop on my twenty-seventh birthday and join my family in vampirism. As did my siblings. But to see my older brother with red eyes and fangs, standing next to my dad who had always looked like that, was disheartening.

Did it have to be this way?

Was there a way to stay human?

To be with Scout?

"What's the good news?" I crossed my arms and forced a smile. I hated Gianni, just as much as he hated me. I didn't give two fucks about his news. But I needed his help, so I pretended to be interested.

"Gloria is pregnant."

"Pregnant? As in…" I struggled to even consider my brother becoming a father.

"As in a new bat baby into the Amato family!" Dad boasted! "Come, have a drink with us, Desiderio, and celebrate your brother's news!"

"Where is your wife?" I stepped forward as he reached for a glass on his bar and poured me a drink.

"Resting. She's been sick," my brother explained. I sipped the bourbon and faked enthusiasm for my brother's future child. My niece or nephew. What a thought. After an appropriate amount of time, I sat my drink down.

"Gianni, could I have you help me with something?" His expression darkened. However, he knew he couldn't say no in front of our parents, so he followed me outside. I went straight to my trunk and opened it. We peered down at it, and he whistled when he saw the contents.

"When was this?" he asked.

"Early afternoon. I needed a favor." I gulped.

"It's a big one. I didn't have my first until after I was already dead."

"Really?" I was surprised at that, as my brother was much colder than I was.

"Really," he confirmed. "Congratulations, I suppose. Cutting your fangs early."

"I'm not going to—" I grimaced at the thought.

Gianni snickered. "What a waste. His blood is poison now."

"Okay, so now what? What the fuck am I supposed to do with him?"

I hissed and pointed to the dead guy in my trunk. Gianni reached for the handle and slammed it shut, nearly catching my fingers.

"Welcome to the family, baby brother." He turned and started up the stairs, and without looking back, he added, "Figure it out."

"What's that?" Deanna asked me as she rounded the corner and saw me pinning up a flyer to the corkboard that sat just inside the doors of the diner.

"I need a new roommate." I had tried to figure out a way to financially cover the house myself, but I'd have to live at the diner to even attempt it.

"Did you paint the walls?"

"The room for rent? Yeah."

"What about the rest of the house?"

"Are you applying?" I asked.

"In that neighborhood? No thanks." She rolled her eyes. "No offense, but didn't your bike get stolen a few weeks back?"

It had.

"Are you looking for anyone specific?" she asked as we walked back into the restaurant. "I might know someone."

"Someone with a job, preferably. A legal job," I clarified, thinking about all of my former crew and the stuff they did to earn money. I didn't need my house raided while I was at work. Or worse, robbed.

"Man, woman, kids, no kids, pets, no pets?"

"It's one room, so no kids." I grimaced. "Dogs are fine."

"No cats?"

I shook my head.

"Perfect, I'll call my friend, Luis, he's been looking for a place, but he has a Rottweiler."

"A Rott?" Those things were huge.

"Brucey is super sweet. Gentle giant. He lets me cuddle him all the time. You'll love him more than Luis."

We went to the back and began tying our aprons on and putting our hair up. "I'll call him if I get a break tonight and see if he can come up here. You'll love him."

"Thanks," I said and hoped she was right. Having a roommate would be such a load off my plate. I could afford to eat again.

"So, tell me about your date. How did it go with Desiderio?" she asked as we walked to the hostess podium.

"It was amazing. He took me to an art gallery." My entire mood soared just thinking about him.

"An art gallery?" She cocked an eyebrow. "Fancy. Which one?"

"Greco's," I revealed.

"I know that place. Wait." She squinted. "What did you say he did again?"

"He works at the dirty movie theater. I know, it's an expensive place but he seemed to know the owner." I shrugged and looked at the hostess's chart. "We'll talk later," I told Deanna and started waitressing tables.

The monotony of taking people's orders and bringing them their food helped me forget about my financial worries for a little bit. Soon, three hours had passed in a blink. I was taking a quick water break in the kitchen when Deanna rushed in.

"Hey, Luis, your potential new roommate came to have dinner and talk to you. I'll cover you for fifteen if you want to go meet him."

"Already?" I gulped down my glass.

"Come on, I'll introduce you two." She led me out to the restaurant and to a table where a tall, bald, dark-skinned man sat. He looked up when we came by, smiled politely, and extended his hand.

"Scout, this is Luis. Luis, this is Scout."

"Nice to meet you." Luis spoke with a thick accent that I thought could be African.

"Luis is from Ghana," Deanna explained. "He came for college and just stayed." She grinned.

"College? What did you go to school for?" I asked, sliding into the booth.

"English. I'm a playwright."

My eyebrows shot up.

An artist?

I glanced at Deanna, who was grinning wildly.

"Do you want a Coke, Luis?" she asked.

"Yes, please."

She left us to talk.

"A playwright. That's impressive. Deanna said you're looking for a place?"

He nodded and folded his hands over the table. "I am. I haven't had much luck because of my dog, Brucey."

"I heard about that. Is he mean?"

His eyes lit up with almost a look of shock. "Oh no. Just large." He motioned with his hands. "Very large. But once he knows you, he will not harm you."

"What made you pick that breed?" I had met a Rottweiler

or two, and they were always scary. Barking and drooling so much their bodies shook. But those dogs had always been owned by people who wanted them to act that way.

"I wanted something to protect myself. You see, I'm..." He paused and leaned into the table. I did the same, curious as to what the seemingly kind man had to say. "I prefer the company of gentlemen." He watched for my reaction carefully.

"Oh. Okay." I smiled warmly. I didn't care, but I also understood why he'd want a little extra security.

"I've found that my dog keeps people away from me when I walk at night."

I knew exactly what he was referring to. There was so much hate in this world, and people were ruthless. He was right to have something to protect himself, but it didn't make it any less sad. Deanna came back with a pop and told me I had ten more minutes. I cleared my throat and returned to the interview.

"Do you have a job?"

"I do. I currently work at Catalina Private School across the town. I teach Great Literature."

Catalina was where Desi went to school. I remembered.

"You like it there?"

"It has its benefits. It is helping to pay my bills and save for my citizenship. I'm this close to becoming a United States citizen," he boasted proudly.

"That's great, Luis." I was sincerely happy for him. Something about him just radiated positive energy, and I was already loving it. To imagine it at my house all the time? Yes, please.

"I have a one bedroom for rent. We share all the bills, right down the middle. Food can be negotiated. If you want to go half or separate. I like to draw, and my art is all over the walls. Except your room, of course." I paused to smile.

He was nodding eagerly, so I continued.

"Take care of your dog's mess naturally. I'll try to keep it down so you can sleep at night. I work the night shift." I raised my arms and motioned around me. "I'll be quiet coming in."

"And I will be at work while you sleep!" he added excitedly.

"Yes!" I slapped the table. "Exactly! Why don't you come over on my next day off and you can tour the place?"

We made plans to do so. I shook his hand just as Deanna returned to take his food order. When she returned to the kitchen, she was dancing.

"I told you I knew someone. What do you think?"

"He's incredible. Perfect. Thanks so much, Deanna."

"Anytime, girlie. Plus, you'll need Luis and Brucey there now that you've got a boyfriend in the mafia."

"The what?"

"Why are you trying to ruin this for me?" I sighed, wiping down a table that had just been bussed.

"I'm not!" Deanna protested with a smile plastered on her face. "It's just… tell me I'm wrong." She put her hand on her hip and stared at me from across the room where she was mopping. "He's got money. He's Italian, you know, because of the weird name. Then he did his friend a favor?" She put up air quotes with her fingers. "What favor?"

"I don't know, maybe he got him a private viewing at the theater or something. You always do this." My shift was almost over, and I was exhausted. "You get these crazy ideas and then ruin things for me."

"When was the last time?"

"Uh, I don't know." I laughed. "Maybe when you were convinced Prince had come in wearing a disguise."

"It looked just like him!"

"It was a woman with a mustache!"

"Okay, but all the purple? Come on, that was an easy mistake."

"Not for everyone else in the restaurant," I reminded her.

"Fine, whatever, but I'm not wrong with this one. I know that gallery. It's a front. That's why it's only open at night."

"Or it's just upscale," I suggested. "Who knows what rich people do."

"Rich people in the mafia." She wagged her finger in the air. "Mark my words." She put her hands up in innocence. "Do what you want. He is extremely good-looking, but I think he's too good to be true."

Desi did feel like a dream. He was perfect, in every way. Well, except for being late all the time.

"If it will make you happy, I'll ask him about the favor," I offered.

"Hey, it's not me I'm worried about. Just be careful. He's hiding something."

I thanked her, even though I didn't mean it. Then, I glanced at my watch and saw I could clock out. I hurried to change and get moving. I wanted to take a hot shower and relax in bed. As I was stepping off the steps of the diner and pushing play on my Walkman, I thought about the conversation with Deanna again. It was absurd. Desi, in the mafia? Never. He was too adorable to be a criminal. He wouldn't hurt a fly. Or would he?

I brushed those thoughts away and focused on The Gap Band singing "You Dropped a Bomb on Me". I gripped the straps of my backpack and started home.

Maybe once Luis moved in, I could start saving for another bike. And two chains with locks this time, instead of just the one. Riding a bike saved me half an hour each way every day. And my poor feet.

I tossed and turned in bed and woke up at ten-ish, still tired. There wasn't enough coffee to revitalize me this morning. Still, I drudged to the kitchen to brew a pot to try. I was sitting at my table, sipping my coffee, when there was a knock on my door. I went to it, still dressed in an oversized teal shirt and cotton shorts. My hair was a mess of curls and I hadn't done my face yet, but I was too tired to care about who was on the other side. I opened the door and immediately regretted my previous opinion on my appearance. Desi was on the other side with a brown cardboard box under his arm.

"Hey! You look tired."

I ground the sleep from my eyes. "Little bit. Long night at work. What are you doing here?" I asked, stepping back to let him in. I tugged at my clothes but sighed. It was too late. He had already seen me looking rough. *And he still came in.*

"Well, that was kind of what I was here about. Work. It sucks, doesn't it?" He went straight to my kitchen. "It smells good in here."

"You want a cup? I don't have any sugar or cream." I prayed he wouldn't take liberties and look inside my empty fridge.

"Sure, black is fine." He set the box on the table. "I got you something."

"You got me something? Why?" I poured him a cup of coffee and set it on the table for him.

"Well, I tried to call you last night, and it just rang and rang."

"That's what it does when no one is home to answer it."

"Yeah, but with our schedules, that sucks. I want to be able to talk to you whenever."

"About what?" I said as he pulled out packing peanuts.

"About anything. Like, yesterday, I was bored…" He looked up from the box and shrugged. "You know at my job. So I called to talk about if you preferred Freddy Kruger to Jason Vorhees, but you weren't here." He pouted, making my irritation at him gifting me something completely wash away.

"I would have told you Kruger." I reached for my cup and took a sip. "So, what's your solution then?"

He pulled out a black plastic thing with wooden paneling, and I nearly spit out my drink. "Desi, that's—"

"An answering machine!" He beamed.

"That's a ridiculous gift! Do you know how much those are?" I set my cup down and grabbed it from him. Brenda and I had seen these in the store. I couldn't afford that.

"I do, as I just bought it this morning." He put his hands in his leather coat and rocked on his boots. "Do you like it?"

"No. I can't take this." I shook my head and pushed it back toward him. "This is too much. I could never afford this."

"I know, that's why I'm gifting it to you." He was smiling until he saw my reaction to his words. "Scout, that's not what I meant." He set the machine down and tried to reach for me, but I stepped back.

"Desi, this is too much. You spent all that money, just to tell me you like the Halloween movies more than the Friday the 13th series?" I shook my head in disbelief.

"Yeah, I did. I don't know why, but I want to share everything with you. It sucks that we can't just talk all day."

I wanted to be annoyed, but his intentions were so sweet, I couldn't be mad. I shook my head and waved him on. "Set it up."

"Great! There should be directions somewhere in here," he muttered. I sat in my chair as he hooked up the new machine. He spent the entire time going on and on about how excited he was that he would be able to talk to me whenever even if I'd have to catch the messages later. And I sat there, watching and wondering.

What if he's in the mafia?

CHAPTER 21

Desi

"It's getting late." I looked out Scout's kitchen window. Sadness began to sink in just as the sun was —slow and eventual. "I need to get going."

"Yeah, I have to get ready for work." Scout scrunched up her nose. "What time are you going into the movie theater?"

Every time she mentioned the little lie I had told her about what I did at night, I died inside. I had to figure something out. I couldn't keep lying to her about Aleida.

"Uh—" I racked my brain, and then coming up blank, I looked at my watch. "In about a half hour."

"Oh!" Her brown eyes widened. "You need to go!" She stood from the couch we'd been relaxing on. She pulled me up and started shoving me out. "You're going to be late!"

"I've got time."

"No, you don't," she insisted. She went to her front door and opened it. "Come on, I'll walk you to your car."

Reluctantly, I went to the kitchen to grab my coat and headed out with her. We walked down the broken path to my car, and I paused, leaning against it. My hands went to her hips and I pulled her into me as if I couldn't survive without touching her.

"I had fun today."

"Just sitting at my house?"

"Yeah, I mean, that's all I do at my place."

Not a lie. Not an entire lie at least.

"I guess I'll see when you start calling me and leaving me messages." She grinned. "Thank you again."

"Of course. It was more for me, I think, but still. I like being able to do things for you." It was a nice change of pace. None of the other girls I'd been with ever needed things. They were all spoiled rotten. The look on her face told me I had made a mistake.

"What?" I asked.

"I don't need you to do things for me."

"I know that." The tense moment passed almost instantly. "I don't want to go," I confessed, thinking about what was waiting for me once I left. A miserable night, with my fingers twitching, itching to call Scout, and avoiding Aleida as best as I could.

"Work needs you," she said and then cocked her head as if wondering how true that statement was. "How else will dirty old men get their rocks off tonight?"

"I'm doing the lord's work, really." I saluted and hugged her.

"Did you get that body in your trunk taken care of?" she asked.

"What?" My heart stopped for a second.

"The other night, remember? Something was rolling around back there that made a loud thump." She nodded to my car.

I forced a laugh. "Oh, right. Yeah, he's not in there anymore."

"What'd you do with him?"

I decided to tell her the truth. It was ironic, considering that the stuff she wouldn't believe was the only thing I was being honest about. "I have a buddy who knew about a pig farm a few towns over. Drove over there, tossed him in. Took fifteen minutes."

"Perfect," she crooned, then stood on her tiptoes to kiss me. "I can't imagine you hurting a fly, let alone disposing of a body."

If only she knew.

"All right." I chuckled. "I probably should go. Tickets aren't going to sell themselves, and believe it or not, randy men get really hungry during the movie. I go through so much popcorn."

She giggled, which made my heart soar. I gave her one last kiss, taking my time to savor and taste her lips. I inhaled deeply, trying to keep the smell of her perfume in my nostrils as long as I could. Finally, she stepped back, and I got into my car.

"I'll call tonight and test your new setup." I winked as I turned the car on and pulled out of her driveway. On my way home, I chose to go the long way, and in doing so, I passed the movie theater I was pretending to work at.

Maybe I should apply. Would it be terrible to get a job? It'd be terrible to lose Scout because of a stupid lie. I just found her.

I decided to ruminate on the idea and head home. By the time I pulled into my driveway, the sun had long since fallen, and it was night. Disappointment and panic shot through me as I saw Aleida's bright red '94 Mustang in my driveway. The top was up, so I couldn't see until I parked beside her, whether or not she was inside it. I turned the car off and turned to look.

Hello, Aleida.

She leapt out of her car, and I moved out of mine.

"What are you doing here?" I asked. Despite it being the middle of the week, she was wearing a mini dress and her hair was done up in a way that made it look like she was on her way to the club.

"I haven't seen my fiancé in a few days." She rolled her eyes and made her way to my car, her heels clicking on the cement. "I missed you." She tried to hug me, but I shoved her off and wiggled my keys. Despite living way across the town from Scout and her friends, paranoia made me aware of my open yard.

"Let's go inside," I muttered and brushed past her. She followed behind me, and only when we were safely inside my house did I relax some.

"Why are you so stiff? You've been acting odd since I got back from Vegas."

"What do you mean?" I went to the kitchen to fetch a beer.

"Where have you been?"

"I was hanging out with the guys. You know, while I still can." I turned and popped the cap of the bottle. She crossed her arms. Her blood-red eyes were looking me up and down, analyzing me. Could she smell Scout on me? Vampires' senses were enhanced, and Scout and I had spent a large portion of the day entangled in each other on the couch.

Fuck.

"You don't smell like weed or beer," Aleida noted, confirming my worries.

"I'm sorry? You hate the smell of weed."

She scrunched up her nose and looked around my place. Despite my use of candles and the cleaner that came once a week, I couldn't get the smell of weed out of this place.

"Whatever, keep your secrets. It won't matter in a year. I just came to ask how it felt."

Flashes of that night in my car, when I finger fucked Scout's perfect pussy, flew through my mind and made my hand shake.

"How what felt?"

Glorious.

I hadn't even gotten my cock wet, and it was easily the best sexual experience I'd had to date. But that wasn't what she was asking about. Laughing, she strode over to me, placing a long, painted finger on my cheek. She slid it down my jawline and popped my parted mouth shut.

"I heard that you killed Lawson Loren." The grin that curved her red lips turned my blood cold. She flashed her fangs and her red eyes glinted. "I want to know everything."

CHAPTER 22

Desi

"I don't want to talk about that." My mood shifted, and I could feel the heat in my cheeks. I took a sip of my beer.

"Why not?" Aleida stepped back and threw her hands up. "It's exciting! I didn't kill until after I turned, but hey, what does it even matter?" She spun around and laughed.

She hopped around my kitchen in her heels and the tight mini-dress. Just weeks ago, I'd have bent her over the kitchen table and shoved her panties down to bury myself deep inside of her. Now, my cock didn't even twitch.

"Seriously, it's no big deal. I'm hurt you didn't tell me." She turned back to me and pouted.

"There isn't anything to tell." I shrugged. "A guy needed a favor."

That guy being myself.

"Who?" She demanded.

The more lies I put out into the world, the harder it'd be to remember them. There was no harm in her knowing. "Philippe Greco."

"That's weird. Why would he come to you for a favor?"

I finished off my beer and set it in the sink. I grabbed another one from the fridge and then started out of the room. In the living room, I pulled a slim, wooden box from under the couch.

"I probably wasn't his first choice." I opened the box and pulled out a pre-rolled joint. I took the lighter from my pants pocket and lit it quickly. I sat back and reached for my remote.

"I wonder why Gianni didn't take the job." She came to sit beside me. Her hand went to my thigh, and I jerked away almost instantly. "Don't tell me you're jealous of your brother."

I took a hit of my joint and offered it to her. She stuck out her tongue.

"I have no real feelings for Gianni, jealous or otherwise."

"I bet you'll be more bloodthirsty than him or any of your family."

Was that meant to be a compliment?

"It was just a job. Nothing more."

"Job!" She laughed and tried to slide her hand along the inside of my thigh again. I moved away while in the middle of another hit of my joint. I blew the smoke in her face, which I knew would get her to move. "Ugh! You jerk!"

It wasn't cool, but I didn't like her touch. Not anymore.

She shifted away. I turned my TV on and began aimlessly scrolling. I found a rerun of *Quantum Leap* and settled on that. I wasn't a huge fan, but it was a distraction.

"So, if you're taking on those kinds of jobs now, does that mean you'll stop with that?" She pointed to the weed.

"I'm not taking those jobs. It was a one-time thing. And I'm considering quitting altogether," I said, taking a bigger hit, and coughing afterward.

"You? Giving up weed? That would be a dream. I'd be more impressed if you hadn't just gotten high."

"It relaxes me." I snuffed out the joint in my ashtray.

"I know other ways to relax you," she purred and leaned in again.

"I'm not in the mood." I put my hand up.

"How?" Her seductive kitten tone instantly changed to a sharp and pissed-off tiger. "You can't go that long without me."

"I did before I met you," I pointed out.

"Are you feeling guilty for killing him or something? Sweetie, it's perfectly natural for us." She ran a finger down my face. "In fact, it's kind of sexy for you to be diving into death before you've turned."

I brushed her away.

I didn't do it for you. I did it for Scout.

She scooted closer, and despite my annoyance, I didn't push her away. She wrapped her arms around me, using her vampire strength to keep me in place. She kissed my cheek and then moved to nibble and suck on my earlobe. I closed my eyes and tried not to tear myself away too fast. I didn't want to lose my ear.

"Tell me about it," she whispered into my ear.

"About what?"

"How you killed Lawson Loren."

I hadn't been able to talk to anyone. Gianni was completely uninterested in helping me when I asked, so I had to figure it out on my own.

"I followed him. Starting at a deli uptown. Then, he went to work at an office."

"You waited all day?"

"No, just until lunch. He had parked his car in a carport. I jiggled the window down and unlocked the door. I waited in the passenger's seat until he came to take his break."

"Then what?" Aleida stopped nibbling my neck and turned to rubbing my shoulders.

It was as if I were back in his car, reliving it so vividly. My vision glazed over as I recalled how I took someone's life.

"I put the gun to his head, and I asked him if he knew why I'd been sent."

"Did he?"

"He had suspicions," I confirmed. "He listed a number of people, including Greco. He asked how much I was being paid. I told him it didn't matter, and then I cocked the gun and shot him."

He'd slammed into the side of his door, blood smeared all over the windows. I'd stared at him for a long time before I moved. I was waiting to feel something. But… I didn't.

"You shot him in the car?" Aleida pulled her hands away and gasped. "And no one noticed?"

"I had a silencer and it was an empty garage."

Just our two cars.

"Then what?" She put her hands in her lap like a child, eagerly listening to a fairy tale.

"I put him in my trunk, and when night fell, I took him over to that pig farm. Tossed him right over the fence." That was the only moment I wondered if I would be able to kill when I became a vampire. The sound those pigs made while consuming the man was… nauseating.

"I never knew it worked."

"More or less." I shrugged and reached for a cigarette in my case on the table. "I think there were some parts left. But it was too dark to get a good look." I lit it and took a drag.

"You are incredible." Aleida sighed, and before I could

protest, swung her leg around and straddled me. I stiffened as she ground into me. My hands remained outstretched, holding a lit cigarette as she put her arms around my neck and tried again to get me to show her affection.

I couldn't.

It was like looking at Lawson Loren.

Nothing.

"You're going to be an incredible vampire, Desiderio. And I'm going to revel in being your wife."

I groaned. Before, I would avoid thinking about it, as it sounded incredibly dull to me. Now, it was terrifying to imagine.

"But," she continued. Despite my attempts to move my head, she kissed me on the lips. "Until then, I'm going to have some fun."

"What does that mean?" I asked.

"It means that if you won't fuck me, I'm going to find someone who will." She stood and stormed out of my house.

CHAPTER 23

Scout

The red light was flashing when I got home. I desperately wanted to push the phone button and hear Desi's voice, but I wanted to wait. To savor his words, whatever they were. I showered and changed into an oversized shirt and shorts before returning to the kitchen to playback the messages I had.

A moment later, his voice came through the speaker.

"Have you seen this new show, *The X-files*? It's pretty freaky. We should watch it together sometime. A new episode every Friday. Do you always work Fridays?"

Beep.

"What do you do when you're not working? I like to watch movies. I also go to concerts and hang out with my buddies. You've met them. Do you have friends that you hang out with?"

Beep.

"I'm so fucking bored."

Beep.

"You work weekends. I get it. What about holidays? Do

you do anything for those? My family doesn't really do dinners. Maybe you and I could do something?"

Beep.

"Am I getting ahead of myself with the whole holidays thing? I'm not trying to scare you away, I just thought it could be fun. Do you like pie?"

Beep.

"Okay, so maybe I'm scaring you. We don't have to talk about this unless you bring it up. I'll eat just about anything, though."

Beep.

"No, actually. I lied. Not a fan of cinnamon."

Beep.

"When's your next day off? I kind of miss you already. Is that too cheesy?"

Beep.

I pushed rewind and played the messages again. And again. And again. I laughed every single time. I understood now why he wanted me to have the answering machine. I missed him too.

Eventually, the kitchen chair grew too uncomfortable, and I went to bed. I had to wake up early to meet with Luis, who was coming to check out his room.

I dreamed of Desi's words and imagined a life where I cooked him Thanksgiving dinner and baked him Christmas cookies. I had grown up in the system. I was lucky if I had a bed, let alone presents and cookies and Santa Claus. As an adult, I'd struggled weekly. Brenda or whoever I was living with at the time would always invite me to their family holidays, but it wasn't the same as having your own family traditions. I was never comfortable at those things anyway.

I'd like a small Thanksgiving.

Just Desi and I, with a small turkey and potatoes and pie.

No cinnamon, of course.

I woke up to my alarm blaring in my ear. In my dream, he had been hanging out at the diner again while I worked. I sat up and stretched, then looked toward my jar.

Art school.

I don't even know why I started that damn jar. Just looking at it made me depressed, so I stood and got ready to meet Luis. He was coming in an hour. I tossed up my hair and tidied up my bedroom. I had a habit of throwing clothes around when I was getting ready for things.

Like dates with Desi.

Shortly after lunch, a red Ford Escort pulled into the drive. I waved as Luis stepped out of the car, followed by a humongous dog. The Rottweiler, while looking absolutely terrifying, bounced next to his owner.

"This is Brucey." Luis grinned. "I figured you should meet him right away to see if you like him or not." The dog and I stared at each other. He was almost as tall as I was.

"Can I give him treats?" I asked nervously, not taking my eyes off Brucey.

"Of course! Do you have any?"

"No." I frowned. "But we can keep some in stock. My last roommate left her cookie jar here. We can fill it up and use it for him." I reached my hand out and slowly brought it closer to the dog's snout. He sniffed it and then licked me, causing both Luis and I to let out sighs of relief.

"Why don't you guys come inside and check out the place?" I stepped away from the door to let them in. "It's not much. And I work evenings, so if you want to have guests, I won't be around."

"Where is the room I'd be renting?"

I pointed and led him to Brenda's old room. "We did paint

her room for the next person. As you can see, you can decorate. Paint, wallpaper, or you know, scribble."

"I see that." He laughed and nodded. "I have a cage for Brucey. Where could we put that?"

I looked down at the dog who had been following us diligently.

"What size cage would fit him?" Still cautious, I reached down and petted his back. He stiffened, then relaxed once he realized I wasn't going to hurt him.

"It's quite big, but it's necessary for guests. Is there space?"

"Let's check the kitchen." I took him through the rest of the house. "If we move some stuff around, I think we can put it here." I looked at Luis as I waved at the space where I currently had a shelf and the trashcan.

"That should work, thank you."

The phone rang, causing us to startle. "It's fine, I have an answering machine." To get away from the loud ringing, I took him to the living room. "As you can see, there's not much here. You can bring in whatever you want to decorate."

"You really like to draw," he said, looking around the room.

"I know, the landlord says as long as I paint before I leave, I'm—" My words were cut off by a loud beep from my answering machine. Luis and I exchanged a look as a moment later, the person spoke.

"Hey, it's me. Maybe I'm overthinking things. Am I being too presumptuous that you would want to spend the holidays with me? I know we just met, but I mean, I did finger-fuck you in my backseat the other night. Should we have waited? Call me."

CHAPTER 24

Scout

"Do you want to call him back?" Luis was trying so hard not to laugh in my face.

"It can wait," I said through flaming cheeks. The phone rang again, and I flew to it.

"Stop calling!" I hissed as soon as I picked it up.

"Hello?" a female's voice said into the phone.

"Oh, I'm so sorry!" I closed my eyes and took a deep breath. "Who is this?"

"It's Deanna, why are you so jumpy?"

I relaxed. "Sorry, I've just got Luis here and…" I took a step back to look at him in the other room. He was looking around, pretending not to listen. "I'll tell you at work tonight."

"When does he move in?"

"Let me ask." I put my hand over the receiver and called to Luis. "When do you want to move in?"

"I have to pack, but I'll be ready by next weekend if you are."

I gave him a thumbs-up and returned to the phone call. "Next weekend. Look, I gotta go. We'll talk later."

"Okay, fine, but just know I have gossip about your mafia boyfriend."

"Don't call him that. I'll see you tonight." I hung up quickly and returned to Luis.

"Do you get calls like that a lot?" Luis smiled.

"Deanna? Sometimes."

"No, the other one." He rubbed the back of his neck sheepishly. I covered my face with my hands.

"Absolutely not. I just started seeing this new guy and he's…" I lifted my head and rolled my eyes. How could I describe Desi? "He's crazy in the best way."

"Sounds like it." Luis grinned. "So, everything is split down the middle?"

We went to the kitchen where I brewed some coffee.

"I share food, but if you don't, that's fine. Maybe put your name on it though?" I shrugged. Brucey had to go to the bathroom, so I took that opportunity to show them the backyard. Brucey was more than happy with it. He did his business and then ran around in loose circles.

"He doesn't get the opportunity to run around a lot where we currently are."

"Well, consider this space his." I beamed.

After an hour, Luis decided he had seen what he needed to and we made plans for him to move in. I shook his hand, and he started to his car. He put Brucey inside and they started to leave. Just as he was pulling out of my driveway, a police car turned onto our street and crept to a park in front of my house.

Luis looked at me with raised eyebrows, and I made a gesture to tell him I had no idea what was going on. He drove away, watching the house. I groaned. First Desi, and now this? Could this short meeting have gone any worse? Two policemen stepped out of the vehicle and started up my drive.

"Can I help you, officers?" Growing up in the system had hardened me against law enforcement. The people who were meant to keep us safe were often the ones doing the most hurt to us.

"Yes, are you Scout Smith?"

I scrunched my nose up at my last name. Given to me by the state when they found me. My brown eyes, black hair, and tanned skin fit the Smith name apparently.

"Yes, that's me," I replied curtly.

"We wanted to ask you some questions about last Wednesday. Do you mind?"

I nodded.

"Where were you that evening?" The policeman to the left pulled out a small notebook.

"What does this pertain to?" I asked.

"Just answer the question." The second policeman sighed.

"I was out. I came home sometime in the early morning."

"Were you out with someone?" They both looked up at me, and the expressions on their faces told me they already knew and were looking to see if I'd lie.

"Yes. I was."

"And who would that be?"

"I had a date with Desiderio Amato," I declared.

"Where did you two go?" the policeman with the pen asked while writing.

"We went to a gallery and then dinner. He took me home after."

"That's all?"

"Yes."

"How long have you been seeing each other?"

"Is there a reason you're asking? Was a crime committed?"

"We have a missing person case, and we have a reason to believe Desiderio Amato might be involved."

"Who went missing?"

"Lawson Loren. A middle-aged man. Brown hair, average build, average appearance. Does that name ring any bells?"

"No, none."

The policeman on the right pulled out a business card and offered it to me. "If you happen to hear about Mr. Loren, consider giving us a call."

"He's missing?"

"For now. His family seems to think he had gotten caught up in some things he wasn't supposed to. He was a gambler."

"This sounds like a bad mafia movie." I laughed.

They didn't.

I rolled my eyes and waved the card. "Got it. If I hear anything about someone sleeping with the fishes, I'll give you a call."

"I wouldn't be so careless, Miss Smith," the policeman to the right said. "The Amato family and their associates have been rumored to be involved in many dark things."

"Got it." I gave them a thumbs-up and waited for them to leave. I locked my door after they took off. I tossed the card on the kitchen table and looked around. I needed to find a place to put that shelf if Brucey's cage was going to be in the kitchen. I went to work trying to move that on my own and discovered after cleaning everything off that it was way heavier than I originally thought. It nearly crushed me when I tried to move it. I quickly abandoned that idea and pushed it back.

A knock pulled my attention to the front door.

"Hey!" I opened it to find Desi.

"Hey." He smiled back. "I, uh…" He reached up and

brushed his hair back. He did that when he was nervous. Which was often. "Did I go overboard last night?"

"Last night?" I crossed my arms. "No. This morning, a little bit." I sighed. "I had someone over, and he heard the entire message."

"He?" His eyes darkened, and he looked over my head into the house.

I stepped back and let him in. "My new roommate. He was checking out the place to see if he wanted to rent the room. Your message did not help." I went to the kitchen. "You have perfect timing. Can you help me move this?"

"What is this?" The sharp tone in Desi's voice caused me to pause and turn back to him. He was holding the cop's business card.

CHAPTER 25

Desi

I stared at the card. She had spoken to a police officer? When? Had they come here, or had she gone to them? So many questions pounded in my head as the blood rushed in my ears.

"Two officers came by. I didn't tell them anything," she swore. Her eyes were large and the fear on her face was evident. "Desi, I don't know what's going on."

I crumpled up the card and shoved it in my pocket. "Nothing is going on. Just some cops trying to harass me." I took a deep breath, steadying myself. "I'm sorry they came here."

"It's fine." She crossed her arms. "They were just asking about our date, but I kept it short."

"What exactly did they want?" I tried my hardest to be invested in the conversation without looking too insane.

"There's some guy missing. Maybe it's the dead guy in your trunk," she said in a playful tone.

I didn't share her joke.

Her smile dropped.

"Desi?"

The word echoed in my head. The word that had given me such joy in such a small amount of time, *Desi*, was now ruined.

"Desi, why aren't you laughing?" Her voice sounded so far away. As if we weren't even in the same universe. She took a step back, causing me to step out of it. I forced a half smile, but it was too late. She had seen past my veil. She knew the truth without me having to tell her. Her eyes flicked away from mine. She looked at the round table.

There was a fraction of a second where we were both frozen, watching the other. She moved, and I launched for her. She flew around the table, and I followed behind as fast as I could. She reached for something on her countertop and I heard the telltale sound of a knife being pulled from the block.

"Stop!" I cried out, arms outstretched, trying to grab her, but she was quick, and ran from the room. I fell to the floor but caught myself and leapt up. "Scout!"

"Don't come near me!" She walked backward into her living room, watching me with large, terrified eyes. She thrust the knife in my direction with shaky hands.

"I'm not going to hurt you. Calm down." I spoke slowly, trying to relax her. It didn't.

"Why didn't you laugh?" she demanded. "Was there really a dead body in your trunk?"

One.

Two.

Three.

"Yes."

Tears slid down her cheeks. Her chin trembled. "You killed someone?" she asked so softly it was almost as if she was afraid to hear the answer.

"Yes."

"Why?"

How could I tell her the truth? That I had ended some-one's life so that I could take her on a date.

"I don't want to tell you," I answered honestly.

"Why did you kill that man the police are looking for?" she repeated her original question.

"You're just going to yell at me!" I threw up my hands.

"You're afraid I'm going to get mad?" She stared at me as if I were the insane one. "Desi, I'm so far beyond mad right now."

"What are you?" I asked, trying to gauge where her head was at.

"I'm fucking afraid!" She laughed dryly and shook her head. The knife in her hand swung to her side. "I'm sitting here, holding a knife, because my boyfriend murdered someone."

"Yes. But that's no reason to freak out." Why was I so fucking bad at this? She blinked rapidly. Now I was the one who was afraid. "Give me the knife, Scout," I said slowly.

"No." She raised it again. Her hand was trembling. I bet I could grab it from her. I took a step toward her, and she took a step back. She had the hallway behind her that would take her to her room. Or her backyard. Where she could run. And call the police. And put me away.

My future flashed before me in a single moment. Me at my next birthday, dying and transforming into a vampire. Guards and prisoners all around me, witnessing it happen. I'd have to kill them all before they killed me. And killing all those people would cause a stir that humans wouldn't over-look. I could expose the entire vampire community to humans.

No, I couldn't let that happen.

"Give me the fucking knife," I said with determination,

this time through gritted teeth. I reached for her wrist, and she swiped the knife across the air between us.

"Tell me what you did," she demanded.

"I already told you!" I yelled.

"But why?"

Something deep inside of me snapped.

Red.

My vision flashed for a moment, and the person I was before was gone. I stepped toward her again and she turned to run down the hall. I stalked after her. She froze at the fork in the hall that would take her to her room or the backyard. I brushed past her, covering the door to the back. She stared up at me with wide, terrified eyes.

"We just need to talk," I said.

"Desi, please," Scout pleaded with me as I backed her into her room.

"Drop the knife, and I'll explain everything. I'm not going to hurt you."

"I bet that's what you said to him, isn't it?"

"He didn't have a knife."

"I don't trust you." She raised her arm again, but I smacked it back down. The feeling was mutual. She'd end up doing more damage to herself than to me if she tried to use the knife.

"Please," I pleaded once more and reached for the knife. Maintaining eye contact, I bent down and took it from her slowly. She ducked and tried to rush past me. I caught her with my open arm and shoved her back. She landed on her mattress on the floor. Rolling quickly, she tried to kick me, but I crawled to her, pinning her down under me as I did.

Her chest rose and fell with heavy breaths, and mine matched her with the effort it took to stop her from moving. My hands gripped her wrists, while my left still held the knife. Chest to chest, we stared at each other, waiting for one of us to react. It was at that moment that I realized never once did she call me a monster or threaten to turn me in.

She wasn't really afraid of me. Her feelings for me were just as powerful as mine were for her. That was what had her so scared.

My eyes flicked to her voluptuous lips. The memory of them touching my own was too powerful. I was lost in her. Enraptured by her heavy breaths against my chest. Our lips met. For a moment, I wondered if this would be our last. I needed to make it count, so I parted mine just a bit.

And then she kissed me back.

CHAPTER 26

Desi

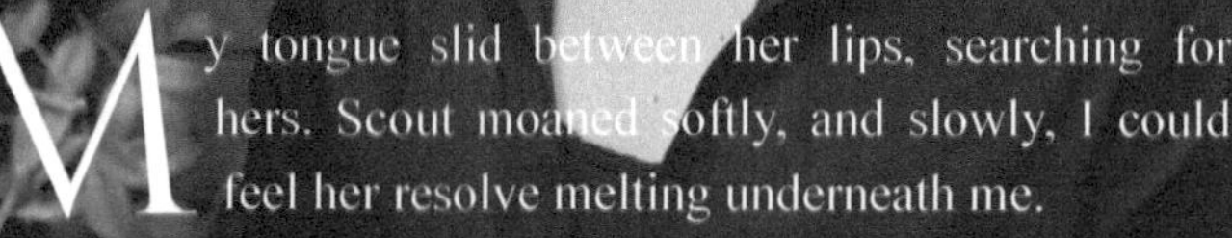

My tongue slid between her lips, searching for hers. Scout moaned softly, and slowly, I could feel her resolve melting underneath me.

"No." She sighed but continued kissing me. I let go of her wrist and squeezed the knife I now held in my hand, putting it to her throat. I pulled away to stare down at her. My adrenaline was shot as her breathing accelerated. The silver blade was so enthralling against her tan skin.

"You aren't going to tell anyone about what I did, are you?" I whispered.

Her eyes flickered to my hand and then back up to me. The look in her dark eyes was different than before. She wasn't afraid of me.

"What if I do?"

My cock stirred in my jeans. What was she doing to me?

"Are you going to slit my throat, too?"

"I didn't slice him." I pressed the knife deeper into her pretty little throat. "I shot him in the temple." I let go of the knife, leaving it on her chest. My lips found hers again, and I dropped her other wrist in favor of exploring her body.

"You didn't answer me." She gasped as I trailed kisses down her neck. One hand palmed her breast, while the other cupped her mound and rolled in massaging circles. She squirmed under my touch.

"What? Do you want me to shut you up?" I slid my hand down her chest, tracing her curves. I slipped under her shirt and pulled her bra down. My fingers found her nipple and pinched it. "Or do you want me to make you scream?"

Where was this sexual prowess before?

"I shouldn't like you as much as I do," she panted. I sat and pulled her with me. The knife fell onto her lap. We both reached for it, but I was faster. I held it up, pointed the tip at her, and shot her a look. I pressed it under her chin and pushed up, raising her head.

"But you do like me, don't you?" I moved the knife lower, reaching for her collar with my other hand. I nipped the fabric and sliced down her shirt. The kitchen knife wasn't the best tool for the job, but I didn't falter. I made a large cut, letting the tip trace her skin underneath as I did so, and then tore the rest of it, pulling the clothing down her shoulders.

"You know what I'm capable of, and yet, you still have me here." I unclasped her bra. I stared down at her beautiful body. My cock pulsed against my zipper. It was painful, but I wanted to savor her. I pushed her back down on her pillows, then I dropped my head to her chest and ran my tongue across her beautiful brown nipple.

"Why is that?" I asked her. "If you're so scared of me, why are you letting me touch you?"

She moaned as I palmed her other breast while tugging her nipple between my teeth.

"I don't know," she gasped. I pushed her legs apart and positioned my hips against her.

"Don't know what?"

"Why…" She sighed. Her hands found my belt, and she fumbled with it, causing me to groan. I needed to be inside her.

"Well, you better figure it out soon," I said, brushing her hands away just as she undid my belt. I pulled it out of the loops and removed it. Her gaze flickered to it and then back to the button on my jeans. "Because I know what you want, but you don't get it until you give me an answer."

Her hands drifted over the fabric of my pants, finding my cock. Her touch was so unraveling.

"Tell me, Scout, how do you feel about being in love with a killer?" My heart beat furiously as I clocked her reaction. She was breathing heavily, her breasts rising and falling. I reached up and played with them. "Does it give you chills, thinking about the hands that give you such pleasure could cause so much pain?" My mouth dipped to her navel, stopping at her shorts. I unbuttoned them, and she raised her hips, giving me permission to slide both her panties and shorts down and off her.

I kissed all the way down as I tugged them off and then returned to the apex of her thighs. She was smooth and wet and completely bare for me. I spread her pussy open and slid a finger inside.

"I don't want that. I want you."

"Well, you don't get me until you explain why you want me so bad, knowing that I've killed a man and wore you like a Muppet while his body was in my trunk." I moved in and out of her body, one finger turning into two.

"I don't care about that," she panted. "You won't hurt me."

"How are you so sure?" I asked, pressing deeply into her and hooking her G-spot.

"Because I think if I die, you would too." She confessed.

Bingo.

Moving furiously, I removed my pants and boxers and the rest of my clothes and found myself again between her thighs.

"Should we use a condom?" she asked.

"Do you trust me?" The question was more than about a condom. It was about everything. I kissed her neck, sucking on the sensitive skin as my cock pulsed against her ready and eager pussy. I wouldn't go any further until she answered me. Did she still want me, knowing the full truth of how evil I was?

"Yes." She took my cock in her hands and stroked. I closed my eyes and reveled in the feeling. She stroked and spread her thighs wider, directing me to where we both wanted this to go. With no condom or anything else between us, I slid into her pussy and froze.

It was the most intense feeling I'd ever felt. She was so wet, so tight, so hot, and so. Fucking. Mine.

I crushed my lips to hers and moved, thrusting in and out of what was mine and would only ever be mine.

If I had felt love before we were together in carnal bliss, this feeling was otherworldly.

It was beyond love, it was beyond passion, it was an explosion of everything!

Together, we raced toward the end. I ground my hips against her, pushing my cock as deep as I could get from this angle into her body, needing to feel her come to reach my peak. She arched her back, cried out my name, and I was done for. A small grunt escaped my lips as I spilled my seed, pumping until I emptied every single drop.

Scout was mine, and I would never let anyone take her from me. Even if that meant another bullet through someone's temple.

CHAPTER 27

Scout

I held my blanket to my chest and leaned against the wall. Desi was to my right, naked, sitting up as well, and grinning at me. He had a lit cigarette between his lips as he turned back to the cards he had pulled out after we had woken up from our moment of complete vulnerability. He had confessed his crimes, and I, in turn, did the same, giving him all I had—my body.

"Which card did I draw again?" I asked, peering over his bare shoulder. I admired all of his back muscles as I gazed. That was mine. He was mine.

"The Hanged Man." He took a drag of his cigarette. "What a card."

"It's a good thing, though, right? It must be, considering where we are now."

"Something like that. I'm not paying attention to the cards right now. Not when they pertain to you and me." He leaned over to plant a kiss on my lips.

"Do you always play with your cards after sex?" I teased.

He looked up at the ceiling, as if in thought. "Yeah, I guess I do. I shuffle my cards any time I'm truly relaxed."

He was relaxed. But how could he be calm? He had murdered someone. If he was bad, what did that make me?

"What are you going to do about the police?"

His head turned quickly and his silly expression disappeared, replaced by a scowl. He leaned back, careful of the cigarette in his mouth, then put his hand on my shoulder and squeezed gently.

"Let me worry about that. The police won't be showing up at your door anymore."

"Why?" My eyes went wide. "Are you going to…"

"I'm a murderer, not an idiot." He tried to laugh, but when I didn't join in, he sighed. "Seriously, I've got this handled. They were just trying to shake you down. It's stupid."

"What if you go to prison?" My stomach tightened. Desi in handcuffs and a cell? No!

"I'm not!" He chuckled. "Honestly, if they hadn't had come here, you would have never known, because they have nothing. Just a hunch. Hunches aren't shit."

"Desi, can you be serious for a minute?"

"No." He finished his cigarette and stretched to put the butt in a bottle, and then returned to me. He pulled me into his embrace and rolled on top of me. "Because it's not serious. It's over, it's done. And I don't stress about the past. I want to live right now." His hands drifted to the edge of my blanket.

"So, it was just a one-time thing?" I asked, hopeful.

"Scout, this stuff with my family is… complicated." He sighed and moved off of me. "But I've got it."

"It's true." My heart sank.

"What's true?"

"That you're in the mafia. Your family is the mafia."

"Are you—" He waited for me to tell him I was joking,

and when I didn't, his eyes crinkled in amusement. "Oh, okay, you're serious." He scrunched up his mouth and nose. "Mafia isn't really…" He tilted his head. "Okay, maybe a little."

"Is that why you're so weird?" I shot at him.

"What do you mean?"

I thought for a moment, choosing my words carefully. I didn't want to hurt his feelings.

"Well, your job. Do you really work at the dirty movie theater?" I pointed out. "Or what about the private school, and the car, and where you live? You could only afford stuff like that if you had mafia money. That's why you're weird."

"That's not weird."

"It's weird that you want to be with someone like me." My emotions got the best of me. I finally said what we had both been thinking since day one. I wasn't good enough for him. I was a charity case, and eventually, he'd get bored and move on to someone from his world. Some rich, mafia princess who could make his family happy.

"Scout, baby." He cupped my cheek. I stared at the blankets and blinked away my tears. Desi grabbed my chin and forced my head up. His eyes were dark and his face was so serious, it made my heart stop. "You can get rid of all those ideas right now. I don't care about money, or my family, or whatever you're worrying about. It's just you and I until the end. Got it?"

My lips trembled, and he stifled them with a scorching kiss. It turned into another, and the blanket between us shifted and his body was moving against mine again. In the friction of his hips against mine, I found total ecstasy and something else I had never truly felt before.

Love.

I woke up from a nap, to find tarot cards scattered all over the room. It was dark now. I rolled over, and my heart sank when Desi was nowhere to be seen. I slapped the bed and a paper crumpled underneath my hand.

I flicked my bedside lamp on and sat up.

I stayed too late and now I gotta run. I am late for something. I'll come retrieve my cards later. Thanks.

Desi.

I cried, despite the note not being anything detrimental. I got out of bed, threw on a shirt, and collected the cards. With each card I found, I reminded myself that he was coming back. He had to. He wouldn't leave his cards behind completely. I reread the note, wondering how true it was. What was he late for? Was he off to kill another guy for someone?

I mindlessly watched Will Smith argue with Carlton while replaying everything that happened today. How could Desi be so… nonchalant? He killed someone. On purpose. That was murder. My boyfriend was a murderer. Eventually, I went into the kitchen to make a bowl of ramen, the only food I could always afford, and the phone caught my eye.

This was the only chance I'd get. If I wanted to confess what I knew and solve that guy's missing person case, his murder, then I would have to call now.

Could I turn Desi in?

"Your new roommate is cute," Catrine admired Luis as he carried another box into the house.

"Oh, are you dropping those cholo boys finally?" I smirked. Together, Catrine, Birdie, and I walked to her car. I wanted to give Luis space to move in, so I called my off-again-on-again friends and asked to spend the day with them.

"Ha! I wish. Get someone who can keep a job." Catrine laughed. She pulled out of my driveway and started toward the mall.

"Or wash his own underwear." Birdie snickered. "I've been having to scrub brown streaks for months now."

"Why do you let these men get away with that shit?" I asked.

"How do you think we can afford to go shopping today?" Catrine laughed.

"My man might not know how to wipe his ass, but he spoils me." Birdie pulled out a wad of bills and fanned them in my face.

"You both need a little more independence. I couldn't imagine wanting a man to pay for stuff."

"See, that's why no one rolls wit' you no more," Catrine jabbed. "You're always lecturing and making us feel stupid."

"You're not stupid," I protested. "But what are you gonna do when Chino and Julio and Creeper and whoever learn to wash their own boxers?"

We all burst into laughter. Like that could ever happen. Birdie leaned forward again, pushing past us to turn the radio up and we sang along to the mix tape she made just for the trip.

"Did you get yours done for what's his name?" Catrine asked when we pulled into the mall parking lot and climbed out of her car.

"That white boy?" Birdie cocked her head. "From Halloween?"

"His name is Desiderio." I rolled my eyes. "And no, I'm still working on the tape. I've been pretty busy at work."

They groaned loudly.

"Fine, I won't talk about work."

We hit a few stores, and both of my friends bought stuff from each one we walked into. They really did have money. I tried not to be envious and remain as supportive as I could as they tried on dresses, pants, and cute shirts, buying nearly as much as they tried on.

"You're not getting anything?" Catrine frowned, as once again, I walked out of a store empty-handed.

"I don't need anything right now."

"I don't need any of this." Birdie giggled. "But I sure do look good when Creeper takes me out and shows me off."

"I want to be more than just some trophy."

"Then do it, fool." Catrine slapped me gently on the shoulder. "Take off, go to art school, before you're thirty."

"I've still got a few years," I defended.

"Until Desiderio gets you pregnant and you end up just like everyone else."

"Except in a different neighborhood," Birdie added coolly.

"Nah, I'm not doing any of that."

"Your man doesn't want kids?" Catrine and Birdie shared a look.

"We just started dating," I reminded them. "It's not like back in the day when you go with someone and you plan your whole life."

"Why not? You should want to be with that person forever." Birdie smiled and her eyes took on a far-off look. "And get married and have kids and—"

"You want to marry Creeper?" I cocked an eyebrow.

"If he ever asks."

We walked to the next store and they tried on shoes while I sat on a bench. *I could use a new pair of sneakers.*

Some day I'd be able to afford shopping just for fun.

"Desiderio should want to spoil you." Catrine clicked her tongue. "You're his girl."

"He bought me a message recorder." Why was I becoming so defensive of Desi?

"How… functional." Birdie smirked. I wanted to comment how the only reason their men could afford to spoil them was because of the shady dealings I'd heard about, but I kept my mouth shut. I couldn't talk. Desi's crimes were far worse than selling some teenagers a little weed.

I continued to window shop while my friends collected more boxes and bags. We stopped at the food court. We ordered Chinese and took a moment to rest.

"Where should we go next? I still have money, and Julio told me not to come home until it was gone," Catrine said.

"Is there anywhere you want to go?" Birdie asked me.

"Not really." I started to shake my head but then I recalled a store we passed by on the way to get lunch. "Oh wait, I want to check out that store with the stars and all the purple curtains."

"With the fortune teller?" Catrine flinched away. "Why?"

Birdie crossed herself. "You can go in alone."

"It's nothing bad. Desiderio likes that kind of stuff. It's interesting."

They shook their heads fervently.

"You go. We'll meet at the fountain when you're done, okay?" Birdie suggested.

We finished lunch and went our separate ways. As I stood in front of the dark store, I was nervous too, but my curiosity got the best of me and I stepped inside.

The smell of incense hit me as I passed through the curtains. Music from some kind of flute played softly through a radio. My eyes had to adjust to the dim lighting. A woman with long curly red hair greeted me in a soft, calming voice.

"Hello, may I help you?"

"I'm just looking. My boyfriend likes tarot cards. I wondered what other kind of stuff there is like that."

"Well, this is the best place for you to start your journey with the mystical world." She beamed. "Have you used candle magik before?" She took my hand and led me through the shop, stopping and explaining things. I learned about different types of sage and the history of tea leaves, and then I was shown the candle selection.

"We also have some beautiful scarves to decorate your altar. Pick one, I'll take it to the counter."

"I don't need all of this right now. I'm just kind of looking."

"Yes, of course. I just get so passionate about my world.

Feel free to explore, and if you have any questions, please let me know."

"How much are the bags for the tarot cards?" I asked, looking longingly at the nice leather pouches. I could imagine Desi holding his cards in them.

"Those are real leather with silk inside; imported from Italy. They are $50."

I didn't even have that much money in my wallet.

"Oh, thank you." I turned away shamefully. I couldn't even buy my boyfriend a bag.

"Your boyfriend, what's his name? I wonder if he's one of my customers." she asked politely.

"Desiderio Amato." I smiled through my tears. It was so stupid to get upset about, but I couldn't help it. We were so different. He probably came here all the time, while I could barely afford to stand in here. "I don't know if he comes here; I just assumed."

"Amato?"

"Is there something wrong?"

"No, I didn't realize he had a girlfriend. Last time I knew, he was engaged."

CHAPTER 29

Desi

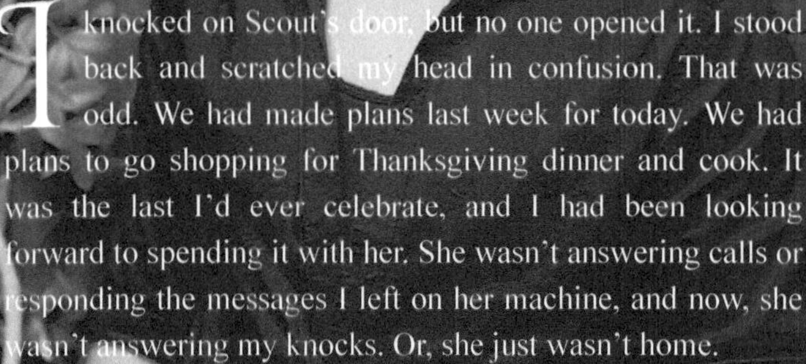

I knocked on Scout's door, but no one opened it. I stood back and scratched my head in confusion. That was odd. We had made plans last week for today. We had plans to go shopping for Thanksgiving dinner and cook. It was the last I'd ever celebrate, and I had been looking forward to spending it with her. She wasn't answering calls or responding the messages I left on her machine, and now, she wasn't answering my knocks. Or, she just wasn't home.

I knocked again and a deep booming bark came from inside. I shrunk away back to my car. Oh, that's right. Her roommate had a dog. There was one last place to try, and relief flew through my body when I saw her in her uniform, serving a table. I sat and waited for her to come over. She froze when she saw me. I waved and smiled, but she didn't do the same.

"What are you doing here, Desi?"

"You're not answering the phone. And you weren't home."

"I picked up an extra shift. I needed the money."

"Why didn't you tell me, then? I don't care, but I thought we had plans."

"Well, we don't. And I don't think we're gonna have any more plans."

I stood quickly.

"Scout, can you take a break real quick?"

She looked toward her waitress friends. They nodded, and she waved me forward. We went outside and walked to my car. She leaned against it and crossed her arms. I shoved my hands in my pockets.

"I'm so confused."

"I know about your fiancée."

Her words were like ice shards. I stared, shocked and panicked.

"Fiancée?" I asked, feeling so idiotic. "What are you talking about?" I took a step toward her with my arms out.

"I was at the mall last weekend with Catrine and Birdie and I went into that mystics shop. I was going to buy you a present when the girl said she knew you, and she found it weird that you had a girlfriend because last she heard, you were getting married!" Scout shoved me away from her.

"I'm not!" I yelled back. "She must have gotten me confused with my brother, Gianni. We used to go in there all the time. He is married now."

"Gianni?"

"Yes!" I said with a forced laugh. "My brother got married this summer. I'm not entirely a huge fan of Gloria, but love is love. The girl at the shop must have gotten us confused. We do look alike."

"So, you're not getting married?"

"No. Now, this is why you were avoiding me? Can we make up now?" I spread my arms out and she leaned in to hug me.

"Yes, please." She sighed. "I've been crying for days."

"You should have come to me about this," I chastised. "I'll take care of everything from now on."

"I gotta get back. I'll make up to you. On your next day off." She pulled away and sniffled.

"Sure. Sounds good. Have a good rest of your shift." I kissed her forehead and got into my car. I gnashed my teeth as I gripped the steering wheel. More lies. The more I lied, the harder it was going to be if she found out. What were the fucking odds some stranger would be the one to expose me?

I turned onto the road that led to the mall and sped up.

The mall was just opening, which meant there were hardly any cars in the parking lot. I parked and stormed inside, heading straight to the mystic's place Scout had gone to this weekend. I pushed past the curtains and my anger shifted. I cooled, knowing exactly how I wanted to play this. I had seen my father, my brother, and even my grandfather on occasion, in action. I could do it too.

"Hello?" A female's voice came from the back.

I looked around, picking up a crystal ball. I turned it around in my hand. "Hello."

She stepped out and froze. "Desiderio, it has been ages since your last visit. How may we help guide you today?"

"I don't need any guidance." I set the ball down and picked up a crystal. "I hear you had an interesting guest this weekend."

"We did. It was a surprise to hear you have a girlfriend. Do the Linottis know?" She crossed her arms.

"They don't need to. Nor does anyone else. I told Scout that it was my brother you mistook me for. And when she comes in next, you'll be apologizing and correcting yourself."

"Oh, will I? Why would I do that?"

I picked up the ball again and slammed it on the ground.

It shattered, and she screamed. I put my hand on the glass counter and hopped over it. My boots hit the ground and I reached into my pocket, pulling out my pocketknife. I popped it open and stalked over to her. She stepped backward, hitting a wall. I caged her against the wall and trailed the tip of the knife on her temple.

"Who owns this store? I can have this entire place in flames. Can you imagine a fire in the mall?" She continued to glare at me, so I decided to push it further. "With the owner still inside?"

She paled.

I dropped my hands and took a step back. "I don't make empty threats. So, this is in your hands. What is your plan when Scout returns?"

Her eyes flicked to the knife and then to me again. "I-I'll apologize. It was your brother, not you, who was engaged."

"And you'll give her a hefty discount every time she comes in. This shit is already overpriced. Got it?"

"Yes. Everything will be on sale for her."

Nodding, I took a step toward the exit. "Good. And if I hear you talking to a Linotti or anyone else about my visit, then you won't have to worry about them finding your charred body in a fire, because they won't find it at all."

CHAPTER 30
Desi

"Doesn't it smell good?" Scout sniffed the air and sighed. "It's the marshmallows." She plopped beside me on her couch.

"I'm starving." I reached for her hand.

"How? You spent all morning eating as we cooked!"

"Yes, but those were snacks. I've been preparing for this day all week. I've barely ate."

Just then, a man came down the hallway with a suitcase.

"Desi, you haven't met my roommate yet. This is Luis. Luis, this is Desiderio." I loved how possessive she was over my name. Whenever I was introduced, she made sure to tell them to call them by my full first name, rather than her nickname for me. I shook Luis's hand and smiled politely.

"Nice to meet you, Luis. I've already met Brucey."

"And you're still in one piece? Must be a good one then." He smiled.

"Where are you from? You look so familiar," I asked. I racked my brain, but I couldn't place it.

"Ghana. I am returning there for the holidays." He motioned to his suitcase.

"I'm still surprised they are giving you all this time off," Scout added. "Kids still have school, don't they?"

"My assistant teacher will be covering me. I have the utmost confidence in her." He turned to Scout and nodded. "Thank you again, for watching Brucey until my aunt comes for him. She'll be here Saturday."

"No problem, he's good dog."

"All right, I'll see you all first week of January then." He started toward the door and then turned. "I think I do recognize you too." He wagged his finger and grinned. "Aleida Linotti."

"Who?" My heart skipped a beat.

"Aleida." He paused for an uncomfortable amount of time. "Her birthday party? That woman is crazy, but she throws a fantastic event. You were there, weren't you?"

"Oh right, over the summer. Yeah, I was there."

"Fun times." He laughed. "All right, enjoy your holidays!"

Scout and I turned to each other. I looked at her for a long moment, trying to assess if she suspected anything.

"He's great, isn't he? He keeps to himself mostly, but when we chat, he's very nice."

"Seems like it."

"He works at your old school, Catalina."

I swore inwardly. Was everyone Scout encountered out to catch me?

"Oh yeah?" I went to the kitchen, where I plucked a deviled egg from the fridge. "So he makes good money then?"

Scout shrugged and went to check the sweet potatoes. "I don't know, probably better than what I do. But you make more than I do at the dirty theater."

"Good." I put my arms around her from behind and pulled her back against me and hugged her tightly. "So when we move in together, he can afford this place on his own."

"Ha! You're already thinking of us moving in together?" She spun around and shook her head. "You are insane."

"Do you not like that idea?"

"Someday, maybe. But we're still new. It's been…"

"A month." So much had changed in such a short amount of time. It felt like weeks and weeks, like my soul had been following hers for years, not thirty days.

"Let's table this conversation for the year mark."

"Are we going too fast?" I asked her.

"With moving in? Yeah."

"I mean, with everything else."

"Oh… I don't know. What do you think?"

I think if you agreed to marry me today, I'd fly us to Vegas.

"I like where we're at," I answered. "I might be a teensy bit jealous of your new roommate, though." I pinched my fingers together.

"Those blue eyes can get you out of anything."

"How do you think I convinced those cops to stop coming around?" I teased.

"Desi, that's not funny." She scowled.

"Oh, come on. You're too sensitive about this."

"About my boyfriend killing someone?"

I sighed. "Can we move on?"

"Fine. Let me stir the mashed potatoes."

This Thanksgiving dinner was by far the best one I'd ever had, and I made sure to tell her so.

"My family has never celebrated. It was always just the kids being served by the staff."

"Your parents didn't eat Thanksgiving dinner?"

Why would they? They didn't need to consume anything other than blood to survive. "Not with us. Now that I'm out of the house, they don't do it at all anymore."

"What about Christmas, do you get candy and stuff?"

"The kids do. Everyone gets presents, we're just not food people. What were your holidays like growing up?"

Scout took another roll off the plate in the middle of the table. "Different in every house I lived in. Sometimes we sat with the families, sometimes we served them. Most of the food was similar, although I did stay with one family that ate fish a lot. I left before Christmas, thankfully."

Our lives couldn't be any more different.

"What about Christmas?" I asked. "Do you have a favorite Christmas?"

She thought for a moment. "There was one Christmas, I was with this family that only wanted me for the money. I lived in the basement and had old things. As their family was unwrapping presents, there was a phone call and then the social worker came. I thought they were coming to take me away, but instead, they brought another girl, Nalida." She smiled, and her eyes took on a distant look. "She was the closest thing I ever had to a real family. Having her with me was the best present."

This year, she would have so many presents her awful childhood would be a distant memory.

After dinner, we made our way to the living room, where we snuggled on the couch. Our bellies were full as we watched *The Wedding Singer* on TV. This was bliss. Halfway through the movie, Scout leaned forward and plucked a fireball out of the candy dish she had on her coffee table. She put her head in my lap and rolled to look up at me. She popped the hot cinnamon candy in her mouth and grinned.

"I don't see how you can eat those all the way to the end."

"They're good!" She'd been eating them for a week now. She plucked it out of her mouth and offered it to me. I turned my head. "Come on." She stroked my cock once, and I throbbed under her touch. "You suck on this… and I'll suck on that."

CHAPTER 31

Scout

I looked up from Desi's lap as he stared intently at the small, red ball of hot cinnamon pinched between my fingers.

"The offer is tempting," he murmured. His fingers went to my hair and began to run through them, tugging lightly at the roots. I moaned softly, which caused him to react. His expression darkened with lust.

"You don't think it could be fun?" I puffed out my lower lip. His gaze went there, as he imagined exactly what I'd do with them if he wanted me to. All he had to do was try the candy.

"Oh, baby, I definitely think it can." He grinned wickedly, and his cock jerked. He urged me up and leaned forward, grabbing a fistful of fireballs from the bowl. He stood and offered me his hand. "Let's go play."

In the bedroom, he flicked the light on, and I swiftly flicked it back off. I closed the door behind us and pushed him toward my bed. He fell back with a low chuckle and propped himself back up on his elbows.

I turned and bent down to turn my boombox on.

"You have a sex mixtape?"

"Only for you," I said, slipping off my jeans. He motioned for me to remove my shirt as well, and I obliged, slow and careful not to mess up my hair. I had taken extra effort today to curl and put it up into two bouncy ponytails.

"You're so fucking sexy," he murmured, as I crawled to the bed. I tugged on his jeans. He shook his head and bit down on his lip. "Nuh-uh, you do it."

My fingers, despite knowing what was waiting for me under the fabric, fumbled as I found the button and popped it open. My heart raced as I tugged his zipper down as slowly as I could.

"You want a taste?"

My mouth watered in anticipation. The memories of his touch and the strength of his desire for me sent my body into a fit of excitement. I had experienced his cock in my hand and inside me, but now, I only wanted him in my mouth.

He shifted his hips to allow me to remove his jeans. I did so slowly, brushing my hand over the bulge in his underwear.

"You tease," he growled low.

"Oh, you want me to touch it?"

His eyes sparkled with mischief. "I want you to put it in your mouth."

"I was just thinking the same thing." Sliding over the top of him, my lace bra tickled my nipples, causing them to rise as they brushed against his warm, bare chest. I reached for the fireballs that he had abandoned beside him. Arousal pooled between my thighs. I put the wrapped candy in-between my teeth and looked up into Desi's blue eyes.

He watched me carefully as I slid the fireball candy out of the plastic packaging and offered it to him.

"We're going to play a game," I told him. "Show me what you want me to do."

He took it gingerly and swallowed nervously. He had told me on more than one occasion how much he didn't like how hot they were. I reached between my thighs and removed his cock from his boxers. It had been barely contained, but now fully out, it hardened even further. I stroked it up and down. He closed his eyes and sighed.

"I think I could come like this," he murmured.

I stopped.

His eyes popped open.

"That's not how the game works, Desi," I warned him.

He rolled his eyes, but finally, slipped the fireball between his lips, and slid his tongue around it.

"This isn't so bad," he said, and then a moment later, he was spitting it out into his hand with a hiss. "Fuck!"

"That was fifteen seconds." I giggled.

"So that's fifteen seconds…" He looked at my hands still on his cock. "Your turn."

I climbed off his lap and slid down the bed, making myself comfortable between his legs. I opened my mouth and, starting at the base, I licked him all the way up to the top of his head and then back down. He groaned as I teased him.

"That was fifteen." I looked up at him. "Want to try again?"

Desi glared at me and popped the candy back in his mouth. His tongue flicked in and out of his mouth and then he blinked rapidly. I grinned wickedly and kept eye contact as my tongue flicked over his cock. He pushed the candy further into his mouth and sucked.

Finally.

I took him completely between my lips, sucking his cock

like it was my own candy. He let out a small groan as I moved up and down, my head bobbing as I listened to him sucking on the fireball. I'd never wanted a cock so badly in my life.

"This isn't so bad," he moaned as he thrust his hips.

I paused, removing my lips from his length.

"Open your mouth."

He did and stuck his tongue out. It was now red, while the candy on the tip was white.

"Change it out," I ordered. His smile fell, but when I flicked my tongue against the tip of his cock, he quickly did as told. Another candy went into his mouth, and I continued performing the best blow job I'd ever done. It was easy to do with him.

I wanted to do this. I wanted to be here, giving him pleasure, taking none in return. I reveled in his thrusts, his moans, and his hips bucking for me to take him further down my throat. I relaxed my body and inhaled, taking him down to the base.

Soon, he had gone through almost all of them.

"Scout, baby, you're beautiful. You know that? With your mouth on my cock? You're fucking beautiful baby, and I-I—" He started panting, and I knew he was close. I sucked him deeper and harder, licking him faster, making tight circles as I went. "I'm in love with you." With those words, his cock exploded. Hot liquid hit the back of my throat and I began to swallow it quickly as he pulsed in my mouth.

My cheeks and lips were swollen, but seeing him splayed out on the bed, his eyes closed, looking so very satisfied, made me feel amazing.

I did that.

I stared for a moment and then it hit me. He had said he

was in love with me. Desi was in love with me. I blinked, trying to process it.

His eyes popped open, and he sat up abruptly. I tried to step back, but he was faster than me. He grabbed my hips and spun me around, thrust me onto the bed, and growled.

"My turn."

Desi was impatient. He ripped my panties down my thighs and his fingers moved quickly, spreading me wide.

"God, you're so fucking beautiful," he said as he knelt between my legs and pulled me to him. I squealed in delight as he ran his fingers along the inside of my thighs, sending delicious tickles through me. His finger slid between my folds, and he chuckled. "Sucking my cock gets you wet? Good to know."

He pushed my legs further apart and leaned in, using his hands to relax me. His tongue rolled around and found my clit, sucking it as he hooked his finger deep inside me. My hands found his dark hair, and I pushed him deeper, begging him not to stop.

He kept going until I couldn't take it any longer, and I exploded. My release came hard and it felt like time had stopped as my body pulsed against Desi's fingers.

He released me and sat up with a wicked grin.

"You didn't have to do that." I sighed contentedly. "I enjoy doing that for you."

He smirked and reached for his pants to pull out his cigarettes. "Yeah?"

"I do." I nodded eagerly and wrapped my arms around him from behind. "I like making you come more than myself."

"You wouldn't say that if you could see yourself." He stood and pulled me up. Careful not to burn me with his lit cigarette, he took my hands and we danced slowly to the music. "I've never seen someone as beautiful as you are when you're coming."

I blushed. His words sent butterflies through my belly. "Desi…" I gulped. "What you said, earlier…"

"You think I said it because we were in the heat of the moment?" he asked, reading my mind. He pressed a kiss on my lips. I could taste myself on him. "No. I said it because I meant it."

"But we barely—"

"Who gives a shit about time?" he huffed and backed away. He took a drag of his cigarette. "Time means nothing. I'm in love with you, and more time isn't going to change how I feel. The better question is, how do you feel about me?"

My heart raced, and my mouth suddenly felt dry. How could I confess to him that I felt the same? We were twenty-six years old. Adults with jobs, bills, and responsibilities. We couldn't be confessing our love like we were fifteen and ready to run away with each other.

Would that be so bad?

I opened my mouth to express my thoughts when there was a loud bang on my front door. We both looked toward it, and the banging came again. Quickly, I pulled on my clothes, and Desi pulled on his pants.

"Police! Open up!"

I froze and turned to Desi. Had they discovered what he had done? Desi's expression darkened, and he put his finger to his lips. I nodded.

"Desiderio Amato, we have reason to believe you are inside. We have a warrant for your arrest."

On Thanksgiving? My chin trembled as the fear set in.

"It's fine. It's a misunderstanding is all. Stop crying," he ordered, tilting my chin up.

I wiped my tears, straightened, and went to the door just as they were knocking again. I opened it quickly and glared at the same two officers from before.

"What do you want?" I surprised myself with how firm and cold I was toward the policemen. Bright red and blue lights were flashing from their car. My neighbors peeked out from their curtains.

"Is Desiderio Amato here, Miss?"

"I am." Desi stepped forward. "And?"

"We have a warrant for your arrest. Now, if you step outside, Miss, we can do this peacefully," the policeman to the left said, waving a small packet of papers.

"What's the warrant for?" Desi crossed his arms. The officer to the right snatched the papers. The look on his face told me they were prepared to send him away for a long time.

"Where were you Monday evening?"

Desi's blue eyes flicked to me. "Why?"

Horror filled my throat. I wanted to scream. What had Desi done? Had he murdered someone else?

"We have you on camera outside Frank's convenience store with your friends, giving your state-issued driver's license to a minor, who then used it to purchase copious amounts of alcohol."

"Seriously?" Desi laughed. "This is what you want to do on Thanksgiving?"

They nodded solemnly. "It is. That minor threw a house party and crashed his parents' car. Now, if you'll come with us."

With a sigh louder than the one I had given when they announced his charges, he turned around and let them put handcuffs on him. He was barefoot as well as shirtless. The neighbors were going to love that.

"Can I get him some clothes?" I asked.

"At least my boots." Desi looked toward them.

They nodded. "Boots are fine."

I hurried back to my bedroom. They allowed me to help him put them on. It was freezing. The October winds had long since gone, and we were now waiting for winter.

Desi gave me one last look, making sure to roll his eyes, grin, and then wink as they shoved his head down and into the back of their car. The officers gave me a quick salute as they left. A moment later, I felt something wet on my nose. I looked up at the bright gray sky and realized that it had started to snow.

That was two things I had missed out on today. Experiencing the first snow of the season with Desi. And telling him I was in love with him too.

CHAPTER 33

Desi

"I bet you think this is real fucking funny, don't you?" I asked the cops sitting up front, grinning ear to ear.

"We do. Gotta be better than that, Amato."

I clenched my jaw tight, trying to remain calm. "What are you expecting to happen?"

"Nothing. We just want to talk."

"Talk?" I leaned forward. "You fucking put me in cuffs!" I thrust forward and back, then kicked the back of the seats. Rage filled me as I recalled Scout's horrified face as they pounded on her door to arrest me. On Thanksgiving!

"You motherfuckers," I snarled. My hair fell over my face, and I blew it back. I closed my eyes and forced myself to calm down. I would make things worse by making a big deal out of this. It was bad enough that they'd be putting my name in the paper. I didn't need to get more charges added.

I was brought to the station where I was fingerprinted and told to stand and get my picture taken. I rolled my eyes as they handed me the placard with my details. My mom was going to love this. I was still fucking shirtless.

"I know you!" the officer taking my mugshot exclaimed

afterward. "My kid went to school with you. Over at Catalina's." He nodded excitedly as I stared blankly at him. "I remember your graduation. I had asked about you because you looked so miserable. Harv, my son, said you were the black sheep of your family." He squinted as he leaned forward to look at me. "Makes sense. You got a different father? It's the eyes." He motioned to his own. "All the other Amatos got those crazy brownish ones."

They weren't brown; they were red. And it'd be a lot more terrifying if he looked into their mouths.

"All your other family members had their pictures taken in suits. They write you off then? What are you the bastard child or something?"

Bastard? That's a new one. If my dad heard him, he'd be torn in two in an instant. While we didn't typically get along, he valued our family name.

It was on the tip of my tongue to mention the fact that they snatched me on a national holiday and that the charges were bullshit, but I bit down and continued to stare at him until he was uncomfortable, and then he backed away and called for someone to take me to a cell.

I sat on the cold, hard bench with my hands crossed over my hard nipples. The charges were such a fucking reach. Sometime later, an officer came by and jingled his keys.

"You want a phone call?"

"Yes." I said through clenched teeth. They took me down the hall and handed me two quarters for the payphone. I dialed my brother's number. It rang twice before he picked up.

"Amato residence," their housekeeper answered.

"I know it's early in the evening." I glanced at the officer who was pretending not to listen but very clearly was. "But can you grab Gianni for me please, it's Desiderio. It's urgent."

The man on the other line grumbled. A few moments later, my brother came on the line.

"Amato."

"Gianni, it's Desiderio."

"You know what time it is? What do you want?" He sounded as if just hearing my voice made him repulsed. The feeling was mutual.

"I'm at the county jail. I need you to post my bail."

"It's a holiday, you fucking—" he hissed. "Who signed the warrant?"

I asked the officer, and he ignored me. "I don't know. Just get me out of here."

"You fucking owe me." Gianni slammed the phone down. I hung up and was taken back to my cell. I was offered a blanket, but it was faded and worn. It did nothing for me. I closed my eyes again and focused on the memory of my last Thanksgiving I'd live as a human. Scout had made all the best food and the dessert was even better.

And I told her I loved her.

I recalled that moment, just before our evening was ruined when I asked her how she felt about me. She looked panicked, but she had opened her mouth to speak. What had she been about to say?

It was deep into the night before Gianni was escorted to my cell by an officer.

"Get your ass up and come on," he snarled. I stood and stretched.

"Jesus Christ," he muttered as he looked me down. His disgust for my acid-washed, ripped jeans and boots was clear on his face. He, like always, was in a gray suit. He stuffed his hands in his pockets and nodded to the officer and then to me. "Get him the fuck out of there."

The officer moved swiftly. He fumbled with the keys and apologized profusely for the misunderstanding.

"Damn right, it was. You'll think better next time you try to drag an Amato down here on a bullshit charge, you got it?" Gianni glared at him until the cop looked away.

"Yes. Of course. Apologies, we just thought—" He slid the bars open and I walked out and joined my brother.

"Thought what?" Gianni asked. "That you could convince him to talk? Nice try. We're leaving."

I followed Gianni out of the station. We didn't speak to anyone else, despite them either glaring at us or continuing to apologize. I was waiting for him to scold me once we were in the car about getting in trouble for such a ridiculous thing, but he surprised me by asking about something completely different.

"Care to explain why they picked you up, shirtless, at some human woman's place?"

"No. I'd really rather not."

He put the car in gear and peeled out of the parking lot. "We all have urges, Desiderio, but duty comes first. You are no exception. Do you know what will happen if the Linotti family finds out you're—"

"I'm what?" I interrupted him. "Like you don't cheat on your wife? I call bullshit."

"I don't sleep with humans. The police said this isn't the first time you've been there. Are you seeing her regularly?"

I didn't respond, which was a response all on its own.

"You know they watch us. You can't keep doing this." Gianni turned to take me back to my house. "Next October, you will be marrying a vampire."

"Or what?" I asked. I felt like a petulant child, but I couldn't marry Aleida. Not anymore.

"What do you think?" He laughed dryly as he turned into my driveway. My blood ran cold as we stared at the car parked in front of us.

Gianni grinned as Aleida opened her door and climbed out. "If the Amato family doesn't kill you, the Linottis will."

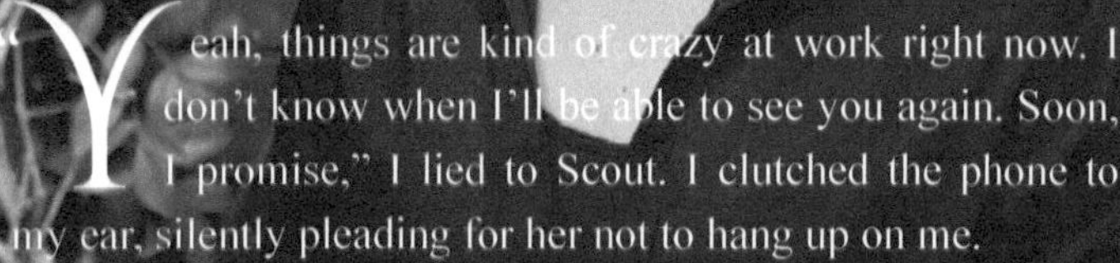

CHAPTER 34

Desi

"Yeah, things are kind of crazy at work right now. I don't know when I'll be able to see you again. Soon, I promise," I lied to Scout. I clutched the phone to my ear, silently pleading for her not to hang up on me.

"You promise this has nothing to do with your arrest?" Her voice sounded so far away, despite just being across the town.

"I swear. The theater gets crazy around the holidays. People are coming home, they hate their families so they come, catch a show and—"

"Take a load off?" She giggled. My heart ached that I couldn't see her right now, but, all in good time.

"Exactly. Are you doing anything on Christmas Eve?"

"No, are you?"

"Just seeing you."

"Please don't make promises you can't keep. You have a tendency to be late." Scout sighed deeply.

"But I always show up," I reminded her.

"Desi."

"No, I'll be there. Christmas Eve. Keep your lights on for

me. I'll be there, on your doorstep, with a present in my hand."

"I don't need a present."

"It's too late, I already bought it."

"Fine. But if you don't come by midnight, I'll consider it your final goodbye."

"I could never say that to you, Scout," I whispered. "I love you."

"I love you too, Desi. I'll see you in a few weeks."

I hoped I'd be able to call her soon, but with Aleida around, I couldn't be so sure.

My shoulders and stomach sank, and I trudged out of my kitchen and back to my bedroom.

"Who was that?" Aleida looked up from the fashion magazine she was reading on my bed.

"Randy," I told her. "He wanted to smoke. I told him I was spending time with my dearest fiancée." I recited.

"Good boy. Come here." She hooked her finger and motioned with it.

"What?" I snapped. She hadn't left my house in a week, except to feed.

"You're so tense, let me rub your shoulders." She opened her arms and made squeezing motions with her hands.

"I'm good. Are you going out tonight?"

"You'd like that, wouldn't you?"

"I would. I'd like that very much."

"You act like me being around is such an inconvenience to you."

It was.

She scooted to the edge of the bed. "What are you going to do when we start permanently living together?"

It was on the tip of my tongue to tell her it was irrelevant because that would never happen, but I kept my mouth shut.

"You know, eventually you'll have to tell me what's going on. Ever since your first kill, you've been acting so… cold." She shuddered. "You can't just close yourself off like this, Desiderio. Human life is pointless to hold on to."

She dug her nails into my shoulders, pulling me to her. "With how you're acting now, I suggest you kill some more before you turn. What are you going to do, starve?" She smirked.

"I have no reason to kill more people."

"No?" She let go of me and motioned around my room. "You think this is an acceptable place to live once we're married? I can't live in this dump. I want a mansion."

"A mansion?"

"Why not?" She crossed her arms, pushing her tits up. The rim of her nipples peeked out, and I quickly looked away. Just a month before, it would have excited me. Now, it felt shameful.

"What makes you think you deserve that from me?"

"I don't care who I get it from. I deserve it regardless. Our parents decided it was you." She glared at me and stepped back, looking at the floor. "Where's my shoes? We need to go before we're late."

"Do I have to?"

"Yes." She gritted her teeth. "My father wants to start going over details for the wedding. I think they are more excited about our marriage than either of us are."

For the first time in months, I agreed with her. During the drive, she lectured me on what she thought I should be doing while I waited my time to turn.

"You have a little under a year to prepare yourself. I bet if you ask my father, he can get you a gig taking care of some of his pesky clients. You know, the ones that don't pay him. Daddy pays people really good money to do that."

"Daddy?" I grimaced.

"I'll talk to him tonight. You can start saving and we can pick out a house together. A bigger house on a better side of town."

"Like your parents?"

"And yours. Don't forget where you come from just because you're slumming, Desiderio."

"What are you talking about?"

"Randy, Mick, and the others," she reminded me.

I let out a giant breath of relief. For a moment, I thought she knew about Scout. We pulled through the gates of her estate and parked in the long, curved driveway.

I got out first, then opened her door for her.

"I wish you had put something nicer on," she complained, eyeing my jeans and boots, as we walked up the stairs. The front door swung open and their butler greeted us.

"Mr. And Mrs. Linotti are in the den, awaiting your visit."

We followed him down the halls, past all the expensive antiques. 200-year-old paintings, vases, and statues from this famous artist or that famous politician. Mr. Linotti had given me a tour once, and the entire house reeked of pretension, much like its owners.

"Hello, Mr. And Mrs. Linotti." I bowed slightly. "How are you doing tonight?"

"Could be better," Aleida's mother, Isabella, greeted us. "How are you, Desiderio?"

"Great." *Fucking fantastic.*

Aleida came in behind me, beaming. "Hello! I'm so glad you invited us. Desiderio and I wanted to ask you for a favor." She ran to her dad and threw her arms over him. He patted her on the back and gave me a stern look over her shoulder.

"Favor?"

"Yes, Daddy." Aleida pulled away and beamed at me, then looked back at him. "Desiderio recently had his first kill. Someone paid him. We wanted to see if you could give him a job so that maybe we can start saving for a home to move into when we get married."

Her father raised his eyebrows with mild interest and nodded slightly. "I see. And you had no issues with disposal or the act itself?"

I shook my head. Honestly, it didn't bother me as much as it should have, taking a life.

Mr. Linotti smiled, and it sent shivers down my spine. "I think I might have a job you can cut your teeth on." He reached into his suit jacket and pulled out a Polaroid. He waved it in the air triumphantly and walked over, placing it in my hand. I stared down at the man in the photo. He was pretty average-looking. Blond hair, relatively good-looking, and… ice-blue eyes.

"Is this a Bloodshed?" I blurted. I'd never seen one in real life, even in photos.

"It is. Do you not recognize him?"

I handed him the photo back. "Who is he?"

Keeping that sickening smile plastered on his face, he offered the photo to Aleida. She took it, and her hands shook.

"He is my daughter's secret lover."

CHAPTER 35

Scout

I bought a calendar to count down the days to Christmas Eve.

Desi promised he'd come. He promised, and I knew he wouldn't break it.

To save my sanity, I threw myself into my work. I took extra shifts as often as I could, and my tips and paychecks reflected as much. I was finally able to put some money back into my art school jar.

After each shift, I'd trudge home in the dead of night, through the heavy snow, wishing that he'd be waiting for me on my porch. I knew that it was a long shot, as he had told me he couldn't see me for a while, but yet, every day, I was disappointed.

With only a week left before the biggest holiday of the year, I reluctantly agreed to take a day off. I hated being alone these days. Luis was still gone, so if I wasn't at work, I was home, staring at the walls and wishing I was elsewhere.

Warm, safe, and wrapped in Desi's arms.

My day off came, and I opted to buy a bus ticket to the mall, rather than ask my friends to come and get a ride from them. The more and more my heart poured into Desi's, the less I wanted to spend time with anyone else. I'd rather be alone than with people who would try to tell me to stay away from him.

They had heard about his arrest and were quick to come around or call me. They seemed happy that their initial opinions about him were right. He was a bad guy through and through.

But I didn't care.

I hung up on them. I shut the door in their faces, and I stopped hanging out with them.

He loved me.

And I loved him back.

I walked to the bus stop, put my coins in the slot, and took a sticky seat in the back. I put my headphones on and listened to the mixtape I was working on for Desi. I had originally planned for it to be his Christmas present, but now that I had money, I decided to wait and continue working on it.

In the mall, I searched through all the stores, looking for the right gift. I found some cool Iron Maiden and Journey shirts I knew he'd like but I set those back. I wanted him to love my gift, not just like it. As I shopped for the perfect present, I picked up a few small things. I found an ornament of a Jack-o-lantern that reminded me of him, and a few other small, spooky trinkets to put in a stocking for him.

Finally, I started toward the mystics store I had visited the last time I was here. I was able to afford the stuff inside now and was looking forward to getting him something really nice for his tarot cards. I went inside and had just started to peruse when I heard wind chimes coming from the back.

"Hello! Can I help—" She stopped short when she saw me. Her eyes went wide with surprise and her happy expression shifted to an angry one. "You are not welcome here."

I looked at the fancy suede bag in my hand. "Excuse me?"

"You!" She stormed over and snatched the bag from my hands. "Get out! Your money is not accepted here."

"Why?" I demanded.

She continued to scowl as she thrust her arm out and pointed to the exit. "Leave."

I swallowed the lump in my throat and steeled myself. I exited the shop empty-handed. My good mood completely deflated; I left the mall with no present for Desi.

The bus ride felt like it was taking three times as long as it had to get to the mall that morning. The longer I rode, the more I thought about what happened, and the fact that I'd have nothing to give Desi on Christmas. I cried into my scarf, wishing I could have gotten him that nice bag.

If I couldn't give him a present, I'd do something else to make our day special. I made a list of all the things I'd cook. Turkey, mashed potatoes, stuffing, and so many cookies.

Every day that week before my shift, I walked down to the grocery store and bought more ingredients to make the perfect dinner. In just days, Desi would be at my door, smiling wide, and wishing me a Merry Christmas.

Christmas Eve morning came, and from the moment I woke up, my nerves were an excited jumble. I flew around the house, lighting candles and starting cookies.

I spent hours curling my hair to perfection and doing my makeup with as much care. I picked my prettiest dress, and despite knowing we'd only be at home, I slid it on. The pencil dress was made of black velvet and was strapless, with a sweetheart neckline. It had a large white bow right in the center where the dip was. I paired it with nylons and heels. I couldn't wait for Desi to see me.

The day dragged on. Eventually, my mood sunk with the

sun. The last words I told him on that phone call a month ago echoed in my brain.

"If you don't come by midnight, I'll consider it your final goodbye."

The clock ticked from six to seven and eventually to ten and eleven. I promised him midnight, and I would honor that. I busied myself with putting the cookies away. I'd bring them to my neighbors tomorrow, I supposed. I wouldn't be able to eat all these if I tried. But then, at 11:52, there was a frantic knock on my door.

I dropped my peanut butter cookies on the floor and flew to the door. I opened it quickly and there he was, covered in snow, grinning wildly at me.

"Hey, I'm sorry I'm late, but I made it." He looked at his watch and then back at me. "I wasn't ready to say goodbye."

I stared at him for a long time, taking him in. He was dressed in a black suit, with a white shirt and suspenders. His hair had been styled back with gel. He looked so dapper, so handsome, and yet…

"Work's been crazy busy." He rocked on his heels, and when our eyes met again, he grinned. "May I still come in?"

"Of course. But… Desi…"

"What?" His smile fell. "Is something wrong?"

"No, I mean, maybe." I paused and raised a finger, tapping my cheek. "Why are you covered in blood?"

"What?" The back of his hand went to his cheek. He wiped the blood off onto his hand and then brought it out to stare at it. His expression changed. The happy Desi turned into one of deep concern. "Oh. That. Is it bad?" He looked at his suit, covered in long slices of red.

I tugged on his jacket and pulled him into the house. "Why don't you come in and explain."

"It smells amazing in here. Did you cook?"

"Hours ago. It's all cold or hard now."

"Look, Scout, I'm sorry. I know I'm late, but I can explain."

"You're in the mafia, aren't you?"

His body stiffened and then he rolled his eyes to the ceiling dramatically. "This again?"

"I'm right, aren't I? It's the only thing that makes sense." I nodded, finally realizing it. "The guy before, the police, the long absence. Your family is into…"

"Into what exactly?" His eyes turned cold. "If you're

going to accuse me of something, you better be confident you're right."

"I am." I glared at him. "You came here, remember?" I pointed to the door. "If you don't want to tell me what is going on, then you should leave now. Say goodbye before I—"

Desi reached out, grabbing my arms. He squeezed firmly and stepped closer. "Before you what? Fall in love with me? Scout, it's too late. For both of us. I came today to prove that I can't say goodbye. I won't. I've been busy, that's all." He wiped a tear off my cheek.

"I… I…" My chin trembled, and more tears came. "I tried to buy you a gift, but I was kicked out of the shop. They told me I couldn't buy it."

"Who?"

"That shop in the mall. It doesn't matter. I just—" I pulled away from him and wrapped my arms around myself. "I wanted to have a gift for you."

"I don't need a gift. I'm just glad I made it in time." He sniffed the air deeply. "I think dinner is gracious enough. Have you eaten yet?"

I'd been too sick to my stomach with nerves to eat.

"Come, let's get some food in our bellies and then we can talk," he said. I followed him into the kitchen and my sour mood lifted instantly when I saw his smile. He lit up like… well, it was Christmas. "You did all of this for me?"

I pressed my lips together and nodded.

"Scout, you're amazing. I'm starving!" He reached for a plate and began grabbing the serving utensils all around, filling his plate. He popped a roll in his mouth and smiled wide. Finally, I reached for my plate and filled it. Not as high as Desi's, but enough to satisfy my stomach.

I sat with him and we ate. Desi talked eagerly the entire time.

"I've had a crazy month. It flew by. I picked up a side gig, and it's kept me incredibly busy. I barely had time to catch that new show I've been watching. *The X-files*, remember?"

"You picked up a third job? I thought you came from money."

"My family has money. I don't." He pointed his fork at me and then stuffed a bite of mashed potatoes into his mouth.

"Are you going to keep being busy? You know, after the holidays?" I didn't want to sound whiny or desperate, but I couldn't help it. I couldn't only see him once a month or less.

"Yes and no. I think my new job might make me more than the other two things combined." He pursed his lips and then slapped his hands on the table. "You know what?" I jumped at the clink of the silverware as it bounced. Desi scooted his chair back and wiped his mouth with the napkin. He strode over to me. He grabbed my chin and tilted me to him, kissing me quickly. "I'm going to do it. I'm quitting the theater."

"Really?"

"Yep." He shoveled more food into his mouth and swallowed. "And I was thinking of giving all my smoke to Randy anyways, so why not do it now? Give me a few weeks to tie up some loose ends, put my notice in, get Randy set up, and I think I'll be able to see you a lot more regularly."

"Are you sure?" I tightened my lips, guilt sinking into my stomach. "I don't want to be the reason you're struggling. I'm not worth it." Desi was mid-bite when I said that. He dropped his fork with a sharp *ting*.

"Baby, you are absolutely worth it. You want to know why I took this other job? Because I was saving up." He stood again.

"Desi, what are…"

With a sly smile, he sauntered over again and bent down. He pulled out a small, black velvet box from his jacket. My heart stopped, my mouth fell open, and my mind went blank. He opened it, revealing a beautiful gold ring with a large round gem in the middle, surrounded by small diamonds. The band twisted around them, making them almost look like leaves, and the gem in the middle, a cloudy, white flower.

"It's Jade." He removed it from the box and motioned for me to give him my hand.

I did, and he slid it onto my ring finger. "But what's more important is that it's a promise. A promise that even if I'm not here all the time, or I'm late, that I'm not saying goodbye. I want you more than anything in this world."

I stared at the beautiful ring. I had never owned something this lovely. All of my jewelry was fake, and no man had ever thought to give me more than dinner or a drink.

"I don't know what to say," I said, finally regaining the ability to speak.

"Say you feel the same." He urged me up with him. "Say you love me just as much as I love you, and that nothing is going to come between us. Say that you want to be my past, present, and future. Say it, and I'll do everything in my power to keep you happy."

I leapt into his arms. "Yes! All of that. Always, Desi."

"Good!" He laughed and then grew serious. "Because now, if you want, I'll tell you why I'm covered in Rock Galante's blood."

CHAPTER 37

Desi

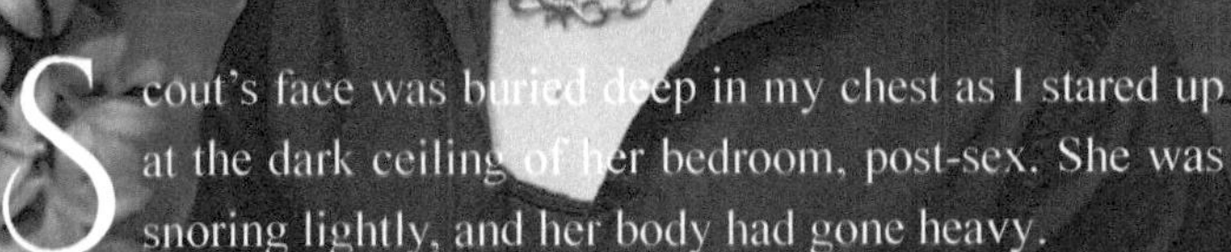

Scout's face was buried deep in my chest as I stared up at the dark ceiling of her bedroom, post-sex. She was snoring lightly, and her body had gone heavy.

We had taken little to no time after I had given her the ring I'd bought her to undress each other and head to the bedroom. I worshipped her body like the goddess she was, and in return, she offered me the most intimate parts of herself, her body, her soul, and her heart.

"I'm sorry I was late." I kept my voice low, afraid to wake her. "I'm sorry for a lot of things lately, but mostly about not seeing you as much as I want to. I'd give anything to be here every day with you."

She sighed and snuggled deeper into my bare body. The look on her face when I gave her that ring was engraved in my mind. She was so surprised and overjoyed. It was a beautiful thing, being able to do that for her. I wanted to see her face like that all the time. Bitterness crept into my mind as the reality of my situation returned to the forefront of my mind.

Aleida.

She was the persistent thorn in my side.

I'd felt nothing when I'd proposed to her.

I thought I had her when her father confronted her about her Bloodshed lover. I had no idea she was cheating on me, let alone with an outcast of our community. I told her dad I'd think about it and left quickly with Aleida in tow. In the car, she confessed everything and begged me not to kill him.

"It's just a fling! It's nothing! Desiderio, please, don't take this job. I'll end it."

I just drove. On and on, past both of our homes, out of the city, until my gas ran out. I filled my tank again and turned back to go home.

"A Bloodshed? A fucking Bloodshed?"

"It's not what you think! He didn't know suicide would make him turn. He was in a bad place and simply wanted out. He was miserable as a vampire until he found me. Just meet him, you'll see!"

"You want me to meet your lover?" The audacity of Aleida was shocking, but not surprising. She was used to getting everything she ever wanted. "I don't associate with Bloodsheds. Where did you even meet one?"

The vampire community was tight-lipped and small as it was. It was rare to find a vampire with ice-blue eyes. The risk they posed to the world if humans discovered they could possibly activate the vampire gene in them by suicide was too high to be welcomed.

"A dance club. He was hiding in the shadows. Most of his eternal life, he's spent in hiding, but no more, Desiderio. They are just like Bloodborns. They're misunderstood."

"What's there to misunderstand?" I pulled into my driveway and shut the car off. "He killed himself. He chose to become immortal, while we aren't given that option. We watch all the people around us grow old and die, and he thought it was fun. I'm not misunderstanding anything."

I stepped out of the car and tossed my hands up. "Go, go see your Bloodshed boyfriend. I don't want anything to do with that sad sack of shit."

"Desiderio!" she wailed. We fought until morning. I wasn't entirely sure why. I begged her to leave me for him, but she was adamant that we could make it work.

"My father would never let me marry him. And I love you! I was just lonely. Turning before you has been miserable," she complained. "Once we're both vampires, things will be different. It'll just be you and me again."

But it wouldn't be. I didn't have the balls to tell her yet, but our future had nothing to do with her secret lover, but with mine.

So instead of telling Aleida the truth, I took the job her dad offered.

I looked at Scout, still so warm and soft. In ten months, this would all be gone. Warm embraces, day dates, dinner at her place. I kissed her hair and smelled the shampoo and hairspray.

"I wish I could take you with me," I whispered. Despite feeling confident in her slumber, I only spoke aloud things that wouldn't give my reality away. To her, I was probably talking about the work I told her was keeping me busy. To me, I was asking her to have vampire blood in her.

Impossible.

Eventually, I managed to fall asleep, and sometime in the morning, I awoke to the smell of sweet batter and bacon. I climbed off her mattress and slid on my discarded boxers. I should have packed a bag, but the entire day had gone so chaotically, I didn't have time.

"More food?" I laughed and came into the kitchen, where she stood in front of the stove, wearing just a T-shirt, and flipping pancakes.

"I can afford food. Sit and I'll get you a plate."

"Merry Christmas." I kissed her and ignored her demand in favor of the coffee pot on her counter. I grabbed a mug and poured myself a hot cup.

"Merry Christmas!" She threw up her hands. Along with her hands went her spatula and a pancake. It flew through the air and landed on the floor with a splat! I went over to embrace her from behind.

"I love you so much," I mumbled into her massive amount of hair. "Best Christmas to date."

"Even with nothing under a tree?" She sighed.

"Trees are overrated. I'm just glad to be here with you."

"It's the perfect hiding place, huh?" She smirked and plated the breakfast. "Hiding where no one would think to look."

"What do you mean?" I looked up.

"We never got to your story. Of why you were covered in someone else's blood? It's the perfect hiding place because visiting my neighborhood makes no sense for someone like you."

"Scout, enough with that self-depreciation shit. I don't care what other people think. And no, it's not the perfect hiding place because the last time I was here, I was arrested." I took the plate and sat at the table.

"Yes, but why would you come back if you were afraid of getting caught?"

"I'm not afraid of getting caught. The guy's dead, gone, and he ain't coming back." A flash of last night's events ran through my brain, and I quickly shook them away. "Is this your way of asking what happened?"

"Yeah, it was. What did you do?" She joined me at the table.

"I told you I got a new job." I picked up a piece of bacon and eyed it.

"You did. And that it made a lot of money."

"It does. People pay me very well to do things they don't want to do."

"People as in?" She raised an eyebrow.

"People."

"And things they don't want to do as in?"

"What do you think?" I took a bite of my bacon and looked at her expectantly.

"Kill people?"

"Bingo."

"And you're okay with that?"

"Are you?" That was the most important thing to me.

"I mean, I don't know. You're being safe, right?" Safe? She wasn't concerned about the lives I was taking. She was worried about mine.

"I am. I've killed three men so far. All scumbags. I had no issue with disposal other than the weight. I'm not built to carry 300-pound men around all day," I joked, but she didn't laugh.

"You're psychotic."

"It paid for the ring on your hand," I said sharply. I set my fork down and sighed. "Would you rather me not do this? I can go back to slinging popcorn at the theater and dope from my car, but that's going to get me in far more trouble than taking out some guys no one's going to miss. I'll do whatever you want me to, Scout. Just say the word."

She thought about it for a long time and then looked at me with her beautiful brown eyes. At that moment, I saw something I'd never seen before. A glimmer, a spark, a hint of something dark. But in her, darkness was beauty. She opened her mouth and said the sexiest thing she could in that moment.

"Just don't get caught."

CHAPTER 38

Desi

"*Just don't get caught.*"

The words echoed through my brain as I drove home later that night. I got home Christmas evening, just in time to meet with Aleida. She was waiting in my driveway, with a forced smile on her face.

"Merry Christmas, Desiderio!" She threw her arms around me, and I stiffened.

"Hi."

"Can we go inside? It's snowing."

I pushed her away from me gently and motioned to the door. "Yeah, okay." We went in, and she frowned at the bare place—no decorations in sight. She slid her coat halfway down her shoulders and stopped. "No tree? No stockings? Not even any lights?"

"Why would I do any of that? I'm hardly here anymore."

"Yes, but…" She stomped her foot. "We're here now. And last year, we decorated the whole house!"

"Last year, I didn't have a job that kept me busy. Last year, I wasn't chasing down guys right up until Christmas." I hung my coat on the rack and walked further inside the room.

"The guy your dad gave me went on the run. Someone tipped him off. I had to go clear across the fucking state to find the fucker."

"But you made it home in time! I was worried when you weren't here last night, but Daddy said you were on the job."

This new career path I somehow found myself going down would hopefully help me see Scout more without people growing suspicious of why I wasn't around as much, once I was more established.

"I was. I don't get a break, I'm always gone. I'm thinking about dropping the lease on this place." I went to the kitchen and grabbed a beer from the fridge. I returned to the living room, where Aleida was still standing by the door, with her coat and boots on.

"What?" I asked.

"Do I not get a gift?"

"A gift? I just got back from a month's worth of hunting down people for your dad, and you think I stopped and got you a gift?"

"Well, yeah. It's Christmas."

"Did you get me a gift?" I asked, knowing she didn't. That wasn't Aleida's MO. She wanted to be the receiver, never the giver. Her very presence in someone's life was the gift. "I don't think I've ever gotten a gift from you now that I think about it. Birthday, anniversary, why would today be any different?"

"You know what? I did, actually." She lifted her head high in the air. "I was going to let you do that thing you've been asking for the last year."

I blinked, trying to remember, and then I laughed loudly. "You think fucking your ass is a gift? When you're giving it to every other guy in town, I think I'll pass. Go, offer it to that Bloodshed."

"Desiderio—"

"You staying or going?" I snapped. I was tired of her already. Before, I could handle her whiny bullshit for hours if I needed to. Now, I didn't even want to look at her.

"I got invited to this vamp party. I thought maybe you could come with me? It's fully decorated and I think they'll be human food, you know, for others like you. It'd be good for people to see us together in public."

No, it would not.

"Why would I want to go and stand in a corner all night and watch you suck on someone's vein?" I plopped on my couch and propped my feet up. "I just got home. I haven't slept comfortably for a month. Consider it my Christmas present from you. Stop inviting me to your stupid vampire parties."

"You act like you're not going to be involved in the scene in just a few months. You don't understand how important it is to get in certain circles as soon as possible."

"I understand; I just don't give a shit." I took a swig of my beer. "I don't care if I'm popular. I don't want to be invited to the blood parties or be involved in the scene. I just want to be left alone."

"You're going to start your eternity on a bad start." A single blood tear slid down her cheek, and she quickly rubbed it away. "But I refuse to do the same. If you want to sit here and mope, fine, but I'm going."

"Good. Go. Don't fucking come back if you can."

"You took that job so you can start saving for a house for us. I thought this was what you wanted, and now, you act like you don't want to be with me."

"I took the job because much like the rest of my life, I don't get any choice. I don't want to be with you. Have I not made that clear enough?"

Aleida stormed over and slapped the bottle from my hand. She was so strong it hit the wall and smashed into pieces. She crouched and then sat hard on my lap. I tried to push her away but her vampire strength overpowered my human muscles. She grabbed my jaw between her hand and squeezed.

"You've always been sarcastic and full of your little jokes, but I'm sick of them. Ever since I turned before you, you've been bitter and shitty and seem hellbent on making me suffer. But it's you, Desiderio, who will suffer in the end. Not me." She forced me to look her in the eyes.

"You think I'd let you off so easily? I'd be stupid to break off our engagement. Despite you being a giant piece of shit, you're the most eligible Bloodborn around. I'm not letting some other vampire take you." She bared her fangs and hissed at me, before letting me go.

It was on the tip of my tongue to tell her it wasn't another vampire she needed to be worried about, but a mere human that had stolen my heart. But I wouldn't put Scout's life on the line like that. She'd be as good as dead.

"I'm going to the party." She lifted her head high in the air. "But next year, when you are a vampire, you will be attending the event on my arm, as my husband."

I stood, my anger rising once again. She may be stronger than I was at the moment, but I had a lot more power than she realized.

"You know, actually, there is one job I still have left to do. It's been sitting on my docket since the night I agreed to work for your dad. Maybe I will go. Is Bradley Donovan going to be there tonight?"

She froze at the door and turned slowly. "Desiderio, you wouldn't."

"I would." I stepped over my coffee table and started

toward her, grabbing my coat off the hook. "And I will. You want to threaten me again?" I stared into her eyes, glaring down at her. For a long moment, we held each other's gazes, before she blinked and looked down.

"No." Her shoulders slouched.

"Good. You wanted a Christmas present? Consider this yours. I won't kill your fucking lover until I have a good enough reason. Don't give me one."

"Why don't you start applying to schools now? You know they have all sorts of grants and scholarships, especially for Latin Americans." Luis asked me one morning in late January, as he got ready for work. I had brought out my art school jug to count and roll coins on the living room floor.

"I know, but you have to be like super smart and write essays and stuff. I don't even think I'll use this for an art school." I waved a roll of pennies in the air. "Maybe I'll just go on a vacation and look at the art there." That would be the more realistic option, but even that was a pipe dream.

"There are some beautiful places all around the world with stunning art." Luis nodded. "Perhaps you can ask Desiderio what places he would go to. Take a trip together." He knew I was missing my boyfriend terribly, and I knew that vacation was the furthest thing from our future. We'd have to see each other to take a trip together.

Every night after I got home, he called me and spoke to me for an hour, even though it was almost always two or three in the morning. With him quitting the movie theater and getting Randy to take over all of his other illegal dealings, he didn't have to stick to a schedule anymore.

"You wouldn't know it, but most of my new job is done at night," he joked one night on a call.

"What if our phone lines are tapped? You can't say stuff like that."

"They aren't, and if they were, I'd take care of it," Desi said so with such confidence, such finality, I felt comfortable. It was an odd feeling, knowing what he was doing now. He had assured me that the people were all criminals.

"I just get paid to stop them from continuing is all. I don't think too much into it. Do I feel bad about getting a known bad guy off the streets? No. Do I feel bad that I'm not making an honest living and am someone you can be proud of? Yes."

"Desi, I don't care if it's honest or not. I love you no matter what your job is." I stared down at the promise ring he gave me at Christmas. The symbol of his love that I had with me always, even when he couldn't be there. If he loved me for who I was, I could love him back just the same.

"Yeah, but what will you tell your friends when they ask what I do, huh?"

"You're a traveling salesman," I repeated what he had told me to say. "You sell magazines door to door."

"Even I don't believe that lie."

We only saw each other four times in January. Every Tuesday, he had made a point to come into the diner and have dinner, but it was just that. Sometimes he didn't even have dessert. The last time I saw him in person after he ate, I took a small break to see him off.

"Maybe we can go out for a movie or something?" I hated that I was pleading for attention, but not being able to touch and hold and kiss him every day sucked. Desi was addicting.

"I'm almost done getting Randy set up," he promised.

"And then I'll take you out for a special Valentine's Day date."

"Valentine's?" My jaw dropped. That was two weeks away. "How much stuff do you still have to do with Randy?"

"Well, he has all the products," he said, with a hint of bitterness. "He had to pay me, which took time, and now I'm setting him up with all my contacts, which I had many."

"I heard."

"I'm working on it, I promise." The front doors to the diner opened and Journey's "Don't Stop Believing" burst into the cold winter air.

"Scout! We need you in here!" Shannon, another waitress, called.

"Coming!" I called back. I waited for the loud music to stop, signaling she had gone back inside, but the song kept blaring. "I hate this song," I muttered, starting away from Desi.

"You hate Journey?"

I spun around and threw up my hands.

"It's too fucking hopeful. Why would I want to hear it when you're leaving again? I stopped believing a long time ago." I stormed back into the diner, not bothering with a goodbye, and went about my shift. For the next few weeks, every time Journey was played through the speakers, I requested we change the song. I stopped answering Desi's late-night calls. I wanted to hear his voice, so I kept the voice machine on, but I couldn't keep hearing him lie to me. It was never 'soon'. It hurt my heart way too much.

Over the messages, Desi promised every day that he'd see me on Valentine's. "I won't miss it. I'm setting it as my deadline. All my loose ends will be tied up by then and I can start living a normal life. Well, semi-normal."

I didn't believe him. Each night I tried to harden my heart

toward him. I couldn't keep waiting for him to come around. With that in mind, I agreed to work on February 14th.

With a few more extra shifts, I might be able to afford a car of my own. I could stop walking and taking the bus places.

I went about my night, smiling and putting on my best face for the happy couples, despite wanting to cry in the back room. I didn't hate Desi for not making it to my house earlier. I hated myself for falling for him in the first place. I was smarter than that. I stared at the ring and thought about what it meant. He promised he'd see me on Valentine's. Desi didn't break his promises.

After my shift, I offered to stay late, so as to not go home and be disappointed. As we shut the neon light off, indicating we were closed, Journey came over the loudspeakers.

"Can you shut that shit off?" I shouted to the cooks, but they ignored me. I steeled myself, and cleaned off the tables quickly, trying not to think of Desi and the last time I saw him. When I was done, I wrapped myself up in my coat and boots and started out the door.

As soon as I pushed through the doors to the outside, I heard a familiar piano tune. I paused and looked around quickly for the source of the music. The cooks had turned theirs off fifteen minutes ago, and yet, I could hear the beginning piano to Journey's "Don't Stop Believing".

Suddenly, someone started singing over Steve Perry. I went down the steps and into the parking lot.

"Randy?" I squinted, seeing a figure standing on top of a car at the end of the parking lot. I started toward him, and Desi's other friends walked out from behind it. Just as the guitar was getting louder, they climbed onto the car's hood and trunk and the music got louder. Soon, they started singing it together.

What was this? They had air guitars and invisible drums and a hairbrush for a microphone. I shook my head. Was this Desi's doing? Why? Could he not come, so he sent his friends to entertain me instead? This was just some stupid game for him. It started to snow again, and I began to walk backward. They didn't understand how hurtful this entire scene was. I was going home.

The long guitar solo came and Randy and the others pointed behind me. I turned, and there he was. Desi, at the far end of the parking lot, holding roses and mouthing the words to the song that had made me cry so much these last few weeks. He started toward me and I broke out into a sprint. My body collided with his and we fell to the ground.

"You said you hated this song," he said after I stopped kissing him. "I didn't want you to associate it with something bad. I don't want you to have any memories about me that are sad. Only good things from now on, okay?"

"Only good memories."

"And this is one of them?" He motioned to his friends still performing their hearts out.

"Absolutely. It completely erases my previous memories of this song." We walked together to his friends, who were now performing "Lights".

"Good," he grinned. "Because hiring a live band isn't cheap."

CHAPTER 40

Scout

"You're getting a car? I can help you get a hell of a deal. Mick's dad owns a dealership."

"I wouldn't know where to start at a dealership. I was just going to check the newspaper. Plus, I doubt I have that kind of money," I told Desi.

"Nonsense. We'll get you something that is going to last. What were you thinking?" Desi glanced at me from the driver's side. He was taking me home after my moonlight Journey concert. "Don't Stop Believing" was still playing in my head.

"I don't know. I just need something that will get me to and from work. Oh, and I need to get a license."

Desi stomped on the brakes, causing us to slide on the icy roads. I let out a scream but he quickly righted himself. "Sorry. Scout, you can't drive?"

"I can drive," I defended. "Just… not legally."

He swore and shook his head. "Scout, do you drive a lot?"

"No, I haven't driven in a few years."

"Okay, well, why don't we start with that, and then get you a car?"

"I can get a car without having a license."

"Yes, but you can't drive it."

"Well, how will I learn to drive without a car?"

"I'll teach you." We pulled into my driveway and went inside.

"You think you have time for that?" I snickered.

"I'll make it work. I promised you I'd have things sorted by Valentine's. It's sorted." We went to my room so as to not rouse Luis or Brucey. I changed out of my work clothes and put on a sleep shirt.

"Are you going soon?" I asked, trying to keep the disappointment from my voice.

"No, I just… I've missed you so much. I'm sorry I haven't been able to see you."

"Well, you're here now, and tomorrow you're teaching me to drive, so I can go get my license."

He slid off his clothes, leaving just his underwear. We got into bed and cuddled, and eventually, it led to an emotional lovemaking, and then, finally, sleep. The next afternoon, Desi put me in the driver's seat of his car and took a deep breath.

"Scout, I love you. I do, I really do, but if you crash my car…"

I laughed, but his lips were in a straight, grim line. I rolled my eyes. "It's fine. I've driven before. It's just been a while. Now, where do I put the keys?"

He scowled and started to show me, but I swatted his hands away.

"Stop it. Let me do this." I started the car and glanced through the rear mirror.

"Adjust all the mirrors," he reminded me. I rolled down my window and pushed the side mirror to my liking. Desi did the same on his side, asking me a dozen times if I could see everything.

"Yes. Now can I go?"

"Can you not hit something?"

"You're an awful teacher," I muttered as I stepped on the break and put the car into reverse. Carefully, I let the car crawl backward down the drive and onto the road. Desi directed me around town, leading me to a middle school parking lot. I stopped the car and he got out and motioned for me to roll the window down.

"Okay, so a big part of the test is parking. If you can't park, you won't even get on the road. So, let's see it. Can you parallel park?"

"No one does that."

"Yes, but you still need to know how to do it."

We spent the rest of the afternoon mastering the art of parking. Only when he was satisfied I'd pass did he get back in the car.

"Okay, now, let's see how you drive on the highway." He directed me again, all the while muttering about how winter was not the best time to learn to drive.

"Well, it was either now or walk another winter. By the time I get to work every night, my toes are purple!" I exclaimed.

"Why don't you ask people for rides?"

"I don't ask for help if I can help it. I don't need anyone but myself."

"There's no shame in asking when you need it." His tone softened.

"Nope. I just figure it out. I always do. I've only ever had myself to lean on, I'm not stopping now."

He reached out and placed his hand on my thigh. "You can lean on me."

"Can I? I've seen you one time this year. You know how I spent New Year's Eve? Alone, drawing in my sketchbook, listening to Mariah Carey, and trying not to cry as midnight hit. All I could think about was all the couples in love and kissing right at that moment, and I was alone. Where were you?"

"Scout." He sighed. I took an exit to turn onto the highway and sped up to match the other drivers.

"Scout!" Desi screamed and threw his arms over my body as suddenly something collided with my side of the car.

The grinding of metal against metal and the sound of glass breaking shattered my ear drums. I clutched the wheel as we rolled one, two, three times. We went down into a ditch, landing on the driver's side. Steam rose from the vehicle, along with the hiss of something coming from the hood. I blinked and only saw white. Snow and broken glass fell all around me. My head was dizzy. I tried to lift it, but everything felt heavy, so heavy.

"Scout! Scout!" Desi's voice was panicked and distant. Had he managed to escape the carnage? I closed my eyes and let the blackness engulf me. If one of us had to be hurt beyond repair, I was glad it was me that had taken the brunt of the collision.

I couldn't survive if he didn't.

CHAPTER 41

Desi

"Scout! Scout, get out of the fucking car!" I screamed. "Wake up! Will you fucking wake up!" I screamed, over and over, as I fought my seatbelt and then hers. My hands were shaking so hard I was fumbling the buttons.

Blood blinded me as I tried to free her and pull her up and out of the car. Someone from outside the car was screaming something to someone else, but my ears were blasted, and I could only hear loud muffles. It was all a blur where time had slowed. Until I knew Scout's heart was still beating, mine refused to.

Giving up on my seatbelt, I managed to get hers off, and I leaned my whole body forward, grasping her shoulders tightly. I shook her hard. Her head bobbed forward, but her eyes didn't open.

No!

"Scout! Please!" Tears mixed with blood fell freely as I pleaded for her to wake up. Suddenly, my door was opened and I was being ripped away from her. Two firemen lifted me out of the car. One of them threw me over their shoulder and trudged to an ambulance.

I screamed as loud as I could.

"Let me fucking go! She's still in there! I can't go without her!" I kicked and screamed.

"Sir, we're working on getting her out too. Just stay put." The fireman released me to a pair of EMTs, who grasped my forearms and pulled me down. I fought, but between the two of them, I wasn't getting out of their hold. The firemen dove in and pulled her out. They rushed her over and put her on a stretcher.

"We've got to get her to the hospital. You ready?" an EMT said to the ones holding me.

"Let's go." They turned to look at me.

"Can you walk? You should probably get checked over too." They helped me into the ambulance and closed the door.

I sat off to the side as they began to resuscitate her. They pressed on her chest, over and over, giving her compressions, but she didn't appear to be moving.

My whole life slowly flashed before my eyes; my future slipping away with each thrust of their hands against her chest. Everything I ever had planned for was disappearing. I thought I had more time, months, maybe years if I could figure it out, but now it was gone. Scout was dead. The love of my life was dead because of me. If she hadn't met me, none of this would have happened.

I bent over, letting my sobs take hold. I did this to her. But then, I heard a beep and a large breath.

"We got a pulse," the EMT said to his partner. "It's strong."

I stared at the pair in uniform. "She's okay?"

"She's alive. That's the first big thing, okay? We got her breathing in time for no brain damage. She was only out for one minute."

One minute?

It felt like an eternity.

I scooted closer to her, reaching for her hand. I squeezed it tightly, but she didn't respond. Her eyes were still closed, but her chest rose and fell.

"We'll be at the hospital soon," they assured me.

Soon, we were being removed from the ambulance, and despite my best efforts to stay with her, they insisted on taking us separately.

I hadn't noticed, but during the trip, someone had cleaned my cuts up. However, the gash on my head and my forearm needed stitches. I waited impatiently to get them taken care of, all the while asking about Scout's condition.

"Are you her husband?" a nurse snapped at me after I asked her too many times.

"No, she's my girlfriend. She has no one else."

The nurse glared and pursed her lips. "They are working on her."

I was admitted against my will for the night.

"You lost a bit of blood, and you've got a concussion," the doctor told me after I argued with him about it.

"How do you know?" I demanded.

"We gave you the tests. Do you not remember them?"

I rolled my eyes but then realized I didn't.

"Why don't you lie down, rest, and we'll get you something to relax you."

I looked at the hospital gown I was wearing. I hadn't remembered putting it on.

"Is there someone you'd like us to call for you? An emergency contact?"

"No!" I threw my hand out. "No one can know I'm here. Don't call anyone."

He raised his eyebrows but then nodded. "Okay. Do you know of anyone we can call for her?"

"Me," I snarled. How did they not understand that I was the person that should be handling things? If I had it my way, she'd be my wife already. The doctor motioned for me to climb into bed.

"Okay, well, Mr. Amato, I assure you, the woman you came in with is in the best of hands."

"Is she going to be okay?" I asked, climbing into the bed and shifting to sit up. He nodded and said nothing else. He left, and I swore at him as he closed my door. A nurse came in and pushed an IV into my hand. I tried to protest, but my eyelids grew heavy and I couldn't speak. My head bobbed and then I closed my eyes. I awoke in the morning. There was ice water by my bed.

I swung my arm out and sent it flying across the room. I then grabbed my remote and pushed the buttons, calling for a nurse. One came a few moments later, visibly annoyed.

"Good morning, Mr. Amato. How are you feeling?"

"Fine, I just want to see my girlfriend."

"As soon as the doctor releases you, you can head to her room. Just sit tight. I'll send him in."

I waited for three hours until finally, the doctor sauntered in with a smile that made me want to murder him.

"How are you feeling today?"

I went through the same quiz from before, quickly assuring him I was fine.

"You'll have to come back in a few days to remove the stitches, but otherwise, just take it easy the next few days. Your concussion may make you a little dizzy and sensitive to light." He went on and on about what I'd be experiencing the next few days, but all I could hear was Scout, Scout, Scout!

He signed my papers, and within the hour, I was released and running down the halls to figure out what room Scout was in. I took the elevator to the floor the nurse told me and flew down the hall. I threw the door open and called out.

"Scout!" I looked around the room frantically and found her in her bed, her arm in a sling. I stormed over and she opened her eyes.

"Desi." Her lips twitched upward, but she was groggy. "You made it."

I laughed and tears slid down my face again. "I did. I did and so did you. How are you feeling?"

"Like someone hit me with their car." She tried to sit up but winced. "I did something to my arm." She nodded to the sling. There was a red, long, thick scar, sewn neatly.

"I guess I had surgery." She chuckled low. "I don't remember much." She closed her eyes.

"Well, you did get hit by a car." I smiled through my pain. "But we're alive, and that's all that matters." She nodded, and a moment later popped one eye back open and grinned.

"You think I'm ready for my driver's test?"

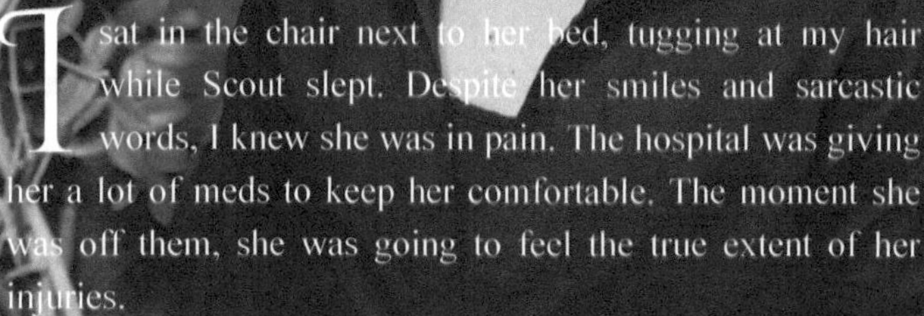

CHAPTER 42

Desi

I sat in the chair next to her bed, tugging at my hair while Scout slept. Despite her smiles and sarcastic words, I knew she was in pain. The hospital was giving her a lot of meds to keep her comfortable. The moment she was off them, she was going to feel the true extent of her injuries.

I slumped in the chair and rethought every moment since I met her. For three days and nights, I replayed every single day I'd had the honor to spend with her. I didn't realize how precious each minute was until I almost lost her. I couldn't bear it.

What was I going to do come October?

On my twenty-seventh birthday, my human heart was going to stop beating, and the vampire blood in me would take over and transform me into a monster of the dark. I would no longer be able to see her.

She'd know something was up. My eyes would turn from the human blue into a red as bright as the blood I'd crave. I'd have fangs, and every time I saw her, I'd want to drink from her until she was limp and dead in my arms.

As I sat there, watching her chest struggling to rise and fall in the medically induced slumber they had put her under, I tried to figure out a plan.

My rational brain was screaming for me to leave while she was sleeping and never come back. I needed to write one of those 'Dear John' letters and say goodbye forever. She'd find someone else; I was sure. She was beautiful, funny, smart, and talented. God, could she draw. I'd never met someone with her level of natural skill with the pencil. Most people had to go to higher education and pay thousands and thousands to get as good as she was just by existing. She was born with a gift that I wasn't deserving of.

But could I let her go? Would I be able to walk out of her hospital room and not look back?

No.

If I left before she woke, I'd never stop watching over her. I'd know when and if she found someone else. I'd torture myself by watching her fall in love with someone else. I'd follow her as she got married to some chump, grew swollen with his babies, and lived her happily ever after. All from my cold, dark, loveless mansion across town.

Like a bird trapped in a beautiful golden cage, I'd observe the world around me, knowing I'd never be free to experience it myself.

It was selfish to stay in that chair and continue to love her the way I did. But my feet were frozen to the floor. There had to be another way. I knew many a vampire who had familiars, humans they fed on regularly, but those only lasted so long. I'd never met a vampire with an aged human.

We had to live under the radar as best as we could. Having a young man with a ninety-year-old woman would draw suspicion, and even if it didn't, at some point, Scout's aged body would become too tired to move constantly, and the longer I remained young, people would notice.

It wasn't until the nurses commented about me going home to change clothes that I moved from that room.

"She'll still be here when you get back, sweetie. Go home, shower, get clean clothes, and come back. She'll probably still be asleep."

"My car is totaled. I don't even know where it is," I told her.

"Hm… is there someone you can call?"

Who could I trust to not ask too many questions?

"Yeah, I can figure it out."

I stood by the phone, debating my options before finally dialing Randy's number and explaining quickly that he needed to come get me. As soon as I got into his car, I was thrown question after question.

"This is the chick we did that thing on Valentine's for?"

"Yes," I answered through gritted teeth. "And I told you not to keep bringing it back up."

"Yeah, yeah, I know. You handed over all your weed and clients and all that for my silence. Blah blah blah. This is just… not you. I didn't peg you for—"

"For what?" I leaned over and pulled a cigarette out of his jean jacket. It wasn't until I got into the car that I realized I hadn't had a smoke since the accident. I pushed the car lighter in and once it was hot and popped back out, I brought it to my cigarette. "A cheater?"

Silence followed for a beat.

"Yeah. Why don't you just end it with Aleida?"

"Have you met Aleida? She'd kill me." I took a long drag and blew smoke toward the window. Literally.

"And you think she'll be happy-go-lucky when she catches you?"

"She won't catch me, because you're going to keep your fucking mouth shut."

"You don't gotta worry about me or any of us," he said. "But you're not good at the whole secret thing. You totaled your car, man. How are you going to explain that?"

"Do I have to?" I was trying to play it cool as if none of this was bothering me, but he was right. I was toeing the line dangerously.

"You don't think your dad, who bought that car, will want to know what happened to it?"

"All I have to say is it was just me in the car. Problem solved."

"Yeah, but don't they do accident reports? For the insurance."

Fuck.

Fuck fuck fuck fuck.

"I'll call in some favors or something. Maybe my brother can help."

"Seriously? You must really be in love with this girl." Randy pulled into my driveway and I got out.

"I am. Thanks, man, I owe you one."

"No, you don't." He laughed, pulled a joint from his coat pocket, and wiggled his eyebrows. "Just keep sending your old clients my way."

"You got it." I went into my house and peeled off my clothes to shower. I winced as I got a good whiff of myself. I was much riper than I had realized. I had just stepped into the shower when I heard a voice clear their throat from behind me. I spun around and snatched my towel to cover myself. Aleida stood in the doorway with her arms crossed.

"Where have you been?"

"On a job. What are you doing here?"

"We're about to be married in a few months. I should be allowed to come and go as I please."

"Well, you're not. Why don't you go spend time with your little Bloodshed boyfriend?"

"You're focused on something so trivial."

"It's not trivial, it's—" I trailed off as an idea sprung to my mind.

The way to keep Scout in my life. It was a risk. There was a high chance I could lose her forever. She either had the vampiric blood in her or she didn't, and we wouldn't know until she…

"Desiderio!" Aleida snapped her fingers to get my attention. "Did you hear me?"

I nodded.

If I wanted Scout forever, she'd have to become a Bloodshed. Which meant, I had to convince her to kill herself.

My eyes were heavy, but eventually, I blinked them open. The meds they'd been feeding through my IV for the last few days made me so groggy.

"Desi?" I croaked. A loud sniffle came from a dark corner of the room. I turned my attention to it, only to find Desi sitting in a chair, wiping his cheeks.

"Hey, babe." He stood and shoved his hands into his leather jacket. "How do you feel?"

I tried to sit up, but I only had one free arm and my body felt so heavy. Desi moved quickly, coming to help.

"Don't push yourself. You had some damage done to you."

"I know." I sighed. "What exactly happened?"

"A reckless driver."

"What about your car?"

"That's gone. We'll go get me another one when you get your license. We can pick out his and hers." He reached for my hand that had the IV attached to it and squeezed gently. His and hers? My belly fluttered. I swallowed, and I realized my throat was ridiculously dry.

"Water?" Desi quickly moved to my side table, picking up a Styrofoam cup and bringing it to my mouth. I took the straw and drained it. Desi chuckled.

"You want me to get you another cup? How about food? Are you hungry?"

"Just water, please."

He nodded and left the room, returning a moment later with a nurse, who asked the same questions he did.

"I think you may be well enough to go home today. The doctor has to do one last check."

I started to sigh in relief but flinched as something sharp poked my ribs. The nurse nodded. "You're going to be sore. You cracked some bones in your rib cage."

I felt like she'd already told me this, and yet, it still felt like new information at the same time. She patted my leg and told me a doctor would come and confirm in a bit whether I could go home or not. Once we were alone again, I turned to Desi. He had returned to his dark corner.

"How are you feeling?"

"Fine. How do you feel about going home?"

I took a deep breath and smiled. "Good. I need to get back to work ASAP. I'm sure they think I quit." It was a decent job. I couldn't lose it.

"Fuck that place." His smile suddenly slid off his face and turned into a snarl. "You almost died and you're worried about your job?"

"Yes. I have bills to pay. I don't even know how I'm going to pay for this!" I threw my free arm up and gasped at the pain. My head fell back onto my pillow in exhaustion. Desi reached out and stroked my bruised cheek.

"Scout." He sighed. "I love you so much. I thought..."

"That I died?" I smirked and closed my eyes.

"Yeah. Look, I can call your work for you. I'll ask if they

can give you a break until you're better, and still keep your job."

"But what about my bills?"

"Scout." His tone became agitated. "Stop worrying. I'll cover it all. Stay here as long as you need. I'll have them send me the bill."

"I have more bills than just this."

"Don't. Worry. About. It." Desi's words were final. I relaxed and fell asleep again, only to wake when the doctor came by to release me, with the warning to take it easy and not to work for at least a month while my arm and ribs healed.

I opened my mouth to protest, but Desi shot me the dirtiest look, and I closed it. Whether I liked it or not, I was taking a break from work. As I was being wheeled out of the hospital, I wondered how we were getting home. Right then, one of Desi's friends pulled right up to the doors and helped me inside his car.

"How are you feeling, Scout?" Randy asked from the driver's seat. All I could muster was a thumbs-up as he drove us back to my house. When we got there, Desi lifted me out and took me inside, placing me gently in bed.

I thanked him but was beginning to struggle with the pain radiating from my arm. While they had given me pills to take home, it wasn't nearly as strong as the stuff they pumped into me there.

"You all right?" Desi asked. I pressed my lips tightly and nodded. "Let me go say goodbye to Randy and I'll be back. Just rest, please." He disappeared and returned an instant later, just in time to see me trying to roll off the bed.

"God damn it, Scout!" he yelled, hurrying into the room to catch me right as I was falling to the floor. "What is your problem?"

"I don't want the help," I protested through the pain. "I need to be able to do this on my own."

"Why? I'm here."

"But you won't always be!" I cried out. Desi cradled me in his arms and tried to soothe me as the hot tears sprung from my eyes. He rocked me as I sobbed. "I have to make sure I can do this."

"Do what?"

"Live! Walk, eat, go to the bathroom. Eventually work. I'll never heal if I don't try."

"Do you have to try on day one?" he asked, exasperated. "I'm not going anywhere, Scout. Get it through your fucking skull."

I closed my eyes and pressed my tear-stained face into his warm, hard chest. "But you will. You always do. You make all these promises, but the only thing I can expect from you is a recording on my answering machine every night. I need to be able to handle this on my own." I tried to push myself out of his arms, but I was weak and he was stronger.

"I know I've been really bad at things," he admitted. "I'm late. I postpone constantly, but not anymore. Scout, you are my biggest priority right now. I can't live without you. If you're not in my life, I don't know what I'd do. Please, let me take care of you."

His breathing became choked, and tears glistened in his beautiful eyes. Suddenly, his jaw tensed and his eyes hardened with what I could only describe as… determination. "I can't exist without you."

Scout

Two months later

"I passed!" I leapt out of Desi's rental car and threw myself against him. "I'm getting my license!"

"That's amazing, baby! I knew you would. You had the best guide," he teased, lifted me off the ground, and spun me around once before setting me down softly. He was careful gripping my still-healing arm.

The tester climbed out of Desi's car and gave us a little wave. He scribbled something on his clipboard and ripped off the paper, handing it to me. "Just take this down to the DMV, and they'll take your picture. Good job." With a tight smile, he walked back to his car.

"How does it feel?" Desi asked.

"Amazing. So good!" I spun around on my own again. "And just in time for spring."

After the accident, Desi begged me to let my body heal instead of trying to continue learning to drive and risk another accident. While it hadn't been my fault, a drunk driver had hit us.

"Yes," he agreed. "No snow to be had. Perfect for driving solo."

"Yeah, yeah. You know, I drove Luis and Brucey around town the other day and neither had any complaints."

"They don't want to be evicted," Desi teased.

"Ha-ha. Okay, let's go before the DMV closes."

We got the picture taken and my license came in the mail that next weekend, which was perfect timing because Desi was free and ready to go with me to buy a car.

"His and hers, remember?"

"I doubt we'll find matching ones with our two vastly different budgets," I reminded him. When we got there, Desi informed me that his friend Mick worked there with his dad. "I think we'll be able to get a deal on something for you."

I walked through aisle after aisle of cars and frowned. "I don't think even a deal will help me afford any of these."

Desi put his arm around me and kissed the top of my head. "We'll find you one. Come on, I think there are some over here in your price range."

My budget had been something we'd argued over almost every day since the accident. He was already paying my hospital bills and helping me cover... everything. I didn't need him to pay for my car as well.

"Desiderio, is that you?" Mick waved to us.

"Hey, man. Yeah, we're both looking for cars today." Desi tugged me forward to greet his friend. Mick gave me a funny look, but it was so quick I wasn't entirely sure I hadn't imagined it.

"That's great. You and..."

"Scout," Desi reminded him. "My girlfriend."

"Right, yeah, from Valentine's Day."

"Scout is looking for a reasonably priced car to get her to and from work," Desi told him.

"Wonderful." Mick turned to me and smiled. "Scout, why don't you take a look around, and Desiderio, why don't we discuss your budget." He put his hand on his back and led him away. I watched them for a moment before turning away. That was weird.

Now that I had a smidgen of freedom, I took off toward the cars that I could realistically afford. I grimaced, as I started to examine them more closely. No wonder they'd been placed in the back. Almost all of them were rusted, dented, or over twenty years old.

I glanced back to where Mick had taken Desi. He was throwing up his arms, all the while Desi seemed his normal, cool, and collected self with his hands in his pockets.

The music being pumped in from megaphones all over the lot was too loud for me to hear what was being said, but it didn't seem like Desi was happy about it. His hands came out of his pockets and he grabbed Mick's suit jacket. He tugged him and said something close to his ear. To which, Mick nodded and Desi let him go. Mick straightened his suit and motioned toward my area of the lot.

I quickly dipped behind some cars and feigned interest in a few. As they drew closer, I was able to pick up their voices.

"How are you going to explain that to your folks?" Mick asked Desi.

"I don't have to, I have my own money now," Desi said.

"You really like her then?"

"I think I might be in love for the first time. She's every-thing to me."

My stomach fluttered at his words. He didn't know I was listening, and he still said them.

"What are you going to do then? About the pesky little thing coming just around the corner?" Mick asked. I frowned and peered from behind the car I'd tossed myself under.

"I don't know yet. I'll figure it out. Until then, just keep your mouth shut."

"You got it, boss." Mick snickered.

"You want to make some money off me today or not?" Desi snapped.

"Hey now, let's not get crazy. You may be a piece of work, but your money's good here. Now, about a vehicle."

I stood and pretended to be just seeing them. "Hey, I think I found one." I put my hand on the hood of a white car.

"That's a 1983 Oldsmobile Regency. Fine car. Real fine. You want to take a peek inside, maybe test drive it?" Mick flashed a smile at me. I nodded and climbed inside once he opened the door for me.

"What's your budget?" he asked.

I glanced at Desi and blushed. "It's kind of low," I admitted. Mick shot Desi a look but then smiled again.

"I think we can make it work. How about that test drive?" While Mick gushed about the car during the test ride, all I could think about was their conversation about the *pesky little thing*. When we got back to the dealership, I agreed to take the car. I signed the papers, and despite Mick claiming the car was under budget, I couldn't help but wonder if he and Desi had worked something out to where I got the car regardless. More and more it felt like I was dating a mobster. I mean, I was, I guess.

On the way home, I couldn't shake the unsettling feeling. I knew Desi had killed people, and I had been sort of okay with that. But seeing him in action, threatening people? Would people come after me for dating him? If they did, what would Desi do, and how would I feel about it?

CHAPTER 45

Desi

"Do you believe in soulmates?" Scout intertwined our fingers together and lifted them to the ceiling of her bedroom. I gazed at them. Her soft, tan one, and my pale, calloused one.

"I don't know. Do you?"

She turned and propped up on her elbow, wincing instantly as the scar on her arm stretched tightly. "I'm not sure. I read this story once about red ribbons and people being linked to each other. They would die and continuously find each other in every life. Every time they met, their souls knew before their minds did, making them fall head over heels instantly."

"Hm, maybe. I did feel something the moment I saw you." I reached up and tapped her chin. "But I'm sure I'm not the only one to be hypnotized by your eyes."

"Desi, be serious. This all feels so unreal. And fast." She tossed a pillow at me.

"Is that an issue?" I said, my gut tightening.

"I don't know. When you're not around, I get grumpy and

sad. I want more of you, but at the same time, I feel like I'm too clingy. We barely know each other, and yet, I'm…"

"Obsessed?" I chuckled and then shifted to push her back down onto the bed. "I am too. It's fine. We can be crazy together."

"I want to be here with you. Obsessed. Forever." She sighed as I rolled on top of her and began planting gentle but intentional kisses on her jaw, neck, and top of her breasts.

The dark thoughts began to creep back in. Flashes of the life I'd been wishing swept through my brain.

"What?" Scout asked.

I looked down at her. She was so beautiful just the way she was. Could I dare voice my deepest, darkest thoughts with her?

"What if we could…?" I whispered. I wasn't even sure I had said it aloud.

"Could what?"

"Be here, like this, forever?" My breathing suddenly took on a more ragged rhythm.

"What, like me not going back to work? I have car insurance now, remember?"

I relaxed and rolled off of her. While I didn't feel anything but disappointment now, I knew once I got back to my place, the guilt would set in. I almost asked her to do the unthinkable.

"You're right. Although, if you just let me, I'd make you a kept woman." I decided to return to her, rolling back on top and kissing her body in all the places I knew she liked. "All you'd have to do is greet me at the door wearing only an apron and those cookies you made at Christmas every time I come over."

"Ha! I'd go crazy. I'll keep my job, thanks though. My art school fund is kind of low anyway. I need to refill it."

I glanced at the jar sitting by the bed. "How many times have you refilled that jar and used it on stuff that's not art related?"

She looked away guiltily. "A few times. There's just never a good time."

"They'll never be a good time," I reached for the jar. "Next time it's full, you should apply."

"I don't even know where to start. All I can do is draw." She motioned to the walls.

"Everyone starts somewhere, and I think you could make a great career out of your art. You're really good, Scout."

"Thanks, but can we get back to you kissing me and telling me how much you love me now?"

She always hated talking about her art. I set the jar down, and just as I was about to honor her request, I spotted something. A stack of books. I picked the top one up and read the title. My blood ran cold.

"What is this?" I turned to her with the book raised. "Is this a fucking joke?"

Scout's eyes widened as she stared at the book. She shrunk into herself. I grabbed the rest of the books, tossing them on the bed. I stood and threw the first book I'd picked up onto the top of the pile.

Psychopaths and the people who love them.

"Desi, I—"

"You went to the library?" I shook my head. "You think I'm a psychopath?"

"No!" She leapt up and tried to touch me, but I stepped out of her reach.

There were so many, all with the same theme. Criminals and their mental status.

"Well, I don't know," she answered honestly, finally finding words. "You just seem so cool and collected about—"

"About my job?" I sneered. "That pays for everything? That keeps you comfortable?"

"I'm sorry, I just wanted to understand you more."

"There's nothing to understand." I grabbed my shirt, pulling it on. "I'm not fucking psychotic." I stormed out, not waiting for her to follow me. I put my shoes on and fled to my car. I pulled out of her drive and got onto the road. I drove with no direction in mind.

She thought I was crazy. Heartless.

How could I be heartless, when everything I'd done, I'd done with her in mind? Every bullet I'd put in someone's brain, I was thinking of her and the money I'd spend on her. The life I was saving up to give her. And yet, she was worried that I was psychotic?

I drove until the gas light came on, and then I stopped and refueled. I pulled out and found a park nearby. It was dark and empty, much like my soul. I sat on the hood of my car and tried to process everything.

Scout thought I was psychotic because of how quiet I was about my new career path. But I was only quiet because I didn't want to involve her. If only she knew what I was saving her from. Not just police or other humans, but my family, Aleida's family, and any other vampire clan that I may have pissed off.

How could I prove to her that I wasn't cold and unfeeling? That this was just a job and nothing more? I needed to show her what it was like. Only then could she realize it wasn't as scary as she imagined.

I got back in my car and started the trek back to her house. It was nearly four in the morning when I pulled into her drive. Her living room light was on, which gave me hope that I wasn't waking her up. I knocked, and after a long moment, the door flew open and Scout threw her arms around me.

"You came back!"

"I did. And I'd like to talk about the books."

"Desi, you're not a psychopath." She hugged me as tightly as she could.

"I know that, but I don't think you do."

"What are we going to do then?" She pulled away.

I nodded to my car. "Come on, I'm going to take you on a job."

CHAPTER 46

Desi

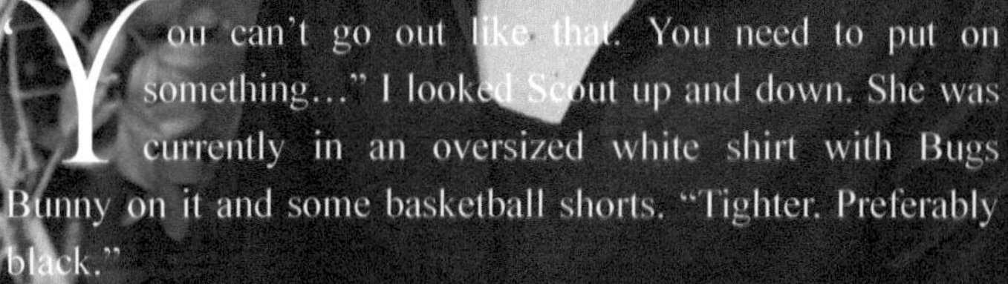

"You can't go out like that. You need to put on something…" I looked Scout up and down. She was currently in an oversized white shirt with Bugs Bunny on it and some basketball shorts. "Tighter. Preferably black."

"You're serious? You want me to go on a job with you?"

"Yes. Now, get dressed, before I go into your closet and start picking things for you."

"Okay." She turned, and I followed her to her bedroom.

"Where are we going?" She pulled out a black shirt. "Will it be cold?"

I sighed and moved past her. "Here, put these on." I handed her a pair of black stir-up tights. "And the shirt, and some shoes that tie. I want to get this done."

"If you're so impatient, then why did you come for me?" she snapped while she quickly changed.

"Because I want to show you how it is. I think you have some misconception about me and I want to change that."

Once we were in the car, she asked, "Where are we going?"

"Michigan. Kalamazoo."

"Michigan?" Her mouth fell open. "That's hours away!"

"A little under three each way." I nodded. "This is a close one. I've been going all across the country," I revealed.

"Wait, shouldn't I leave Luis a note? We're not going to be back by morning."

I looked through the rearview mirror. We were only ten minutes out, but I didn't want to take her back home just yet.

"Why don't we make this a whole mini-vacation? We can get a hotel, do the hit, and then relax for a few days. You haven't gone back to work yet. This might be our last chance for something like this."

"I didn't pack anything. I only have my wallet, and I'm broke."

"It'll be fine. As soon as we're checked in, you can call home." I gripped the steering wheel a little tighter and started off toward the freeway.

"What's in Kalamazoo?" she asked.

"Yorick Sideris."

"Who?"

"Scout." I glanced over and her mouth curved into an O.

"I see. Why are we going to see him?"

"He killed someone he shouldn't have, so now we're going to go kill him."

"Is that usually what's going on? Retaliation?"

"No, usually it's money-related," I confessed. I had originally told her that these people were hardened murderers. But if I was going to bring her into this world, she needed to be told what truth I could tell her.

"Desi, I thought—"

I put my hand up to stop her. "I know. I lied. I didn't want you to judge me. Maybe you're right, I am a little…" I gulped. I hated that word.

Psychotic.

I wished with all my being that I could confess that I wasn't completely coldhearted. I had feelings. I was trained my entire life to not care about human mortality. Humans died. We didn't, and we couldn't care about them. I only cared about one human.

Her.

"Uncaring. I was raised in this world. People come and go. They do crime and then bad things happen to them. I'm just part of the cycle."

"But what if someone comes after you?"

"No one would dare. My last name keeps me pretty safe."

"Amato?"

"That's the one." The bitterness seeped out slightly in my tone. "It has its occasional perks."

"Were you doing this before we met?"

"No. I wasn't lying about that. I sold a lot of weed. Which would probably land me more jail time than anything else." I smirked. She asked me questions until finally she closed her eyes and drifted off to sleep, leaving me to finish the drive.

The sun was starting to peek out from the darkness when I pulled into a hotel off the freeway. I parked and sat back in my seat, watching her sleep. She had been crying before I had picked her up. Her eyes were still puffy and her nose just a little pink. My heart fell slightly, knowing that I was the cause of her tears. I had done that to her.

But no more.

I clicked my seatbelt off and shook her slightly, rousing her.

"Are we here to kill the guy?" she asked groggily.

"You seem to be almost excited to do this."

"No!"

"Sure." I grinned. "But no. We're just at the hotel. Let's

go see about a room for the next few days." There were plenty of rooms, and I offered a credit card to get us booked.

"Is having a card with your name on it safe? What if they trace us?" she asked as soon as we entered the room. I slipped off my boots and flopped onto the bed.

"They won't."

"How are you so sure?"

"Scout, stop worrying." I patted the empty spot beside me. "Come, lie down, we'll take a long nap, and then we'll get going later."

"To Yorick?" She slipped off her shoes and laid beside me. I rolled and pulled her into my body, spooning her. I inhaled deeply, savoring the smell of her shampoo.

"Why are you rushing this?" I groaned. "We're on vacation. Relax."

She scoffed. "Relax?"

"Mhmm." My cock stirred. I bucked my hip and pressed myself against her ass. "We can play and work."

She sighed and wiggled deeper into my hold. "I've never had a real vacation before."

The idea saddened me. My family had taken us on vacations all during my childhood. Paris, Greece, New York, Hawaii. Even with the difficulty of them being vampires and not being able to touch sunlight, we still took lavish holidays. Scout, a simple human, thought this was impressive? This was nothing. I dove my head back into her mess of hair.

"This is just the start, baby. I'm going to take you on so many vacations all over the world. Once you get a taste, you won't want to go back."

"A taste of what?"

I kissed her instead of answering.

"Let's fuck, and then get some rest. When we wake up, I'm taking you shopping."

CHAPTER 47

Scout

"Desi, I can't. This stuff is too much!" I flicked the price tag on the red cocktail dress he had pulled from the rack. "This costs almost as much as my car."

"So?" He smirked. "I'm paying, what does it matter?"

I shook my head. We'd been over this a dozen times if not more. He glared at me and pulled another dress off the rack.

"I'm buying you stuff today, so either you tell me what you want, or I'm going to dress you how I want."

I considered his words as he switched to another rack of dresses.

"Yeah? And how do you want me to dress?" I crossed my arms and followed him around the store.

"As a rule, I'd rather not have you dressed at all." He grinned, to which I blushed furiously. "But I don't know. I think you look pretty fine as you are."

"Really? When we go out together, people give us weird looks."

"Yeah, because they're thinking, *what's this piece of shit doing with this total babe?*" Desi teased.

I rolled my eyes. "You're funny. I think it's the opposite way."

These weren't my style. I wanted something more laid-back, but I also wanted to look like I belonged with Desi. "Maybe I should try your style. I could wear some plaid."

"You do look incredibly sexy in my Iron Maiden shirt. Let's get you a new wardrobe. Ripped jeans, some plaid, and boots?"

"So, no dress?" I raised my eyebrows. He had insisted we go here first, as he wanted to go to dinner tonight.

"Let's start here and then get you some more casual clothes somewhere else."

Something in me shifted that day. Desi had finally worn me down and convinced me it was okay sometimes to let someone else pay for things. I didn't need to be completely independent at all times. I just needed him.

He made me try on every single item he bought. When we dumped all of our bags onto the bed in the hotel, I found almost thirty pairs of new underwear and a dozen new bras. All lacy and various shades of black, red, and gray. In fact, everything we'd bought today were those colors.

"I bought these while you were trying stuff on," he admitted.

"I think we went a little overboard." I cringed. My closet didn't have space for everything.

"Nonsense. I can't wait to see you in everything." Desi wrapped his arms around me from behind. He brushed my hair back, pressing a soft, tender kiss on my neck. The heat of his breath sent shivers down my spine. "And I can't wait even more to take them off you."

He trailed his hands up and down my body, finally slipping under my shirt. "Let's get in the shower so we can get to dinner. I'm famished."

"I'm nervous," I admitted, slipping the dress he had picked out for me over my head and down my body.

"Why? You look sexy," he admired me from the other side of the room where he was drying his hair. We had showered together, but every time I tried to touch him in a more intimate place, he would direct me elsewhere, claiming he wanted to wait. It had left me incredibly frustrated and wanting.

He tossed the towel down and began to pull on his clothes. He was wearing a simple, all-black suit tonight. My dress was more of a nightgown than a cocktail dress. It was black and low cut with spaghetti straps. But it was incredibly sexy.

"Where's those strappy heels I bought you?" he asked and then smiled wide. "I love buying you stuff, you know that?"

"I realize that." I laughed as I went to grab the shoes. "I'm getting used to it. It's not terrible," I teased.

"Keep that up and you'll be getting a boat for your birthday."

"You're so presumptive." I slid my feet into the six-inch heels. "What makes you think we'll still be together in October?"

Desi flicked his gaze at me and stopped tying his tie. He stalked over to me and pushed me back onto the bed. Then he kissed me long and hard, bringing the hand with the ring he'd bought me up for us to look at.

It was a promise.

"You think you can get rid of me that easily? I want you for eternity, babe, and I'm going to do everything in my power to make that happen."

The butterflies in my stomach fluttered excitedly.

"Eternity seems like a long time for a woman you've only known for a few months." I closed my eyes and reveled in his kisses he was pressing on my bare skin.

"I know what I want."

A small moan escaped my lips, and it seemed to pull him from his thoughts. He cleared his throat. "Come on, we gotta go. Yorick will be at dinner soon."

"Wait, we're having dinner with him?"

"Not with, but we're going to the same place. The menu looked good when I scoped it out."

"When did you scope it out?" He'd been with me all day. We hadn't gone to anything but a Burger King to eat for lunch.

Desi walked back to the mirror he'd been tying his tie at. "These jobs are not as quick as a bullet to the temple and done. You have to make sure the timing is right. I've been watching Yorick for a while now. I actually spent some time in his office, studied his schedule. Then, I drove up here, checked out the hotel, the restaurants, and other places he was going to be."

My lips parted but I said nothing. His career was so… fascinating.

"You ready?" He finished dressing and turned to me. I fluffed my hair and took a second look to make sure my makeup wasn't smeared.

"Let's go."

Desi drove us to a beautiful restaurant. I'd never been somewhere this fancy. They had cloth napkins and candles at all the tables. The menu was in French, so I asked him to order for me. We were served wine and some appetizer I couldn't pronounce. It tasted good, whatever it was.

After the waitress left our table, I leaned in to whisper to Desi, "Is he here? Yorick?"

"Behind you, to the left. Don't turn."

My head twitched and I had to force myself not to do exactly that.

"I need an eye on him at all times," Desi muttered low.

"Why?" I asked. Desi knew his schedule. If we missed catching him here, couldn't we just pick him up at the next spot?

"Because he knows we're here for him, and he's trying to figure out how to run."

CHAPTER 48

Scout

"He's watching us just like we're watching him," Desi said, looking behind me. He raised his wine glass and nodded to someone, presumably Yorick.

"So, we are going to have a nice meal, pretend everything is perfect, and you will relax. Understand?" he said.

I nodded and raised the menu to cover my face. None of the words made much sense to me.

"Do you want me to order for you again?" He chuckled brightly.

"Yes, please. Uh, nothing…" I frowned and tilted the menu down. I wasn't even sure what I didn't want.

"It's fine, I'll pick something traditional, something simple. How about steak au poivre, it's got a red wine sauce."

"I like steak."

"All right, we'll try that. And if you don't like it, then you'll have more room for dessert."

"I don't think it's a good idea to stuff ourselves, considering…"

"Stop it. Or I'll take you back to Ohio tonight."

The waitress returned to refill our glasses and take our entree orders. Desi ordered for us, and the conversation resumed to more pleasant things.

"There's a movie I saw posters for the other day. I want to take you to it. It's got Bruce Lee's son in it. It looked pretty good."

I nodded but for the most part of the evening, I was distracted. I felt as if eyes were on my head the entire meal. Desi tried to keep the conversation flowing. He poured me more and more wine, insisted I eat despite my nerves, and talked about things he wanted to do with me this summer.

At some point, I blinked and came out of my fog. "You have a lot planned for the summer. Why are you trying to get all of this stuff done in a few months? Didn't you say something about eternity just back at the hotel?"

His Adam's apple bobbed. Chuckling nervously, he looked at his drink, stirring it slightly. "Yeah, of course. You're right. I just..." He reached for my hand over the table. "I've never had someone I wanted to live for. Do things with. I don't want to miss out on a single thing."

I squeezed his hand. "I don't either. But after this little vacation, I've got to go back to the diner, and you will have… this."

"Right. About that…" He grinned. "Are you sure you want to go back to the diner? I mean, really?"

"Yes."

"How about this." Desi sighed and removed his hand from mine. "I won't ask again until your birthday. By then, maybe I'll have convinced you to leave that place and—"

"And what?" I laughed. "Be your kept woman?" I reached for my wine and took a long gulp.

"I was thinking wife, but—" I choked and spat out my wine, cutting Desi off.

The wine went all over the table as I tried to cough and get the liquid out of my nose. He stood and stared at his suit, which was now splattered in red wine.

"I'm sorry!" I gasped but he wasn't looking at me. He swore and reached into his pocket, pulling out his wallet and a fistful of bills. He tossed them on the table and stormed off.

"Fuck. He's leaving."

People were watching us curiously, but I quickly followed him out. He was running to his car, and I stumbled after him in my heels. We jumped into his car and Desi quickly turned it on and pulled out of the parking lot.

"Shit, shit shit!" he screamed and slammed his hand on the steering wheel. "He saw the opening and fucking took it. Fuck!" Desi sped through the unfamiliar city, eyeing every car, every building, every man on the street.

"What's he look like?" I asked, looking at the sidewalks as well.

"Old, glasses, mustache. I'll find the fucker," he growled. We drove in silence until finally, Desi stopped abruptly at a rundown hotel. "Bingo."

"What makes you think he's here?"

He pointed to a red car in the alley.

"Yorick owns a large number of hotels all over the Midwest. I bet he owns this hazard of a building too." He climbed out of the car and went around to my side to open my door. "You ready for this?"

My heart hammered. Was I? I swallowed the lump in my throat and took his hand with my sweaty palm. Desi pulled me out and put his arm around my waist.

"Come on, we need to get in and get this done quickly," he muttered. We rushed into the abandoned building, and as soon as we got inside, we could hear someone rustling loudly somewhere on a higher floor.

I looked around. The outside was far more worn than the interior. It just looked like a lobby, only dusty with no electricity. Desi pointed to the stairs, and we started up them.

"Yorick," Desi shouted, "there's no point in running. I'm not leaving until this is done."

"Fuck you, Amato!" the old man who I had yet to see spat from the second floor. "I'm not going out without a fight. Come, get me, you pussy! I'll carve you and that pretty girl up!"

"Isn't there a saying?" Desi shouted back, the snark in his voice loud and clear. "It's not smart to bring a knife to a gunfight?"

"In the old days, we didn't use guns. Fight me like a real man, Amato."

Desi looked over at me and rolled his eyes. "The guy he killed, the reason we're here in the first place, he shot with a gun."

As we climbed, so did Yorick. He shouted down at us with threats until we caught up with him. My blood ran cold when I finally reached the murderer we were here to kill. He was as Desi had described, old, glasses, and a mustache. Only, he was a lot larger and more muscular than I had imagined. He was twice the size of Desi and me.

My gaze flickered to the large knife grasped tightly in his fist. Yorick laughed.

"Scared, sweetie?"

"Don't talk to her," Desi snapped. He reached behind him and into his jacket. The sly grin on his face suddenly fell, and he began to pat his back furiously.

"What?" I asked softly.

"I dropped my gun."

CHAPTER 49

Desi

Fuck.

Fuck, fuck, fuck.

Yorick had led us into a den on the fifth or sixth floor of this rundown hotel. The only light came from the windows, but it was enough to see the oversized dagger in Yorick's grip.

I didn't have time to wonder where my gun had gone. I had to get that knife.

"Desi…" Scout's soft, scared voice brought me back to the room.

"Get behind me." I pushed her back, keeping my eyes locked on the old man I'd come to kill.

"Aw, so cute." Yorick laughed. "See, that's where you fucked up, Amato. You shouldn't bring distractions to your job. That's how innocent casualties happen."

I took a deep breath and steeled myself, taking a step forward. "Your time's up, Yorick. You know that."

"Ha! Because of the boy with the red hair? What was his name? Robert. It was an accident! Like it hasn't happened to everyone. It was just a random kid!"

"His name was Robert Vannucci."

"No, Robert Vannucci sells insurance. This kid was just a—"

"Junior."

His head tilted to the ceiling and he sighed deeply. "Fuck me. That's why they're upset? I killed Vannucci's son? Let me call him. I'll pay him for his loss." He took a step forward and tried to go around me, but I blocked him.

"He doesn't want a phone call. He doesn't want a check either. He wants you dead. You shot that boy and left him in the alley to be found in the morning by some drunks. That doesn't sit right with his family, Yorick."

"I didn't know it was his kid!"

"I'm not doing this all night." I slid my hand into the inside of my suit jacket and paused. There was nothing in there to remove, but he didn't know that. "Can we stop running now?"

"I'm not going down without a fight, Amato. You want me dead, work for it." He stormed past me, and I grabbed his suit jacket.

Yorick swung back with the knife and sliced through the air. "I suggest you don't fucking touch me unless you want to get cut."

Keeping my eyes on the knife, I ducked again and shoved him back as hard as I could. He stumbled back into some chairs and crashed to the floor. I leapt over the chairs and fell on top of him. I grabbed both of his wrists and pinned him to the carpet.

Despite his age, he was larger than me and stronger. But I was faster, and I counted on that. Forcing my weight down on him, I worked on prying his hand open. If I could just get the knife…

Suddenly, a blur moved to the left of me and my head jerked.

"Scout, no!" My attention was diverted just long enough for Yorick to take advantage and shove me off of him. Our roles were reversed in an instant, with him pinning me to the floor now.

"What did I tell you?" He laughed in my face. "Don't bring what will distract you. I should tie her up and make her watch me carve you like a ham. Or should I do it the other way? You want to watch my cock sink into her ass over and over until I get bored and decide to put two bullets in your head?"

I fought against his hold and looked from side to side. The images Yorick described were gruesome, but I didn't let that detract my focus from finding Scout. Where had she gone?

"It doesn't matter." I spat. He pushed on my chest, and he wasn't even putting his full weight on me. If he did, he'd crush me. Panting, I shook my head and snarled. "You wouldn't fucking dare."

"Dare what?" He let go of my arm, instantly replacing his hand with his shoe, crushing my bones. He took the knife in his hand and slid it across my throat.

I winced as the blade went through my skin. It was barely a scratch but stung nonetheless.

"I know about you and your family. I know about all of you. The ones who only do business in the moonlight. Powerful families with so much money and influence they can't be touched. We've all heard the stories of those who have tried to kill people like you." Yorick shook his head and raised the blade. "I'm not that stupid."

Black clouded my vision as he continued to force more and more of his weight down on me. I was going to pass out if I didn't get him off me. Yorick bent down, his chest pressed tight to mine, and he whispered in my ear, "Vampire."

"Get off of him!" Scout's shrill scream came just as a loud thunk above me caused Yorick to fall to the side.

I inhaled and tried to sit, but I was dizzy and swayed.

"Scout, stop!" I put my hand out, but she was moving too fast. She kicked him and shoved her sharp, six-inch heels I had bought her just this afternoon into his thigh. He screamed as she put all of her weight into it.

"Stop!" he screamed. Then, as if suddenly we were in slow motion, Yorick opened his hand and the knife clamored to the floor. Scout was faster than me. She scooped the knife up and held it out with a shaky hand.

I stood, finally regaining my footing. She sunk down onto Yorick's lap, her heel still stuck in his thigh. The wound in his leg was distracting him. I watched, too stunned to move, as Scout pulled the knife from behind her and shook her head.

"You don't threaten my man."

"Or what?"

"Or this." She held her arm up and swung down, sinking the knife deep into his chest. He tried to stand, but Scout quickly leaned over and used all her strength to pull a chair to her. The chair squealed, and Yorick fell back, scrambling to pull the knife from his chest. Scout pulled again, and the chair fell over, right onto his head, squishing him. Blood and brain matter splattered all across Scout's face, dress, and exposed skin. She tried to step back but her heel was stuck. Her eyes went wide as she stared down at it. I hurried to her, bending down to unstrap the shoe and set her free. I stood and pulled her to me.

"Are you okay?" I asked.

"I…" She gulped.

"Sshh." I pulled her tighter, kissing her hair over and

over. "It's fine. I told you, we were going to do a job, and you did. It's over. We're done. You did it, baby. See, it's nothing. He was a bastard, and now he can't hurt anyone ever again," I whispered to her over and over, trying to reassure her everything was going to be fine. "How do you feel?"

She looked up, and when our eyes met, I was surprised to see no tears. She pressed her lips and then answered me.

"I feel… good."

"
re you hurt?"

She had to be in shock. Surely, there was a delayed reaction. Scout had just stabbed a man and then pushed a chair onto his head. His guts were splattered all over her face. And yet, here she was, wrapped tightly in my arms, asking me if I was alright.

"No. Do you want to talk about what just happened?"

"He was going to hurt you. I couldn't let that happen."

"Well, thank you." I smiled and kissed her.

"What do we do now?" she asked, nodding to Yorick's body. "Do we have to bury it?"

"No. They prefer for the bodies to be discovered. So they can boast about how they got the job done." I waved it off. "It's a whole thing. Office politics, all that. Come on."

"You aren't afraid of getting caught? What about fingerprints?" Scout gulped, and her eyes widened. "Or steps? My heel!"

Ah, there it was. The panic I'd been waiting for.

"Scout." She'd begun to pace, and I caught her, holding

firmly to her upper arms. "It's fine. The police aren't going to investigate this."

"How do you know? Why wouldn't they?"

"Because the police are in my client's pockets. They are going to find him, report the death, and rule it an accident. Actually"—I glanced at the limp body— "you smashing his head in with the chair helps that. He was drunk, fell, and reached for the chair. It tumbled and squished him."

"Desi." She blinked. "I stabbed him."

"Yorick's head was knocked in. I'll make sure to tell my client that, and when it comes out in the paper, I'll show you. This isn't my first rodeo."

"Well, it's mine!" She pointed to herself.

I noted that she hadn't added anything else.

Had I sparked something deep and dark inside her? Would this benefit me in more ways than one? I stared at her, gorgeous as usual, pacing. The blood and brain matter she was covered in only made her more attractive to me. Was my vampirism starting to reveal itself early?

In six months, I'd be drinking blood and craving it daily. Up until now, I'd never thought about it one way or the other, but now... I wanted to lick every last drop off of her naked body, right here, right now.

"Why are you looking at me like that?" she asked, bringing my mind back to the room.

"I... I didn't think I'd ever say this, but this is the sexiest I've ever seen you."

She looked down at herself for the first time, seeming to only now realize she was covered in blood. "Really?"

"You don't know how much I've worried that you'd run and never speak to me again once you found out about my job. Tonight was a test. Are you going to leave me?"

"No? Why would I?"

"Because… I kill people…"

"Am I any different?"

I pulled her deeper into my embrace. Our hearts were as one, beating powerfully, trying to call to each other.

"Desi, I don't know what it is about you, but something in me has changed. I've lived my entire life laying low, making no real attachments to anything, but then I found you, and now…" She sighed. "It sounds insane. I'm lovesick."

"I feel the same. Like I'd been drifting through life for so long and then suddenly I didn't want to do that anymore. I wanted to do more, be more, but if it meant losing you, I'd give it all up to get you to stay."

"Exactly. If this"—she motioned to Yorick— "is what it means to be with you, then I guess it is what it is. He was a bad guy. He said so himself."

I nodded. He was. It took me a moment to digest Scout's words.

"What do you mean by I guess it is what it is?"

"It means, I can't let you do this alone."

I grinned. "You're finally quitting the diner?"

"I don't know yet. I still have to work. I have bills."

"Fuck all that." I lifted her up and she wrapped her legs around my waist. She put her arms around my neck, and I kissed her. "Fuck that stupid diner, fuck your bills, and fuck your worries about money. I'm going to pay for everything your little black heart desires. You're a kept woman now, Scout." I kissed her again as I walked forward, finding a table.

"My little black heart?" She giggled as I set her down and began to unbuckle my pants.

"Mhmmm. It has to be a little dark to love someone like me," I said, raising her dress over her thighs. "And you do love me, don't you?"

"I do," she said, pulling me between her legs. She kissed me, her tongue darting out to play and entangle with mine. I reached for her breast, cupping it, and thumbing over the small nub there.

"Good," I said. Using my other hand, I slid up her thighs and found her lace underwear. I wasn't in the mood for a slow seduction, and instead, I grasped the fabric and yanked. It came off quickly, and she jerked forward. I laughed and pulled her to me, positioning my cock at her entrance.

"Oh, Desi," she gasped and pushed me forward, plunging me inside her. She was incredibly soaked and so tight. I wanted to live here, right between her thighs for the rest of eternity.

I leaned forward and cradled my head against her neck. The blood was starting to dry and become sticky. I pressed a few kisses on her collarbone and slowly licked the blood that had splattered there. It had a metallic taste, and I found it otherwise unappealing. I wondered what Scout's blood would taste like. Would I like it as a human, or would it only taste good once I had fully shifted into my vampire form?

"Desi," Scout moaned as I thrust inside her, reveling in how good she felt and how hot this entire night had been. I'd watched her kill someone, get up, and want to fuck me afterward. How sexy was that?

She tightened her grip on my shoulders, threw her head back, and screamed. Her pussy tightening around my cock in short quick bursts caused me to follow an instant later with my own explosion. I came into her needy pussy with an eagerness I'd never felt before.

Our kids would be so fucked up but so beautiful.

Finally, our breathing slowed, our bodies separated, and we looked around the room. Scout turned to me and grinned.

"Now what?"

"If you don't want to do the actual killing, at least just come with me."

I considered Desi's request while we drove home from our vacation. The idea didn't seem so bad. I didn't have to be in the room for the… killings. I had gotten a little tease of what our life could be this week. Would letting Desi spoil me for a while be so bad? Could I let go of my independence to join him on the road?

"When do I have to decide?"

His jaw tightened and his eyes turned to slits. He stared hard at the road. "Yesterday."

"Desi."

"Fine. I've got some things I need to take care of once we get home. You have until I return in a few days to decide whether you're coming with me or not."

"I need more time. I have to get my bills figured out."

We rode in silence for a long time before he said, "How about this? My schedule will keep me away for a few weeks. I go, do what I gotta do, and when I return, you should be ready to decide."

"Are you saying if I don't murder people, we can't be together?"

"I'm saying I'm sick of missing you every night." He reached for my hand again and pulled it to his lips, planting a kiss on the top. He ran his thumb over the ring he had given me for Christmas. "Soon, I plan on changing this promise ring into an engagement ring."

"Desi!" I yelped and pulled my hand away quickly as if he had stung me. I shook my head and cupped my hand. "We have time for everything. Stop rushing everything!"

"What if we don't?"

"What do you mean?"

"Nothing. It's stupid. I'm—When I know what I want, I want it all. Scout, I don't want to wait for my future with you."

I wanted the same, but my rational brain knew that if we went too fast, we'd burn out.

"I like the pace we're at. Let's keep taking things at a medium pace, okay?" The word felt like such a lie. In the little time that I'd known him, we'd fallen in love, murdered people, and he'd given me a promise ring.

Desi dropped me off and helped me bring in all my bags and bags of clothing and other things he had bought me. Luis was home and watched in bewilderment as the bags kept being brought in. When we were done, Desi took his leave, citing some errands he had to run.

"I'm a part of a wedding in the fall. They want me fitted for a tux."

"Oh? Whose wedding?" I asked.

He shifted and looked down at the ground. Luis interrupted his answer.

"You look different."

"You like it?" I asked, spinning around. I had opted for

shorts, fishnets, and an oversized plaid button up over my black tank top. He chuckled and turned the other way to give us privacy.

"Do you still have to go?" I looked back at Desi.

"I do. I'll call you later and let you know my schedule."

I stood on my tiptoes and pressed a swift kiss on his lips. "Sounds good. Have fun at your tux fitting."

Desi nodded and left.

"Tux fitting?" Luis came back out once Desi was gone.

"Yeah, he's in a wedding, I guess."

"I see." He eyed me cautiously. "How long have you known Desiderio?"

"A few months. I know, it's soon to be taking vacations for."

"Not really." Luis grinned. "I had a friend over this week. It was like a vacation."

"Good for you!"

"Thanks. Now, you want to show me all the things that man bought for you?"

The rest of the day was spent showing off my new wardrobe and toiletries. I had lotions, perfumes, shoes, accessories, makeup. Desi had wanted to buy full stores!

"When do you start work again?" Luis asked as he tested out a lotion.

I didn't really want to go back, but the other option had major drawbacks.

"I haven't decided yet. Desi doesn't want me to go back. He wants me to travel with him this summer while he works."

"And what will you do?"

I squinted. He had a good point. What would I do? I'd never had time to just do... whatever before.

"Maybe I'll do art."

"What an image. By the time you come back in the fall, you'll be barefoot and pregnant."

"Ha!" I laughed. "Even Desi couldn't convince me to do that."

"You'd be surprised at how good a man like he is with his words." The way he said it made it sound like he knew something I didn't.

"What does that mean?" I asked.

"It means, have a good trip. I'm going to be very happy in an empty house."

Scout

Luis seemed more excited than I was to quit my job and travel with Desi for the summer. He had grand plans for fancy book clubs and things I had never put a stop to but he never wanted to intrude on me by hosting them.

"I just like to remain respectful of my roommates," he told me when I asked why he waited until I wasn't around to do these things.

"You don't have to be. I know we are obnoxious sometimes," I blushed, thinking about the few times Luis had knocked on the walls to shush us during the throes. "If the time comes when I move in with Desi, do you want this place?"

"I would need a roommate to help with rent," he admitted. "But yes."

"Great!" I grinned. "Well, until then, I'll keep paying my half and if it ever happens, we have a plan."

"I wouldn't go that far," he warned me. "Something's up with that man. But I am enjoying the spoiling too."

Ignoring his vague warnings, I went to the diner and

turned in my notice. Deanna was in when I came to speak to our manager. She waited for me just outside the office and when I came out, she followed behind me.

"Long time, no see, girlie. You forget your apron?"

"Actually, I officially put in my two weeks. Although Stanley said I didn't really need to, as they've already replaced me after the accident." I waved my arm with the large scar up.

Deanna rolled her eyes. "Yeah, Kelly. She sucks. I kind of figured you weren't coming back though. I mean, I don't blame you, landing a guy like that."

"Yeah? Desi is kind of great."

"I don't know. Something about him still strikes me as off." She scrunched up her nose. "Like, he's got a secret family or something weird. He got kids?"

"No. And he's perfectly normal," I lied. "Stop trying to make me paranoid just because I finally met a decent guy."

"Fine. You want to run off with a handsome man and let him pay for all your stuff by all means, but can you stop throwing it in my face so much?" She grinned and reached out to hug me. "Best of luck, Scout. You deserve some good in your life."

"Thanks, Deanna. I really appreciate it. I think while he's working, I'm going to spend the summer working on my art. Maybe I'll actually get better."

"Thank god. I can only watch you scribble for so long." She laughed. "And when summer's over, then what?"

"Stanley said I can come back at any time. I might, who knows. I really want to make this thing with Desi work."

"You should. You're what, twenty-five?"

"Twenty-six. Twenty-seven in October."

Barely a week apart from Desi.

"That's a good age to settle down. You better invite me to

the wedding. I wanna see what kind of dough that mafioso puts out for you."

I nudged her. "Don't go saying that stupid shit too loud."

"All right, he can keep his secrets. But if he's got a single cousin or something…"

Now that I was mostly healed and had my license, I took long rides just to be by myself. I had a handful of tapes in the center counsel and would listen to them on full blast while I drove.

Tonight, I had the tape that I was making for Desi in my player.

I had decided that I'd be giving it to him as a birthday present and to celebrate our one year since we met. I couldn't afford much, even more so now that I quit my job, but I knew that he'd love the sentiment.

I was about halfway through picking songs. The A side was full, so I just needed to choose some more for the other side.

I was so in the zone, I hadn't noticed how far I had gone outside of the city. It was nearly two in the morning, and I had no idea where I was.

I found the nearest gas station and refilled my tank. As I was paying the clerk, I asked where I was, and discovered I had somehow driven almost two hours away from my house.

Shit.

"You lost?"

"No, well, kind of. I'll find my way back, no big deal. Thanks." I paid him and hurried back to my car.

I started back the way I came. As I drove, I slowed at all the places with lights on, looking for a payphone.

The more I drove, the less hope I felt about finding a payphone. I was surrounded by nothing but trees.

I practiced breathing slowly and tried to focus on the road instead of my worries, and eventually, I found my way home.

It was nearly morning as I pulled into my driveway. The sun was just starting to rise, and I saw a figure on my front porch.

I climbed out of the car and called out to the guy, "Can I help you?"

He turned, and it was Mick, one of Desi's friends. He was holding a manila envelope. He turned and his eyes widened in fear, as if I caught him in the act of something treacherous.

"Mick? What are you doing here?"

He hid it behind his back. "Nothing. I don't know. I should go." He kept his head down and tried to brush past me but I raised my hands and held him back.

"What's going on? What do you have?"

"Nothing, I didn't think I'd see you here this early. I didn't want you to know it was me. I… I gotta go. I'm saying a lot of stuff I shouldn't."

"Mick!" I demanded. "What is going on? If you don't tell me what is in that envelope, I'll have to ask Desi why his friend was here at five in the morning hanging something on my door."

He froze. His long dark hair hung over his eyes, shielding them from my scrutinizing gaze. He began to tear it into pieces.

"What are you doing?" I scrambled to try to collect them but he shoved me away and picked them up, shoving them into his pocket. "Are you nuts?"

"I was stupid to come here. I shouldn't have. Desi is going to kill me if he finds out."

"Well, he's going to know." I put one hand on my hip. "Unless you tell me what the hell is going on."

He stammered again until blurting out something I never expected.

"I-I'm in love with you!"

Desi

I shoved Mick to the floor and stepped on his chest. Randy, Eric, and Tommy circled us as I crouched down and sucker-punched him straight in the nose.

"You think your little stunt was funny?" I asked. He sat up and scooted away.

"I panicked! I'd already torn the invitation up!" Mick's nose bled as I shoved him back down when he tried to sit up.

"You shouldn't have been there in the first place. Now she's thinking you're a fucking weirdo trying to sleep with her." I stood and backed away, but not without kicking him one more time in the ribs.

He yelped and rolled over. "Why am I taking the fucking beating when you're the one with two women?"

"No one asked for your fucking opinion or judgment." I spat on the ground near his face. "Now, do you want to get up and try swinging at me again or are you done playing the fucking hero?"

All of our friends spread out as I circled him. While they didn't agree with me not telling Scout about the situation with Aleida, they sure as hell weren't going to rat on me like Mick tried. They were all more than happy to watch me kick his ass in his very own garage.

"She deserves to know. She's a good girl." He stood back up. "When do you plan on telling her? When she sees your announcement in the paper? Or what about when you and Aleida have your first kid?"

"I'm working on it." I tightened my fists. Who the fuck did he think he was, showing up to Scout's house and trying to tape an invitation to the wedding to her door?

"When? Before or after we got fitted for tuxes?" He scrambled up and lifted his fists. He bounced slightly on his heels, waiting for me to swing again. "I spent a hundred bucks on that stupid suit."

"Is that what's got you so bent out of shape? A fucking suit?" I spun around to face the rest of my friends. "Do you all feel this way?"

They grumbled and muttered various forms of… yes.

"Fine. You want money for the fucking suits? Here." I pulled out my wallet and removed four hundred-dollar bills and handed them each one. "Now you can shut the fuck up and let me handle this."

"Desiderio, how?" Randy shook his head. "You're getting in deeper and deeper with this chick and the longer you wait to tell her, the worse it's gonna get. Aleida Linotti doesn't play. She'll take you for everything you've got."

"She'll rip your balls off if you embarrass her at the wedding," Tommy chimed in.

"I won't let it get that far. I'm working on it, okay? I'm leaving for work after Memorial Day and I won't be back 'til sometime in September. While we're gone, I'm going to call Aleida and tell her we've grown apart and the wedding's off." That was the plan. It wasn't a good one, but it was all I had right now.

"We? Who is we?" Randy demanded.

"I'm taking Scout with me."

Their eyes bulged and jaws fell as they took in my statement.

"It'll be fine."

Tommy shook his head. "You're fucking insane, Desiderio. You know that? We've always known you were a little quirky, but dude, you've gone off the rails. Ever since you met her, you've changed."

"So?" I flipped him off and reached for a cigarette in my pocket. "I want to do more with my life that smoke dope and hang out in front of the liquor store."

"You think Aleida's family will let you off easy? You know what they do." Tommy's expression darkened as he looked to our friends for support.

"Mafia." Randy cleared his throat. "You know, they say the same thing about your family too."

"They do?" I raised my eyebrows and feigned surprise. "What?" I finished my cigarette and flicked it to the ground, smashing it with my boot. "You all watch too many fucking movies." I took a deep breath and adjusted my jacket. I stepped toward them and stopped near Mick. "Mind your own fucking business, and we won't have a repeat of this."

I stormed out and drove home. I had to call Scout as soon as I got home to explain Mick away. I got into the house and tossed my jacket on the couch. My shoulders fell as I stalked to the kitchen, only to stare at the phone on the hook for far too long before finally picking it up and dialing her number.

My stomach twisted in knots as I waited through each ring, praying she didn't pick up. But finally, her voice came through, and I stiffened up and forced a giant smile.

"Hello?"

"Hey! It's me. I just wanted to let you know I talked to Mick. He was embarrassed about the entire thing."

"I bet. I'm embarrassed for him too."

"He won't be visiting you in the early morning hours anymore."

"Did you threaten him?"

"No, of course not," I lied and then instantly recanted. "I'm sorry, I don't know why I said that. I did a bit. I was pretty pissed off. I didn't realize I was the jealous type."

"Don't be mean to your friends. It's not like he actually tried anything. I didn't even get to read the letter he wrote me."

Thank god for that. It was mine and Aleida's wedding invitation. She had sent them out without my knowledge a week ago. The date was set for a week after I turned into a full vampire.

"When am I seeing you next?" she asked.

I looked over at the calendar I had on my wall right beside the phone. Aleida had written all over it. She had me booked for all sorts of wedding shit for the next three weeks. She wanted to pick flowers, register for gifts, select a band, and even try cakes. Why we'd care about what food was served when we would both be vampires by then confused me, but I knew I'd be expected to do these things anyways.

"I have Friday the 13th off. I think that movie I've been wanting to see will be out. What do you say. Movie date?"

"Sure. But what do I do until then? I quit my job, remember?"

I thought for a moment.

"You said you want to do more art, right? Tomorrow, expect a delivery."

CHAPTER 54
Desi

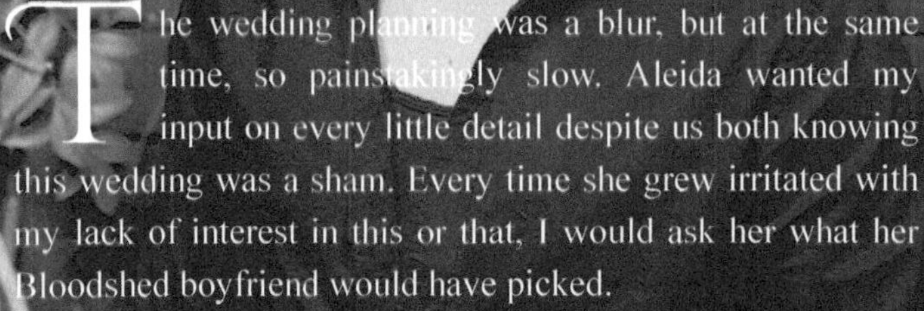

The wedding planning was a blur, but at the same time, so painstakingly slow. Aleida wanted my input on every little detail despite us both knowing this wedding was a sham. Every time she grew irritated with my lack of interest in this or that, I would ask her what her Bloodshed boyfriend would have picked.

"I wish you would stop calling him that. And I wished you cared more to fight for me."

"I guess I'm not the jealous type." I pointed to some plain-looking orange flowers. "What about those?"

"Tigerlily's? In the fall? Jesus, Desiderio. Remind me to never let you decorate our future home."

My eye twitched at her words. There would never be a home that we would share.

It took everything in me not to end the engagement then and there. Each and every night that I was dragged out to another place for planning the words sat on the tip of my tongue. But keeping Scout safe and alive was more pressing.

I had it all planned out. Once I got her out of the state, I'd break it off with Aleida, and Scout and I wouldn't return home for a year or so. By then, the Linottis would have found some other vampire to marry her off to.

There was only one problem with my plan.

Scout was still human.

I had no choice but to turn when my twenty-seventh birthday came, but Scout would remain as she was, aging each and every day past me.

That left few options for us. I could reveal the truth, and we stayed together until she either died of old age or found a human to grow old with, or, I could convince her to attempt to become a vampire.

No one knew exactly what it was about humans that allowed some to become vampires. We only knew how to do it. But the penalty for failure was death, and the community frowned upon that. How could you encourage someone to kill themselves in the random chance it worked? Was I prepared to gamble with Scout's life? If she didn't have vampirism in her blood, I'd lose her forever.

But if we didn't try, then eventually, we'd have the same outcome.

Every single day since the car accident, I went over our options. I thought long and hard about the speeches I'd give her. I acted it out in the privacy of my living room. I would get down on my knees and recite the words I'd memorized, and yet, I still hadn't gained the courage to say them to her.

After weeks of feigning even a slight interest in wedding planning, Friday the 13th came and Aleida left. I showered, shaved, and dressed in clean clothes. Toward the end of our wedding planning, I'd been purposely avoiding all three of those things in hopes that Aleida would stop inviting me. It hadn't worked so far.

I hopped into my car to take Scout out to dinner and then

the movies. The sun didn't go down until much later now, which meant Aleida and all of our family were stuck inside.

I could still walk in the sun; an ability they no longer possessed.

Scout came running out of her house, dressed in all the grunge clothing I'd bought her. I thought she was stunning in anything she wore, but in boots and flannel, she was even sexier. We looked like we truly belonged together.

"Thank you, thank you, thank you!" she squealed and threw her arms around me. "There was so much stuff delivered. I don't even know how to use most of it!"

She was referring to the art supplies I had paid to be delivered the day after we had talked.

"Did they keep you busy while you waited for me?"

"Somewhat. I started painting the walls. Luis is not entirely enthused."

We jumped into my car, and she directed me to a burger place. We sat outside on the hood of my car and ate fries and burgers, catching up on what we'd missed. She told me all about the new art she'd created and I… lied.

I told her I was away, off in New York, getting things done. I made up some guy and how I had killed him. "I had to stalk him for a while, he was smart, but eventually I caught him."

"Well, I'm glad you got back in time to take me to the movies." She leaned over and gave me a kiss. "I would have had to go without you."

"Like hell you would have." We finished eating and hurried to the theater, where we were lucky to get seats before it got packed. "I want to see The Crow just as much as you do."

"That was epic!" Scout gushed after the movie ended.

"And Brandon Lee in that makeup?" She pressed her hands to her heart and sighed. "That man was gorgeous."

A small twinge of jealousy poked my ego. I frowned, and she nudged me with a grin. "Oh, don't tell me I can't admire a movie star. A late movie star." She crossed herself quickly.

"I keep surprising myself with how much I don't want you looking at anybody but me ever again."

She laughed and kissed my chest. "Well, in reality, I don't see that ever happening, but a girl can fantasize about a man in makeup knocking on her door in the middle of a thunderstorm and ravaging her when she opens the door."

How… specific.

I took her home, and despite wanting to stay the night, I feared that Aleida would show up at my house and demand I do something with her, so I left, promising to see Scout soon.

Aleida spoke to my father, who called the next evening and demanded I stay in town and finish up wedding plans.

"I've got marks lined up all summer," I complained.

"They can wait. Get this done, boy."

I was grounded. May came and went, and I had to continue lying to Scout about where I was and what I was doing. Each night, I went to bed feeling more and more shitty, and each night, I wrestled with my morality. Could I ask her to do it? Spend eternity as mine?

Scout's disappointment over my absence was clear more and more each time we spoke on the phone. It killed me each time I had to lie about where I was, and I hoped that soon the wedding planning would be over.

Toward the end of June, Aleida declared that everything was ready.

"Just show up and say your vows and you're done," she snapped when I asked if I could leave.

The next day, I woke up to the weather absolutely

gloomy. The sky was gray and the clouds poured rain. All day, I slunk around the house, feeling just as miserable as the clouds pouring rain did. I wanted to see Scout, but I knew she'd be angry at me for being gone so long.

And then, suddenly, I had an idea. She'd told me exactly what she wanted, and I could do that.

I drove over to the pharmacy and found the makeup aisle. I had to ask a clerk what to get, and they sent me on my way with foundation, a bunch of eye stuff, and black lipstick.

I spent all afternoon working on my face, all the while, the weather grew worse and worse, as if the planets were aligning for me to do exactly what Scout had requested the last time I saw her.

I finished and took one last look in the mirror. I didn't have the hair, but I thought my makeup looked pretty damn good.

Careful to not get my face wet, I drove to her house.

The rain had turned the night sky completely black, but I pushed through, finally making it to her doorstep. I ran the doorbell and then straightened.

I counted my heartbeats as I waited for her to open the door.

One.

Two.

Three.

The door unlocked and creaked open. Scout looked up and then froze.

"What are you doing here?"

Desi glared at me, in full makeup, looking very much like Brandon Lee, from the movie we'd watched well over a month ago. His chest heaved and his broad shoulders rose and fell.

Desi stood frozen, his smoldering gaze penetrated my soul.

I lost my breath. Suddenly, my brain shifted from shock from seeing him, to curiosity about the time of night.

I opened my mouth but he lurched his arm forward, grabbing onto my shoulder. He tightened his grasp and pushed me backward into the house.

The lights flickered and then went out completely. Ringing silence filled the air, and Desi reached for my hips, pulling me into him. I stared up at him, seeing the sexy mix of Brandon Lee's character and Desi. I was living a fantasy.

He leaned in to kiss me, pressing his lips hard onto mine, crushing any questions I had about his intentions tonight.

Desi wasn't here to simply tease me, to play a game. He was here to ravage me.

I stumbled as he led me through the house in the pitch dark. The rain beat down against the house and onto the roof, but it was muffled by the blood pumping through my ears.

We reached my room, and Desi shut the door behind him quickly. He stripped off his rain-soaked shirt and tossed it onto the carpet. The lightning that went with it lit up the room, and I lost all train of thought.

Desi was beautiful.

He continued to dip his head down so his eyes looked even more dangerous. He could have been in the movie rather than Brandon Lee.

"Desi."

He stormed over to me and lifted me in the air. I wrapped my legs around him, and he cupped my ass, pinning me to him.

Our mouths found each other's, desperate and eager to reconnect. It had been so long. I needed him now. My skin grew warm with desire as my dry clothes connected with his damp body.

"I missed you so much." He planted kisses on my jaw, my neck, and then my collarbone.

Desi carried me to my bed.

Lightning crackled again, lighting up his pale body and white-painted face. He raised his arms and my soul left my body.

My face must have revealed my thoughts because suddenly Desi's serious demeanor shifted. He smirked and bent down.

I raised my knees to my chest and he crawled slowly onto the bed and up to me, pulling my legs back down. His hands drifted up my thighs. I savored the feel of his calloused, chilled hands on my soft, warm skin. He found my shorts and underwear and began to tug. I raised my hips to allow him to fully remove them.

His bright blue eyes raked over my naked body, and I, in turn, admired his chiseled frame. He still wore his black jeans, but I was fine with that. Paired with the makeup, it was intensely sexy.

Desi spread my legs apart and pushed himself through, finding my lips and parting them. His tongue probed me, discovering how wet I was in the mere five minutes since he'd arrived. He slid a finger inside me and began to fuck me as he lapped at my arousal.

I gasped and squirmed as he sucked hard on the bundle of nerves there.

I closed my eyes and threw my head back.

How I had missed his touch.

A full month of self-indulgence didn't come close to even a single touch from the real thing.

I came barely a minute later, and Desi kept licking until my body stopped shaking.

He tweaked my nipples. He kissed me then, shoving his tongue into my mouth. I tasted myself and groaned. He was so good with his mouth.

We continued kissing, and he ground his body, still half-dressed, into my naked one. He kept a finger inside me, thrusting his hips in time with his hand.

"Desi, please, no more. I need the real thing. I need you!" I begged.

Tears streamed down my face as I recalled every night I had experienced without him. Nothing compared to him being here, and I wasn't sure I could face another night alone.

He growled and pulled his finger away. He stood and tore the rest of his clothes off. With a swift thrust, he slid inside me, and I gasped. It felt foreign and familiar at the same time. I rolled him over and straddled him, taking every single inch of him into me. I choked on my breath as his cock shoved against my G-spot.

I ground into him, rotating my hips as he played with my breasts. The pleasure was almost too much, and I was struggling to hold on. I wanted this to last.

Otherwise, I risked losing him again.

"Scout—" Desi's face took on a pained look, and he moaned. "You need to hurry, baby."

And with that, I gave my body permission to come.

I exploded.

Every nerve in my body quaked and warmed as orgasm overtook me. I ground into him again, wanting every ounce of ecstasy his cock could give me, and then I collapsed.

Desi kept moving, bucking me up and down until a moment later, his thick mast began to pulse inside me, and he cried out.

We held each other, and I cried.

"Please don't." He wiped my tears.

"I thought you'd never come back."

"Ssshh, of course I would. I always will, baby. Please don't be sad. I won't be leaving without you anymore. We leave tomorrow."

I looked up into his still painted, albeit makeup-smeared face.

He seemed so confident, so sure of this.

"Are you sure? I can't keep getting my hopes up."

"Thank you for holding on, but the storm is over. And you know what they say."

"What?"

"It can't rain all the time."

I surprised Desi in the morning by already having suitcases packed and ready to be loaded into his car.

"I decided to come with you weeks ago so I..."

"You are so fucking amazing, you know that, right?" He grabbed my bags and took them outside. Luis was just coming out of his room, groaning about not having power all night.

"I hope it gets turned on soon. All our food is going to spoil."

"Your food. We're leaving here soon."

"Oh?" Luis turned just as Desi was coming back in. My roommate eyed him curiously. Desi still had half of his makeup on. It had smeared from our long night of love-making and eventual sleep.

"Um, maybe we should shower first," Desi suggested.

"No running water," Luis reminded me.

"Right. Well, maybe just a rag or something."

"Hopefully, when we reach a hotel, they'll have power. You ready?" Desi asked. He shifted on his feet, and I could feel the eager energy radiating off of him.

"Yeah, all right. You good, Luis? You'll get a check in the mail with my half of the rent each month."

"On time!" he called as Desi pulled me out the door.

"On time!"

My excitement was bubbling over. I had spent the last month fighting with myself over if I should do this, but it was really happening. We were going to spend the entire summer together, with him… working.

It had taken a lot of mental gymnastics to justify what I had done to Yorick, and what Desi had planned for the summer, but it still hung over my head like a dark cloud.

"What's wrong?" Desi reached for my hand once we were on the road and traveling far, far away from town.

"It doesn't feel right to be happy about this."

"Those people on my list will die whether I do it or not," he pointed out. "It's all a matter of who gets the money afterward. Why not let it be us?"

"Karma, heaven, all that stuff."

"There is no heaven for me."

"I wish I had your confidence about not getting caught. I think if we did, I'd just kill myself," I muttered and looked out the window.

"That's not—Scout, please don't say stuff like that."

"Why not? You don't think I've thought about it on and off since that night with Yorick? Why do I deserve to live but he didn't?"

"Because he was a monster. You are the opposite." His jaw tightened.

"Maybe to you. Not so much to the people he left behind."

I closed my eyes then and forced myself to sleep. It was draining to go from such a good mood to such a low one in minutes. When I woke, Desi was pulling into a gas station.

"You want a donut?" He looked genuinely concerned for me. I could almost read his thoughts.

Was this a mistake?

"Donuts sound good. Nothing with sprinkles though."

"Why don't you go in and pick out your own while I pump gas? I'll join you inside in a bit." He reached for my hand again, and I squeezed it tightly. "Are we okay?"

"Yeah, I just have to get used to this. I know if I want you, I have to accept this. So, I do."

"Scout, you know I love you. I'm only doing this to give you the life you deserve."

"I don't need all that, Desi. I just need you." I climbed out of the car. "I'm starving. Let's get some bear claws and get back on the road before I think too hard about this." I rolled my eyes and gave him a goofy grin. He relaxed and joined me outside the car.

I grabbed donuts and poured coffee into two Styrofoam cups for us.

"Who's our first… guy?" I asked during the drive. The coffee perked up my mood and my eyelids. I sat forward and turned up his radio.

Journey played through, and I sighed happily. Despite the dark parts, the good parts were really good. And this was a good part.

"I've got names all over the country. Just pick a state."

"Do you have a list?"

"I do, actually." He shifted in his seat and tugged a spiral notepad out of his pocket. "If they aren't crossed out, they are available."

I gaped as I started flipping through the pages. "You did all these?" There were so many names, and pages of them were crossed out.

"No!" He chuckled. "I did some, but others I either

declined the offer or someone else was faster than me. Go to the last page, that should have some good ones."

I flipped through.

"Hmm…"

"Pick one, that's who we'll kill."

My stomach tightened. I was determining someone's fate.

"Okay. What about Bradley Donavon? What did he do that made him get put on this list?"

Desi's smile fell instantly. "We're not doing him. Pick another name."

"Why is he on your list then?"

"He's only—It's complicated."

"I've got time." I wasn't trying to irritate him as much as I was interested in the politics of it all.

"That person was put on that list because my boss's daughter is seeing him. It's stupid. Until he gives me a reason, he lives."

"That seems dumb."

"It is," he agreed. "Another name please?"

I looked back at the list. "Okay, oh, this is a woman's name. Ida Persner. How old is she?"

Desi scrunched up his nose. "I'll have to look at my other notebook. She's old. I think she's way up north. That could be fun. You ever been to the Great Lakes?"

"I barely got out of our town, let alone travel the country."

"Great!" He beamed. "I love being able to show you new things. Let's go to a hotel and we'll plan our schedule." He reached for my hand again and squeezed. "Let's go kill Ida, the rich woman with a passion for dating and killing younger men."

CHAPTER 57

Desi

The first leg of our trip hadn't gone as I'd hoped. In fact, it was the exact opposite. Scout was having trouble dealing with the truth.

I was losing her already.

But I refused to let it happen. This summer, I was going to show her the glorious life she could have with me if she stayed… forever.

I was still trying to find the words to explain what I needed her to do to accomplish that.

I was worse than a normal hitman. I didn't just kill bad guys. I convinced good girls to kill themselves.

I drove north. Petoskey, Michigan, was almost six hours away, and Scout and I felt every single minute of them in my car.

We rotated through all my tapes and stopped for bathroom breaks and snacks, but by the time we reached the scenic, almost storybook-looking town, we were exhausted.

"Why don't we just rest today and start up tomorrow?" I offered.

She stood by the car outside, taking in the light lake breeze drifting in as I went inside and booked our room.

"What's there to do here?" she asked.

"Petoskey? I don't know. I can ask the hotel clerk."

We went inside and did just that.

"There's tons of restaurants and landmarks. But my favorite thing to do is go look for stones." The clerk said when we asked.

"Stones?" Scout cocked her head.

"Petoskey stones." The clerk leaned over his desk and snatched up a rock with circle designs all over it. "It's our state rock. Go down to Lake Michigan Beach. Wear shoes, though, it'll bruise your feet. There's millions of rocks. Just dip them in water and it will reveal what they are."

I turned to Scout. "What do you think?"

"Sounds fun. Let's go."

The clerk gave us directions and after we put all of our things in the room, we took off toward the beach.

"Are we sure this is the right place? No one's here." Scout frowned as we parked and started over a small bridge.

"I'm not entirely sure," I admitted. The bridge ended, and a small path had signs telling us to keep going.

"Why does everything look like it's still the 1950s?"

"I kind of like it. It's like, this town has been saved by the modern world. It's frozen in time."

"Hopefully, not the people too," she muttered.

"What do you mean?"

Would it be so bad to be frozen in time?

"Like, with views, you know. Segregation and all that? My friends and their families had to deal with that. Probably my parents too."

She was right. I was surrounded by so much protection, so much... privilege.

We reached some trees and passed through them, finding the lake.

"Where's the sand?" Scout asked.

"Under the rocks?" The beach went on for miles and was about a quarter of a mile from grass to water, and it was nothing but rocks. "We might wanna get a move on." I walked forward, reached for a rock, and put on it, rubbing the face.

Nothing.

"Shouldn't we start by the water?" Scout asked as we started down the bumpy, rock-covered beach.

"He did say that you had to get wet to find them," I said, following behind her. When we reached the water, I rolled my pants up. Scout did the same, and then we started searching for rocks.

"I think I found one!" Scout yelled with delight after twenty minutes. She was a foot in the water and waving wildly to me.

"Oh yeah? Let's see it."

She showed me the wet rock, and I put it close to my face. "I don't see anything." I shook my head. "No go."

She tossed the rock down and kept looking. I was having terrible luck as well. It was nearly another hour before finally we were able to agree that we had found one. It was a pebble at best.

"That was so much fun!" She laughed as we sat on the rocks to rest.

My feet, despite having kept shoes on, were bruised from walking on the unbalanced terrain. "It was. And now you have a souvenir." I handed her the tiny stone.

"Yes, I do. I wonder what other things I can get from other places. Natural things, of course."

"Hmmm. Why don't we try to find one in every town?"

"I'd like that," she said and leaned into me, resting her head on my shoulder. "What now?"

We stared out into the water until the sun went down. It was the most beautiful sunset I'd ever seen. I doubted I'd ever experience another one like it.

I wanted to blurt out exactly what I wanted to happen. I wanted to turn and shout.

Now we get engaged and I marry you in some small ceremony and then on our birthdays we die and turn and then we travel the world as vampires.

But I couldn't. Instead, I chose to hold her tight.

She stared off into the distance.

"What are you thinking about?" I asked.

"Ida," she said simply. "This time tomorrow, she'll be dead. No more wind in her hair, no more sunsets, no more nothing."

"I doubt she cared about those things every time she killed one of her twenty-something boy-toys."

"What?"

"She's a black widow of sorts. She finds young men, seduces them, and when they realize they don't want to be her slave, they suddenly disappear. She made the mistake of picking up the wrong boy. Kyle Wong." My eyes glazed as I recalled the conversation about Ida. "She doesn't care about death as much as you think."

"And you're saying I shouldn't either."

"Yes. You shouldn't. Mortality is just a concept. If we put in the effort, we can live on long after our human bodies fail us."

"Since when did you get so deep," she teased, elbowing me.

"Don't you want to live forever?" I asked.

"I guess it depends. If you're talking about a legacy, if it's a good one, like Rosa Parks, then sure. If it's someone like John Wilkes Booth, maybe not."

"Not legacy." My hands began to sweat as I considered my words. "Like, for real. Eternal life, as you are right now?"

"Hmmm…" She tapped her finger on her chin. "Would you be there?"

I grinned and wrapped my arms around her small frame. "I wouldn't miss it."

I gripped her hand and pulled her back to the bridge. "Scout, I have something I need to tell you."

And then suddenly, she collapsed.

CHAPTER 58

Desi

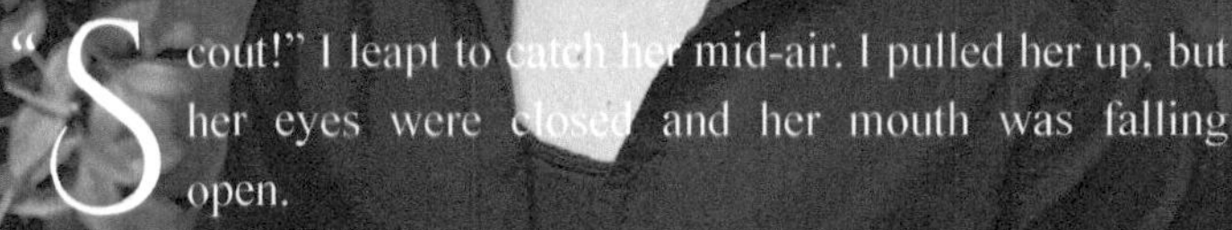

"Scout!" I leapt to catch her mid-air. I pulled her up, but her eyes were closed and her mouth was falling open.

Fuck.

Shifting my weight, I hauled her into my arms and started back to the car. Resting her in the back, I dug for water. I poured a smidge into my hand and wiped her face. She blinked and then groaned loudly.

"Are you okay?"

She gulped down the bottle. "Yeah, just a little light-headed. It was so fast, I'm not sure what happened."

"Well, it's been a bit since we've ate. Let's go back to the hotel and I'll order in."

"What about Ida?"

"Fuck Ida, she can die tomorrow." She passed out and was worried about our kill?

When we got back to the hotel, Scout insisted on napping instead of waiting for food.

"Just a little nap, and when I wake up, I'll scarf down everything." She fell asleep almost the exact moment her head hit the pillow. I sat in the chair by the table, watching her sleep until midnight. I wasn't tired in the slightest. I was too worried to sleep.

I was going to ask her. By the end of the summer, I was going to do it. Beg her to hear me out, understand my situation, and ask her to commit suicide on the off chance she'd change and be with me for eternity. And either one of three things would happen.

She'd leave.

She'd do it and die.

She'd do it and turn.

I needed to ask her though because I couldn't imagine a life without her in it. I didn't want to live if she wasn't in my life.

If she died, I would kill myself too. It was only fair.

I bounced my leg while watching her. The piece of paper with a phone number scrawled on it weighed heavy in my wallet. I couldn't take it anymore and left the room and went down to find a payphone. I walked down the block, slid a few quarters into the machine, and dialed.

"Hello?"

"This is Desiderio Amato, we've spoken before. Xerxes?"

"Ah, yes, the Bloodborn who thinks my kind is inferior yet is still interested in knowing how we operate."

"Yes. We spoke about an interview."

"How Anne Rice of you."

"Who?"

The man on the other side cackled dryly. "Nothing. Where are you currently?"

I looked around me. "Up north. And you're in Kalamazoo, right?"

"I am. When can you come this way?"

"Tomorrow."

We set up a time, and I hung up. I looked at my watch. I had time to take care of Ida and come back to Scout and sleep.

I caught the old bag doing what she did best, putting a body on her boat to dump out onto the lake. I joined her, and together, we tossed her last lover overboard and then I did the same to her. She deserved to drown.

I was glad my father had taught me how to work a pontoon boat when I was younger. I made it to shore, abandoned the boat, and drove back to the hotel room.

The next morning, Scout seemed in good spirits. I informed her that Ida was gone and we'd be going back down with a small stop tonight.

"I have to meet with someone."

"Can I come?" she asked as we popped back into my car. "Who is it?"

I thought about it. Perhaps I could tell her then, confess to the darkness that consumed my soul, but something held me back. "No, it's too dangerous. I'd rather you not."

She wasn't happy with my answer, but I didn't budge. I got us another hotel and when the sun fell, I gave her money to order food and kissed her goodbye. "I'll be back in a few hours. Stay put, please."

I drove to Xerxes's house. It looked relatively normal. I knocked, and he answered. I blanched when I saw his startling blue eyes. They were unnatural.

"Should I wear sunglasses?" He smirked.

I grimaced and looked away. "No, I just don't see vampires like you."

"That's because there isn't many of us. We're accidents."

I rolled my eyes. "Yes, that's what they say."

"I can make you leave at any time. Or kill you if I wanted," he threatened.

I laughed. "You'd be stupid to try. You know how quick you'd be dead after killing a Bloodborn with my last name?"

"I don't follow their politics," he said and allowed me entrance.

He brushed past me and took me to his living room.

"You should. You never know when they'll decide to change their minds about your kind." It took me only a moment to realize what I was doing and quickly apologized. "I'm sorry. I shouldn't be treating you this way."

"You're right. I'm only here, in this state, because I wanted to end things. This was my eternal punishment, my hell, for what I did."

"How did you do it?" I asked, morbidly curious.

"Well, back then, I had a passion for flourish. I had read in a book once about torture. I won't go into specifics, but I set up a trap so that I would be devoured by mice."

"And it worked?"

"Oh yeah, I felt every bit of it. And then I got to feel pain again when I was reborn, healed, and transformed into this." He waved his arm dramatically at himself and then sat on the opposite couch. "Now, what do you want to know?"

"You had no idea you were a Bloodshed?"

He shook his head. "None. Didn't even know vampires existed."

"So you have no clue what triggered it? Did you have any illnesses as a human? What about others like you? Did they have anything they think caused you to turn?" I fired off questions, and he raised a hand to stop me.

"Hold on, one question at a time." He lowered his gaze. "Why are you so interested in us?"

I stared at him. Neither of us had anything left to lose.

"I am going to turn in a few months, and I'm in love with a human."

Xerxes blinked and let the words settle. "Are you proposing she..."

I looked away guiltily. "I've considered it. I've never felt this selfish before. I just want to know the risks before I go through with it. It has to be suicide with no help from anyone else?"

He nodded grimly. "You cannot assist her. I'm sorry, Desiderio. I don't know how or what in my blood triggered the change. I don't have a history of suicide in my family. I just know what happened to me and the consequences."

"What were the consequences?"

"I'm a pariah. I'm not welcome into any Bloodborn company, yet I bleed from every orifice if the sun touches me. I am hated simply because I didn't know. If I had known, I would have figured out a way to be murdered rather than to have done it myself."

"And you have no other differences, besides your eyes, to Bloodborns?"

He shook his head. "Only the eyes. Oh, and we can't sire children. That was a gift only the Bloodborns have. Not that I wanted any, but I know many a Bloodshed who have mourned for children they cannot bear."

Interesting.

Did I want children?

Not really.

"Is it still worth it to you? To create a Bloodshed lover, knowing all that she will endure for eternity?" Xerxes asked me.

I licked my lips.

Good question.

CHAPTER 59

Scout

I sat in the bathtub in a hotel, eyeing the razorblades I had bought at a gas station when Desi wasn't looking.

It had been one week since we'd left Ohio. Since I made the conscious choice to follow Desi across the country while he murdered people for money. I was a part of his killing spree. I had wanted that. What kind of a monster was I?

I didn't deserve a life of happiness.

Desi didn't either. Sooner or later, it would all catch up to us. We'd be a modern day Bonnie and Clyde. I wasn't a big history buff, but I knew how their story ended. I had a dreaded feeling our end would be a lot more torturous.

I couldn't go back to my home, with Luis and Brucey and all my friends, with my conscience as heavy as it was. How could I go about living a normal life, knowing I'd put people in the ground? People who were parents, children, and had people who loved them. People that missed them and wondered what happened to them.

I reached for the razor blade. My heart raced as I bit down

my lip and nerves. With a shaky hand, I brought it to my right arm and pressed.

"Scout? You all right? It's been a while." Desi banged on the door.

I stared at the red line spilling from my skin.

Desi's pounding began to get louder and more frantic. "Scout? Scout, will you please fucking answer me?" His voice came out tortured, and I began to cry.

I closed my eyes and leaned my head back. I slid my bleeding arm into the bath, letting the warm water coax the blood to move. Please, just let me go fast.

I took a deep breath and prepared myself for the other arm. I lifted my hands and switched the blade from one hand to the other. Just as I was pressing it into my skin, the door burst open.

Wood splintered as Desi fell to the ground. He caught himself with his palms and looked up at me. I blinked and tried to sit up, but my head was dizzy.

"Scout? Oh my god. Fuck!" He scrambled and ripped me out of the bath.

I was too weak to fight him, so I remained cradled in his arms, all the while, pleading for death. He snatched a towel and pressed it against my bleeding arm. He swore as he tried to save me. I closed my eyes, trying to work past the fuzz in my brain. Something wasn't right. What had I done?

Desi was crying. I had hurt him. I couldn't die, knowing his heart was breaking.

"We need to get you help," he choked out. "Fuck, I don't know what to do."

I felt myself being lifted and taken out of the steamy bathroom. Desi placed me on the bed. The click of the phone being taken off the hook caught my attention. I tried to focus on what was going on. Had he called an ambulance?

"Do you have a sewing kit? I tore my shirt," he said to someone.

When had he ripped his shirt? Oh wait… he was talking about me.

He hung up and came back to sit beside me. He pressed his hands over my cut and squeezed the towel again. "Sssh, it's going to be all right."

Someone knocked, and Desi stood to get it. I swiveled my head and tried to open my eyes, but everything felt so heavy.

"Thanks. Here, for your troubles." Desi spoke to the person and quickly shut the door.

"I-It hurts," I murmured when he returned to my side.

He brushed my hair, wet and matted, off my face. "I know, you're hurt. But I'm going to fix you, okay?" He continued to apply pressure to my arm before finally unwrapping it. "I'm going to sew you up. Thankfully, you missed all the important parts."

"How do you know?" I asked through the fog. I managed to crack my eyes open just a touch, and saw his eyes darken.

"Because if you had, you'd be dead."

He propped me up on pillows, and I tried to focus on what he was doing.

I watched, as an observer, and not an active participant in the room as he prepared the needle, threading it and tying it. His eyes held a grave intensity in them.

He took my arm and seeing it smeared with blood, he got up and returned with a cold, wet rag. He cleaned me up and then brought the needle to my skin.

"Try to relax, Scout," he said as he pierced through.

I gasped and shrieked as I felt every inch of the thread being pulled through my skin. And then, he pierced the other side and did it again.

"Scout, you need to relax," he repeated. I pressed my lips

and closed my eyes. A moment later, my brain went black. I awoke sometime later. I hissed with pain as I hit my arm when I sat up.

Desi's voice from the other side of the room caused me to jump out of my skin. "How do you feel?" His hands gripped the arms of his chair as he glared at me.

"I… I'm alive." I blinked, considering what I'd just said. That wasn't part of the plan. I was supposed to be dead.

He nodded grimly and sat forward, resting his chin in his hands. "Yes. You are. You want to tell me why you were trying not to be?"

My chin trembled as the tears welled up in my eyes. I shook my head. "Desi, I don't deserve to live. I'm a monster. I came with you to kill people. Lots of people." My hands covered my face as I sobbed. "I'm alive, and I shouldn't be. I need to pay for what we've done."

Desi flew from his chair with such force it hit the wall with a loud thud. He pulled me into his arms. "That's not true. You're not a monster. You deserve to be alive. Stop thinking like this!"

How could I think otherwise?

"People are dead because of us, Desi!"

"And if it weren't us, it would have been someone else. Scout, we've been through this. Why are you letting yourself think about them? They are nothing. They were worthless scum. They were—"

"Murderers?" I laughed through my sobs. "And what are we?"

"If you go, then I go too. You know that, right?" Desi whispered. "If you kill yourself, then I will do the same. I can't live without you, Scout. I love you."

"Is that a threat?"

"No, it's the truth. You think I want to live without you?

Every day that I've been stuck traveling or doing something that keeps me from seeing you has been hell. All I do is think about you, our future, and how to get there. If my future doesn't include you, I don't want it." Desi paused and gently pushed me off of his lap. He climbed off the bed and went to his knees. He reached for my undamaged hand and squeezed. "I want you to make me a deal. A promise. Okay?"

"What?"

"Stay alive until our birthdays. Fight this sadness. Fight it and when you turn twenty-seven, we'll decide together. If you want to die, we'll do it together."

Was this some trick? Did he think he'd be able to convince me that what we'd done was okay? He rubbed the ring he had given me for Christmas.

"Just wait until your birthday, okay? It will get better, and if it doesn't, I'll follow you to hell."

"Hell?"

"That's what you think, isn't it?"

Only to avoid causing Desi any more pain, I agreed. I'd stay alive until my birthday and then decide for the both of us.

Would I take us to hell, or were we already there?

Desi and I did everything he promised we'd do that summer. We went to movies, to every zoo, amusement park, and roadside attraction we came upon on our journey. Nothing was off-limits because we had the money, the means, and time.

All across the country, Desi and I traveled, killing people we were told deserved it. Despite what he seemed to expect, I couldn't pretend there was nothing wrong with what we were doing.

Desi assured me each and every time that I only had to be as involved as I wanted to. I could stay in the hotel and wait for him to return, or go out with him and take the person out.

"I can't sit around and wait," I protested every time. "I'll worry too much. At least with me beside you, I can help protect you."

Desi snickered at that, but I reminded him of Yorick. Desi could have died if I hadn't been there. I refused to let that happen again. Each night, when we returned to whatever hotel we were in, I'd lock myself in the bathroom and stare at the walls.

What had we done?

Desi had begun inspecting the bathrooms and my bags, looking for razors, pills, and anything I could use to hurt myself while in there, but I couldn't help it anymore.

It had become a compulsion, the desire to slice my skin open, to bleed, to hurt, to feel. I deserved to hurt for what we were doing. I found ways and places to hide razorblades. Sometimes, I'd sneak off while he was dealing with a mark and do it. He was too busy making sure the person didn't get away to make sure I wasn't hurting myself.

But every night, when we were back in our room, he'd bow his head, sink his shoulders, and politely, ever so softly, ask me where I hurt myself.

"Do you need more bandages?" he asked, not looking me in the eye.

"It'll heal."

"Scout, let me see, please." Desi dropped to his knees and he reached for me.

I tensed as he buried his head in my lap and cried.

"I hate what I've done to you," he said, lifting his head. "You were so beautiful, so pure, and now, you hate yourself."

He lifted my skirt and found the slashes on the inside of my thighs, still bleeding a bit. He stood and went to his bag, pulling out his kit. I lay there, numb, as he worked. He cleaned my cuts, bandaged, and wrapped what he could, and the deeper ones, he took his suture kit at and sewed what I had sliced too deep.

And then, he cried.

My arms, my legs, my stomach, my breasts, were covered in bandages and stitches and scars. The outside matched the inside.

Desi and I embraced each other tightly. At first, he tried to hold it together, but at some point during our journey, he lost his will to fight right along with me. He and I cried every night, and in the mornings, we'd pack up and continue as is.

He asked me every single day if I wanted to go home, and I'd refuse.

While I had taken to carving into myself as penance, Desi had started to chain-smoke. It felt like in an attempt to give ourselves a better future, we were creating a rift that would inevitably break us up. Eventually, he wouldn't be able to take my miserable moping and leave me. Finally, after a particularly long night of cleaning me up, Desi threw up his hands.

"We're done. If we go on one more day, I'm going to lose you."

I sat up and blinked through my tears. Was this it? Was he breaking up with me?

He climbed onto the bed and straddled me. He brought his face inches from mine and bore his beautiful blue eyes into me.

"What do you mean?" I whimpered. He ripped open his dress shirt, then pressed his lips against mine. This was the first time in weeks that I had felt any true passion between us. Was this our goodbye kiss?

"I can't lose you," he murmured, pulling away from my lips. He kissed my chin, then my neck, then my collarbone. He lowered himself and began kissing every inch of my skin he could, even the scars. "I've taken everything from you, but I need to give it back. Scout, I'm sorry for what I've done to you. I don't want this for you. For us. I need you back."

He sat up and removed his clothing. I admired his perfect, unflawed body. I had taken all the pain so that he didn't have to.

"You're still beautiful, you know that, right?" He reached out and held my head between his large, warm hands, forcing me to look at him. "Stop it. You are the most beautiful woman I've ever seen. And tonight, I'm taking you back. Taking us back."

I didn't know what that meant, but then he kissed me again.

I didn't want to lose him either. In an attempt to not lose him, I lost myself.

But not anymore.

I kissed him back. My body relaxed into his as we kissed, our tongues mingling with intensity. We both knew what was at stake if we didn't do something. He needed the skin on skin contact just as much as I did.

I thought there'd be a pause when he saw me fully naked. I thought he'd stare at me, horrified, disgusted. But no, Desi bent down and kissed every single mark I had made this summer. And with each kiss, he gave me a different promise.

"I am devoted to you completely."

"I'm going to give you the life you deserve."

"I'm going to marry you."

As he kissed my scars and wounds, his hands moved over me, finding my breasts. He cupped them and brushed his thumb over my nipples. They pebbled under his touch, and it felt so good. It had been quite long since I'd wanted to feel good like this.

Desi reached my feet and then came back up, finding my core. Looking up at me, he eyed me cautiously. I nodded, allowing him to touch me more. Gently, he slid my thighs apart. His tongue found my arousal and lapped at it slowly, testing the waters.

When I began to respond with moans, gasps, and tense movements, he slid a finger inside of me and began to move in and out, coaxing pleasure from me.

"Oh, Desi," I moaned.

"Yeah? Come for me, baby." He dove back in, focusing hard on my clit.

I gasped and exploded. My orgasm rolled over me. Warmth and good feelings flooded my body. I pulled his hips down, welcoming him inside me.

We made love with an intensity that only he and I could feel for each other. We cried as we rode the feelings, the pleasure, and finally, the tandem explosions of our love for each other.

Desi held me in his arms afterward, and finally, I made a promise I intended to keep, much like the ones he had made to me tonight.

"I won't hurt myself anymore. As long as I have you."

CHAPTER 61

Desi

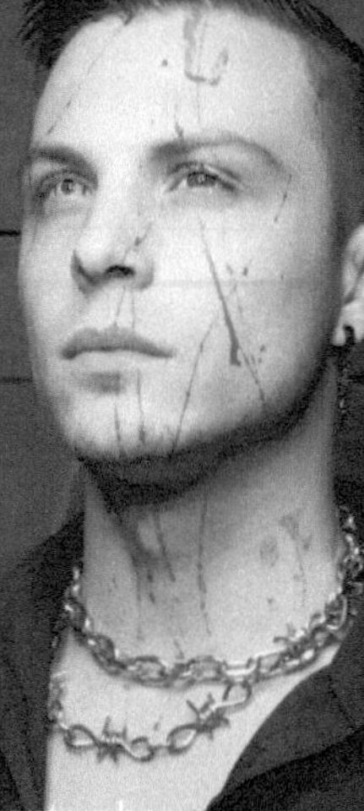

September

While I dreaded returning home, it was necessary. September was here, and I was expected by several people who would hunt me down if I didn't show. I knew this because I had called a few times to get my money, and each time I was reminded to be home in time for the wedding.

Scout and I had spent the last few weeks of summer not taking on any more jobs, but instead finding each other again, touring beaches and watching the sun set and rise together.

The last ride home was a long one. I held her hand and we sang Journey at the top of our lungs over and over until we drove past the city limits, and we were back where we started. It felt weird to drop her off at her house.

"I was serious. I want us to move in together," I told her as I held firmly onto her hand. The idea of being away from her wasn't one I liked. "Let's go pack up your stuff right now."

I had no idea what I was saying. I couldn't move her into my place. Aleida had keys, she knew where I was, and the hours I kept. She'd see another car there. How could I move Scout in? Thankfully, Scout shook her head. Relief, yet a twinge of disappointment, wafted over me.

"Soon. For now, I want to go inside and rest in my own bed. Alone," she clarified when I made a suggestive face.

"Are you going to be okay alone?" I asked. While Scout had kept her promise during the rest of the trip to not touch another razorblade, I still worried about her mental state. If she was alone, would those dark thoughts return? If I wasn't there to sew her up, it could be disastrous.

"I'll be fine. I'm mostly going to stretch, shower, and then get a good night's sleep with my comfortable blankets and pillows."

I only dropped her hand when she forced me to. She started toward her house but then spun around and waved. "I'll be fine! Go, unpack, and I'll call you in the morning, okay?"

Reluctantly, I got into my car and took off toward home. I turned onto my drive and hit the brakes sharply. Aleida's car was in my driveway, and the lights in my house were on.

Fuck.

I stared at my house, trying to figure out what was about to happen and how to get out of it.

She had to know.

That was why she was here. She knew about Scout and was going to confront me, and… then what? She couldn't kill me. To kill a Bloodborn before they turned was not just frowned upon, she'd be hunted down too.

No, Aleida wouldn't kill me, she'd do worse. She would kill Scout. I couldn't let that happen. Gathering up the courage to leave the car, I climbed out, grabbed my bags from the back, and headed up the stairs. My heart hammered as I unlocked the door and opened it.

I stepped inside, looked up, and froze.

Aleida, in full wedding gear, stood in the center of my living room, smiling at me. "Surprise!"

I took it all in. Her dress was large, with giant balls on her shoulders and sleeves that went to her fingertips. It was tight at the waist but poofed out so much I couldn't see the ground. The train was wrapped around the room in lazy circles.

Aleida had curled all of her hair and put on such dramatic makeup it was almost a costume. Her veil went to the floor, and the flowers in her hand looked to weigh about thirty pounds.

"What?"

She jumped up and down excitedly. "Surprise, sweetie! I know you've talked all summer about not wanting a huge wedding, so let's just do it now! We can go to the courthouse tonight and a judge will do it."

"No."

She blinked. "What?"

"No, I don't want to do that."

She dropped the bouquet. "Why not?" Her red eyes hardened, and she bared her fangs. I braced myself.

"Because I'm in love with someone else." The silence that followed was thick. We stared each other down.

"What did you just say?"

"I said, I'm in love with someone else. I don't want to marry you. I don't care what our parents want. I can't go through with it."

"Who is she?" Aleida demanded. "Is it Yvonne? Or Fiona Romero?"

It was on the tip of my tongue to tell her the truth, but I wasn't that stupid. "It's not anyone you know."

"So, it's a vampire you met on the road. During your travels, while working for my dad?" She stormed over to me and poked me hard in the chest. "You've got balls, Desiderio Amato."

"Like you haven't been cheating on me this entire time? How is Bradley Donovan? Last time I checked, his name was still on my list."

"Is that a threat?" She laughed. "You forget you're still human."

"I don't forget shit. I know exactly who I am." I glared at her. "Get the fuck out. Go see your boyfriend. Tell him all about what I did. Then, go tell your fucking father the wedding's off."

Screaming, Aleida lifted her dress and stormed out of my house. I picked up her abandoned bouquet and went to the front door. As she was backing out of my drive, I tossed it at her car. It hit the side with a loud thunk and she flipped me off. I went back inside, slammed the door, and sunk down onto my couch.

God, that felt fucking good.

Fifteen minutes later, my phone began to ring, but I ignored it. My message recorder was full, so they couldn't leave a reply, which was fine by me, as I assumed it was either my parents or Aleida's. I turned on the TV and ended up drifting off to sleep to the news, only to be woken up sometime in the middle of the night, to my door being busted through.

I shot up but was too disoriented to react when a closed fist hit my jaw. I stumbled back in confusion, my eyes still blurry, and then, I saw him. He was a huge beast of a man, twice my size both ways. His muscles tripled mine and his anger radiated through them.

"Who the fuck are you?" I shouted.

"You broke my girlfriend's heart, and you're gonna fucking pay."

It took me a moment to realize what he meant and then I laughed. "Brad?" I stood and shook my head. "You're mad because I'm not going to marry your girlfriend? What do you plan on doing?"

"Kicking your ass," he snarled.

I motioned for him to come get me. "Then fucking do it."

He bowed, and with a scream, ran toward me, catching me straight in the middle.

I lost the air from my lungs as he slammed me into the wall. Managing to shove him back, I reached for his head and shoved it down onto my kneecap. I was no match for a vampire, but I could stun the fucker.

Which, after a few rounds of me ducking and getting punches and hits in where I could, it worked. He fell back against the wall and closed his eyes.

"You're a fast guy." He heaved.

"Yeah, and if you don't get the fuck out of here, you'll be a dead one. Now go and tell your girlfriend to leave me the fuck alone."

"You'll regret this," he warned as he stumbled out of my house.

"Maybe," I replied.

He was right. Telling Aleida the truth might have very well been the worst mistake of my life.

CHAPTER 62

Desi

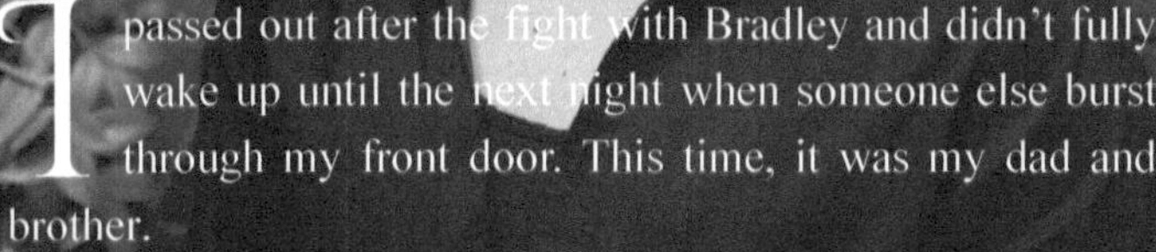

I passed out after the fight with Bradley and didn't fully wake up until the next night when someone else burst through my front door. This time, it was my dad and brother.

I groaned, wincing from the pain of getting the shit beat out of me the night before. While I had managed to get a few hits in, enough to get him to leave, he still did more damage to me than I did to him. I was still very much human, and he very much vampire.

"You think you're fucking funny? Huh?" Gianni kicked my calf hard with his pointed leather dress shoe.

"Fuck!" I leapt up. "What the fuck is your problem?" I stumbled to my feet and looked at them. Frozen in time, we all looked so similar now. We could all be fraternal triplets if people asked.

"Desiderio, what were you thinking?" He slapped me across the back of the head. "You found another vampire?"

"I found another woman," I clarified.

"What's that supposed to mean?" Gianni scoffed. "You mean, like human? A full-blood human?"

I didn't say anything, but the look on my face revealed it all. My father groaned and shook his head.

"No, no, no, Desiderio, what are you thinking? You can't be with a human. It's absurd."

"Why?"

"Because they die!"

"And she will die," my father muttered. "If this gets out, Desiderio, they will come for her. You know how this goes. How many humans did you kill this summer? Huh? You don't think some of their people won't come for her?"

"I know." I brushed my hair back and laughed dryly. "I fucking know. It's stupid. It is, but I've never felt like this before. With anyone. I think she may not be human." I winced, realizing I said too much. My father and brother froze and looked over at me. The same question and realization on their face.

"Desiderio, you can't possibly be thinking of what I think you're thinking," my dad said.

"You're a fucking idiot," Gianni added. "You think she could be Bloodshed?"

"Desiderio." My father came to me and put his hands on my shoulders. He squeezed tightly until I looked at him. "You can't do that. We have rules."

"Fuck the rules. Who cares?"

"The world cares!" he roared. "Suicide is not something to be romanticized. This isn't Romeo and Juliet. It's not something that humans should take lightly or glamorize. Next thing you know, every kid on the block is gonna blow out their birthday candles and then swallow a gun. We'll have vampires everywhere!"

"And what if she's not?" Gianni stepped forward. "What if you get her to kill herself and that's it? She's dead. No one knows what makes one person different from the other. You don't know if she's got Bloodshed blood in her or not."

My dad clicked his tongue. "Do not do this. If you ask that human woman to commit suicide, I'll disown you."

Romanticizing suicide was exactly why Bloodsheds were considered beneath Bloodborns. I couldn't ask that of Scout.

"Fine. I won't. Happy?" I threw up my hands.

"No, not yet." My dad waved a finger at me. "You have me in some serious shit, Desiderio. I've got Linotti calling me, pissed off because the wedding's off. You know how much money he put out for that?"

"I'll pay him back. I've got money." That money had been meant for Scout and me to start a life together, but if paying Mr. Linotti back for the wedding did that, so be it.

"That's not the point." Gianni seethed. "We have a way of doing things around here and—"

"And what? I have never done things the way I was supposed to, have I?" I looked around my small house. "I could've gone to work right away with you, but what did I do? I chose to grow weed and sell dope just for the laughs. I haven't worn a suit in my fucking life outside of formal occasions, and I started killing before I even turned. Do you really expect me to fall in line now?"

"Yes!" my father boomed. He strode back over to me and poked me in the chest. "You are not to see that human woman. Every time you see her, you put her life at risk. You will begin work with me until we can work out a deal with Linotti. Do you understand?"

"This isn't fair!" I protested.

"You think any of what we have is fair?" My dad scoffed. "You think asking your human mistress to kill herself for you is fair? You have always been selfish, but this is a new low for you."

"This is why you should have just stuck to the plan and kept your eyes on the fucking ground," Gianni snarled. "Marry another Bloodborn and move on."

"I can't do that."

"You can, and you will," my dad continued. "Tomorrow night, you will be at the house. We'll start with getting you some suits." He eyed my jeans and leather jacket with disgust. "And then we'll get to work. I'm done with your nonsense, Desiderio. It's time to grow up."

"And growing up means what? Being unhappy for eternity?"

"If that's what you choose."

"But I don't," I argued. "I can be happy and successful. You just need to let me—"

"Don't tell me what to do." His chest swelled and his fists tightened at his sides. "You are my son and you will act as such."

"Dad—" I pleaded for him to understand, but I knew it was useless. He had made up his mind. He turned and motioned for Gianni to follow him.

"Stay up tonight, so you can sleep during the day. Be at the house by sunset."

They left, much quieter than they'd arrived.

I paced all night long, trying to figure a way out of it. To explain it to Scout. I fucked up by telling Aleida, I knew that. Now, to keep Scout safe, I had to do this. So, in the morning, I called her and prayed she picked up so I could lie out of my ass for the millionth time.

"Hello?" she said after the click.

"Scout? Hey."

"Good morning! What are you up to today?"

"Actually, I'm about to go to bed. I, uh, I need to explain some things."

"Okay? Are you okay?"

"Yeah, of course. It's just… I've been thinking a lot about my future, our future. This summer was too much for me. You don't want to do that, and I can't do it without your support so I'm done. I'm getting out of that business."

"You are?" Her voice was so hopeful it nearly shattered me to lie to her.

"Kind of. I'm not going to be on the road. I'm taking a job under my dad. I'll be working with him and my brother, and they do business at night."

"At night? That's odd."

"Organized crime doesn't sleep," I tried to joke but she didn't laugh. "I'm getting fitted for suits tonight."

"You're starting already?"

"I wasn't given the option. They considered the summer my time off."

"But you still worked. We—"

"I know," I cut her off. "But they are kind of set in their ways. They also want me to focus on learning the ropes. I won't be available for a few weeks."

"Weeks?" Her voice cracked, and it shattered my heart. "What happened to wanting me to move in and never be away?"

"I know, I know. This is something I have to do. I'll try to call when I can. But I need to get this done so they can stop bitching about it. By the time our birthdays roll around, we'll be together, celebrating again. Maybe afterward, we can see about moving in together."

"Desi, that's two months!"

"Six weeks," I argued. "Just for six weeks, please, can you do this? I'll send you your half of the money we earned this summer and you can relax, do your art, and get things in order to move, okay?" My stomach was in knots. Would she do it?

"Okay."

"And don't hurt yourself," I added quickly.

"Okay!" she said and slammed the phone down.

CHAPTER 63

I was done.

He had filled me up with such hope, such desire, such… longing, that I couldn't keep spending tons of time with him and then nothing, only to do it again and again.

"Give me a date," I snapped when he called next.

"What?"

"Give me a date when this is all over, or I'm walking away right now."

"Scout, you know I can't—"

"No, Desi, I can't. I can't keep falling in love with you over and over again. I want to be with you permanently. It's nothing or forever."

"Forever, of course." He sighed. "You want a date? Fine. Your birthday. October 22nd. I'll be there, on time, and we'll start our lives together, for real this time."

"No more excuses. I don't care if we're homeless. I just want you."

"Fine," he said curtly. "October 22nd."

My demand must have caused him to forget why he called because he hung up. I wasn't upset at his reaction. I'd expected it. With that in mind, I made plans with Luis to move out.

"Consider my last day October 31st, just to be safe." I handed him a fat check, finishing up my half of the rent.

"How did you get this much money?"

"Desi and I split his earnings this summer."

"What did you say he does again?"

"Debt collector." I shrugged and stood up from the couch. "Now, you need to go start making flyers and putting the space in the paper, and I need to go pack."

I still had five weeks and nothing to do but pack, so I took my time, cleaning everything extra for Luis and his next roommate. I scrubbed the floors and carpets. I bought paint and, with a heavy heart, layered white all over my drawings. I washed windows, raked leaves, and did everything I could to keep myself busy and my mind off Desi.

He called every night before work, but he was still angry at my ultimatum. Our conversations were usually clipped and short. He would ask about my day. I'd ask about his, and then we'd hang up. But then one day, he surprised me by seeming… happy.

We were only a week away from our birthdays, and the ticking clock had been making him more and more agitated. Now, he was almost the same Desi I'd fallen for in the beginning, almost a full year ago.

"Hey, you! I have a surprise."

"You do?"

"I do. Do you have plans for your birthday?"

Was he going to cancel? "Don't tell me—"

"I want to take you out. We'll move you out the day after my birthday, okay?" he rushed. "Do you want to get tattoos?"

"Really? I mean, I've always talked about it, but—"

"Let's do it. This artist is coming in from Germany who agreed to do us both." His excitement was contagious.

"Sure, I guess!"

"Awesome. Okay, come up with something and I'll pick you up in the morning on the 22nd, okay?"

Finally, it was happening. Desi and I would be together forever. "Okay," I whispered.

"Scout, I love you. You know that, right?"

"I love you too."

"Good."

I spent the rest of my week trying to decide what I wanted on my body permanently and where. I didn't decide until the knock on my door came right at seven in the morning on my birthday.

"Happy twenty-seven!" Desi shouted in my face, thrusting a bouquet of roses in my face.

I laughed and took them, sniffed, and then lowered them. I hadn't seen him since we returned home in September.

"Oh, how I missed you."

He offered his arm and grinned. "Hungry?"

We left my house and went to grab some breakfast.

"I have a full day planned for you," he declared after we ordered matching tall stacks of pancakes and bacon.

"Do I get to know?" I put my hands under my chin and rested my arms on the table. I just wanted to look at him and do nothing else. Absence did make the heart grow fonder.

"Sure. After this, we're going to do a double feature at the theater. I rented it out so we can be as loud as we want."

"Two movies?"

He nodded. "Then, we can head over to the shop and get inked. Do you know what you want?"

"Uh, maybe? I don't know."

"Well, maybe Marco will have an idea."

We ate our breakfast and flew over to the theater, where we watched another Freddy Krueger flick and then Pulp Fiction. We were loud, just as Desi said we could be. We laughed, we screamed, and shouted at the screen.

"This has been the best day ever!" I squealed when we were walking toward the car. "See, this is how it should be! Me and you, all the time."

"That's what you wanted, right? Today to be the first and last day of your old life?"

I gave him a weird look. "Why are you saying it like that?"

"No reason. Sorry. Let's go see Marco."

As I didn't have a tattoo in mind, Desi went first. "A crow. Here." He patted his forearm. My stomach fluttered when he looked at me as he said it. That crow was for me. Desi was unflinching as Marco dragged the needle across his skin. After two hours, he was done, and it was my turn.

I shrugged when the artist asked me what I wanted. "I don't know. Do you have anything in mind?"

He pulled out a notebook full of beautiful drawings. I flipped through them as he explained that once I picked one, he'd tear it out so no one else could ever get that tattoo again.

"That one." I stopped at a fat cherub with devil horns, bat wings, and a pointy tail.

He asked me where I wanted it. I glanced at Desi. Most of my body was covered in small, lined scars. Could he tattoo over them? Deciding to avoid it altogether, I chose a spot I'd left untouched. I pointed to my ankle. "Let's do it here."

The needle digging into my skin hurt, but it was bearable. Desi held my hand through the entire process, making jokes and telling me about all the things we were going to do together.

Desi paid the tattoo artist. "Thanks again, Marco."

"Anytime. Are you guys going to Randy's party now?"

I looked at Desi. "Your friend is throwing a party?"

Desi shot a dirty look at Marco and turned to me. "Yeah, but I wasn't really planning on going."

"Why not? He got a band and a few kegs. I'm headed there now," Marco said.

Desi looked like he wanted to murder Marco, which only made me curious. Why didn't he want to go? I tugged on his arm.

"Let's go."

He shook his head but I insisted.

"Are you sure you want to spend your birthday at a party with a bunch of losers? I kind of wanted to spend it with you alone. I had something planned."

"Just a little bit. Let's go for an hour, and then we can do your thing, whatever that is."

"Fine. I'll figure things out."

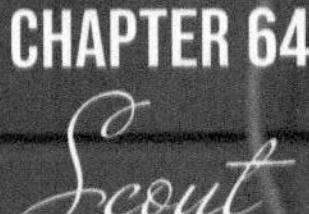

CHAPTER 64

Desi grumbled all the way to the party about how it ruined his plans, and that this was a bad idea.

"Oh stop. I like your friends."

"I don't. They're obnoxious. Or don't you remember, one of them came to your house like a weird stalker and confessed his love on your lawn?"

"Look, are you that against it? This little fight we've got going isn't fun anymore. Why don't you want to go?"

He was silent for a moment and then shrugged. "I just don't think it will be fun. It's fine. We'll go for a bit, talk, drink, enjoy the music, and then go do what I had planned."

"What exactly do you have planned?" It was already seven. There wasn't much time left anyways.

"I want to wait and show you," he said.

We arrived and parked behind a long line of cars. Half the guests were in costumes, half weren't, but everyone had drinks in their hands. Marco saw us and waved as we went into the house and down into the basement. The music was so loud it almost hurt my ears. The band was set up on one side of the room and blasting a cover of The Ramones.

"You want a drink?" Desi shouted. I nodded, and he disappeared into the crowd. I stood awkwardly, looking for someone I knew, and when I didn't find anyone, I forced myself to bob my head and dance a little.

Desi returned with two bottles of ice-cold beer. We toasted and clinked our bottles and drank. People began to recognize him. He introduced me quickly to everyone but there were so many people it was hard to remember names. Despite him drinking a beer and chatting with a few of his friends, he still stood stiffly and looked uncomfortable. He was constantly looking around as if he was expecting someone.

"I've got to use the bathroom," I announced, and Randy pointed me upstairs and to the left. I didn't really have to go, but Desi's mood about the party was starting to make me uncomfortable. As I descended the stairs, the band began to play a familiar tune.

"This song is for the birthday girl, is she down here?" I blushed and looked around for Desi. He was standing by the stage, shaking the singer's hand and smiling at me. The singer returned to his microphone and the band burst into their version of Journey's song, "Lights."

The mood in the room shifted, and couples paired up to slow dance. I went to Desi, and he took me in his arms. We began to sway with the others.

"I'm sorry I made you come," I told him.

"I can't say no to the birthday girl. Plus, it's not midnight yet. I've still got time to get you alone." His smile spread into a devious one.

"Alone?" My belly fluttered. "What are we doing alone?"

Desi whispered in my ear, "If I told you, I'd have to kill you." His words, while playful, held a small edge to it that sent shivers down my body. The song ended and the band decided to play "Don't Stop Believing", which made me remember that I had Desi's birthday gift, resting in my pocket. I planned on giving it to him at midnight.

"Well, I can't wait until midnight," I told him. "I have your present. I've been working on it for almost a year."

"A full year?" He laughed. We pulled apart and went back to his friends.

"Since that night in the park. Do you remember?"

"I do. We stayed out until the sun came up. I think that's when I knew I was in love with you."

"What a line."

We joined his circle again, and no sooner did we stop dancing did Desi resume his weird behavior.

"Dude, what are you doing?" Eric asked when he jerked and spun around quickly.

"What? I thought I heard someone." He was becoming more and more weird the longer we stayed.

"I wonder who Desiderio Amato would be afraid of." Tommy smirked and elbowed Eric. I raised my eyebrows. Did they know about Desi's job?

"Fuck off," he snarled at them.

"Are we still doing that thing next week then?" Mick's eyes flicked to me and then back to Desi's. He grinned, but there was something behind his eyes. Something dark. Desi didn't respond to him. Instead, he tugged on my arm.

"Let's get out of here."

A sliver of warning slid down my spine, and I started to follow, but I stopped when I ran into his back.

"What?" I asked. We hadn't gone that far, so what had stopped him?

"Desiderio?" A woman's voice came through the crowd. I looked around until I found the source. My stomach dropped completely as I stared at the stunningly beautiful woman coming toward us. Tall, pale, and perfect.

Desi's friends circled us, and I felt so incredibly trapped.

"Aleida." He dropped my hand and took a step away from me.

What was going on? The woman, Aleida, smiled at Desi.

"I didn't know you were coming. Why didn't you mention it this morning?"

This morning? Aleida's dark eyes flicked to mine. I blinked rapidly. Were her eyes… red?

"Oh, I think I understand now. Yes, dear, he spent the night with me last night." She extended her hand out for me to shake. "And who are you?"

My lips trembled, my eyes watered, and I backed up. Desi's friends helped me move away from them. It was as if the world around us had become a blur, and only those two existed. I stared at them, and suddenly it all made sense. They looked perfect together.

All of it.

"How long?"

"How long what, dear?" Aleida answered instead. "Him and I? Or him and you? Desiderio, care to answer?" She smiled at Desi.

My Desi.

Not hers.

Or was it the other way around?

He swallowed and looked at me with hardened eyes. "Scout, it's not what you think. You and I have been together for one year, you know that. One year tomorrow."

Aleida cackled. "And we've been together for five. I guess, time means nothing, does it?"

Five?

Five!

Tears blurred my vision, and I shook my head. It didn't make sense, yet, as I stood there, watching the pair glare at each other, I knew it was true.

She wasn't the other woman. *I was.*

My hands cupped over my mouth. I was afraid I was going to burst into tears, but I refused. Not in front of her.

"Oh, come on now, dear." Aleida shook her head. "Don't be too upset. It's about time you found out about the situation, especially now that our special day is next week." She beamed.

Special day?

I looked from her to Desi. He couldn't make eye contact with me.

"I don't understand," I managed to get out. "What special day?"

Aleida rolled her eyes and thrust out her hand again. "Sweetie, I'm not just his girlfriend. I'm about to be his wife." Wedged onto her perfectly dainty, manicured hand, was the biggest engagement ring I'd ever seen in my life.

CHAPTER 65

Desi

"Scout! Wait!" I flew up the stairs after her.

The entire party witnessed the scene. They let her through but stepped in front of me to not let me pass. I began shoving people, screaming for them to get out of my way. By the time I made it outside, she was gone.

I ran to my car and got in, speeding off toward her. She had made it a few blocks by running, and when I caught her, I rolled my window down and yelled for her to get in, but she ignored me.

Frustration gripped me. I sped ahead and crossed her. I leapt out of the car and caught her by the waist. I lifted her and she kicked me the entire way to the car.

"Let me go!" she screamed as I shut and locked the door. I jumped into my side and pulled away before she could jump out. She began to cry silently from the passenger's side.

I tried to talk to her but she refused to hear me out. I didn't stop driving until we hit a bridge and I was forced to slow down and stop. Scout took that opportunity to bolt from the car. I leapt out, following her onto the bridge.

"Scout, let me explain." I put my hand out. "It's not what you think."

"Are you engaged?"

I licked my lips nervously and took a deep breath. This was it. I had to come clean. My shoulders slumped forward as I answered, "Yes."

"When is the wedding?"

"It's scheduled for next week. I wasn't going to go, though."

"Oh okay, cool. Thanks! Get out of here with that shit. You fucking cabron."

"Scout, it's a really long story. If you just let me explain it—"

"Explain what?" She threw up her hands and began to walk onto the bridge. Instantly, my nerves heightened. I watched her every step just in case she tried to jump.

"Fucking leave. I don't want to look at you anymore. I don't want to see you ever again. You lied to me from day one. You convinced me you loved me and to do some fucked up shit in the name of that love. I can't forgive you. Go, be with her. Aleida."

"I don't want to be with her!" I shouted. Tears flooded my eyes as frustration filled my soul. Why now? We were so close, and today, of all days, it exploded! Why couldn't this wait? "I'm sorry." I crumpled to my knees. "I'm so sorry, Scout."

"Don't be." She turned away. "I don't need your pity. I just want to be left alone, thanks."

"On this bridge?" I stood and looked around. "Why? Scout, it's dangerous."

"Oh, now you care?" She laughed dryly. "Fuck off, Desiderio. I'm not interested in anything you have to say."

Desiderio?

She'd never called me that before.

I wasn't Desiderio to her. I was Desi. I was her Desi.

Brushing my tears off, I ran to her and grabbed her shoulders. I gripped her tightly and spun her around. "Scout," I growled and forced her to look at me. "Will you fucking listen to me? It's not what you think." I squeezed her shoulders. I tried to pull her toward me, but she dug her boots into the gravel of the road.

"I don't care." She struggled against me. "If you want to be with Aleida, go for it. I'm not anyone's second choice."

Her lips began to tremble and her eyes grew slick with tears. She turned away from me as they began to slide down her cheek. The night around us was deathly silent as she cried for what I'd done. My hands slid down her shoulders to her elbows, and I pulled her to me.

"I don't want her. I want you," I repeated. Nothing I told her right now was the right thing. She had seen Aleida, the ring, and heard what she'd said. I'd been there this morning like she'd told Scout, but only to plead once again for her to call the wedding off, but that bitch had left that out, naturally. "Scout, look at me."

She ripped herself from me. "No. No. I can't. Desiderio. You lied to me." Her entire body shook as her anger grew. "I'm an idiot. How did I not realize you were with someone? That you promised them forever? Not me. Her." Her voice cracked, and she turned away.

"You don't understand. It's not as easy as you think."

She ignored me. "Thanks for the birthday present." She kicked her leg up and laughed dryly. "It'll be a good reminder for the rest of my life to stay the fuck away from men like you."

"Yeah?" I threw up my hands. "And what's men like me?"

She flipped me off. "Fucking losers."

I saw red. She couldn't just walk away from me, from us. We were so close, all I had to do was have one last talk with her, explain to her who I was, what I was, and how she could be with me forever, and then…

I lifted a foot and then another and I was sprinting toward her. She turned just as I collided with her middle. I hoisted her over my shoulder and turned back to take her to the car.

"Put me down, you psycho!" she screamed as she kicked her legs wildly.

"Not until you listen to me!"

She pounded her small fists against my back, but I wasn't letting her go. "Nooo!" she howled.

I walked to my car and set her down. We stared at each other furiously. Our chests heaving, tears spilling from our eyes, and our hearts shattering.

And then, Scout gasped. Her eyes went wide, and she clutched her chest. She dropped to her knees and began to choke. I dropped beside her and reached for her.

"Scout? What's going on? Can you hear me? Scout!" I shouted, shaking her body. She passed out, and her eyes glazed over. Everything around me started to spin. Blood pulsed in my ears as it hit me. I dropped my head to her chest and listened.

Her heart had stopped beating.

She was dead.

Scout had just died in my arms. Out of nowhere. She was just talking to me, kicking and hitting me. She was crying. We were talking. And then…

I clutched her limp body to me, sobbing over it. I would never get the chance to win her back. Her body jolted in my arms. She gasped deeply and began to scream.

I jumped, and she fell out of my arms, still screaming bloody murder.

How?

Her mouth was twisted in agony as she screamed, and her irises were red.

My blood ran cold for only a moment before I collapsed beside her and took action.

While I'd never seen it before, I'd heard a million times what happened to a Bloodborn as they turned. Scout needed blood. But… I'd always been told it had to be a vampire. Already turned; another Bloodborn. Would my blood suffice her need? I didn't have time to think, because without blood, she'd die.

I pulled my pocketknife out and popped it. I slid my jacket up my arm and sliced my arm. Reaching for her neck, I propped her up and raised my bleeding arm to her mouth.

At first, she continued to scream, but then my blood dripped into her mouth, and she calmed.

We made eye contact, but she didn't seem to see me. She seemed to be looking through me as she lapped and then began to suck on my arm. I gasped when suddenly she bit down. Her fangs were embedded deep into my skin.

Fangs.

My vision blurred as she continued to drink, but I didn't care, because I knew we'd figure things out. None of the other shit mattered anymore.

Scout was a Bloodborn.

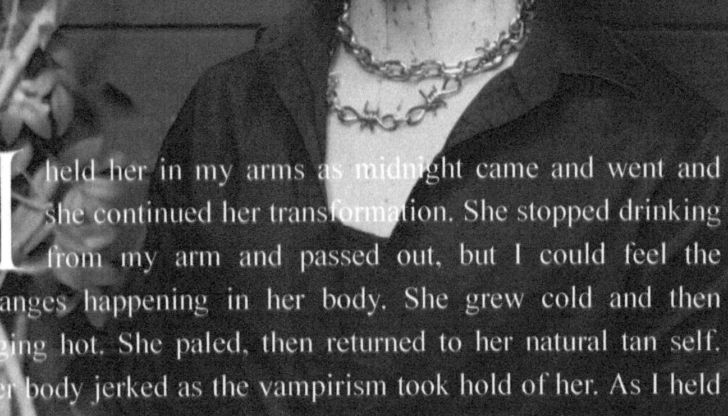

CHAPTER 66

Desi

I held her in my arms as midnight came and went and she continued her transformation. She stopped drinking from my arm and passed out, but I could feel the changes happening in her body. She grew cold and then raging hot. She paled, then returned to her natural tan self. Her body jerked as the vampirism took hold of her. As I held her, I tried to recall the things I knew about the change.

My parents had explained it to me as a young boy. When the clock struck the moment I was born into this world on my twenty-seventh birthday, my heart would stop, leading to my death and rebirth as a Bloodborn. My eyes would turn red, I'd grow fangs, and never be allowed in the sun again. I'd crave blood, although I could eat human food if I so wished, but I'd never age, my body would never change, and I'd live forever.

And now, I'd be allowed to live forever with Scout.

As she turned, I kissed her cheeks and forehead and whispered to her all the things we were going to do together. Sometime during the night, her body grew heavy. So heavy it became painful for me to hold her in my lap. I had to move her onto the ground. Panic set in as I realized we were in the middle of the road.

Using all my human strength, I managed to pull her off the road and set her in the grass. I looked around. There was no way I'd be able to lift her into my car when the morning came if she stayed like this.

I had a few more hours of moonlight. I could run to my parents, grab Gianni, my dad, whoever was there, and come get Scout. Surely, all three of us would be able to lift her frozen form. Making sure she was safe from the road, I left and quickly sped to my parents.

I was such a mix of fear and utter joy knowing that Scout and I had a future now, it was difficult for me to get words out. Finally, they understood me and followed me. We took Gianni's car to the bridge.

"I thought you said she was here." Gianni sneered when we came upon… nobody. Scout was missing!

"She is!" How could this be? I'd barely been an hour.

"We can check the hospitals." My father sighed. "Or the woods." He pointed to the trees nearby.

"I ain't going through any fucking trees." Gianni shook his head.

"I will," I said and quickly ran toward them, screaming her name. Had she awoken? How long did it take to change?

But after hours of calling her name and trudging through thick branches and trees, I knew she wasn't there. I returned to my family and asked them to drive slowly, so as to hope-fully catch her walking.

Gianni threw his hands up. "The sun is going to come up soon. She's probably already dead."

"He's right, son." Dad nodded solemnly. "Her body prob-ably went into survival mode and she went to find blood. You can't finish the transformation without it, remember."

It was on the tip of my tongue to reveal that she had already been given blood, my blood, but something held me back.

"And if she did find someone, she ain't gonna want you anymore," Gianni commented as we piled into his car. "That's why you're supposed to make the turn around family. Drinking your first blood bonds you. It's better to bond with family, than someone you may only love for a moment."

"My love for Scout isn't just a moment." I said. "What do you mean, bonded?"

"Your souls will call to each other. It's nonsense." My dad shook his head. "I've only ever heard about lovers doing it rather than family. They say that they can drink each other's blood."

Gianni gagged. "Drinking vampire blood? Disgusting."

My dad shrugged. "To them, it tastes good. Who knows. This is why we drink the blood of our family. It negates the bonding effect." We drove around the town looking for her. Eventually, we made it back to their estate, and I had no option other than to return to the search alone.

"The sun is coming up, Desiderio," my father said sadly. "I'm sorry."

"Come home tonight!" My mother waved from behind him. "You must be here before ten."

I saluted her and left to continue my search. I went to Scout's house and found it empty. I went to the park, the mall, and all the other places I knew she frequented but no one had seen her. I wanted to keep searching but exhaustion won out, and I fell asleep in my car, parked in a random parking lot.

I was awoken at night by a loud rapping on my window. I jerked awake and blinked. My mood lifted and sank in an instant, when it was Aleida, of all people, looking down at me.

"Heard your girlfriend turned."

I rolled my eyes and turned to focus on the front window. There was nothing but dark outside. "What do you want?"

"Oh, I don't think that's the tone you want to take with me, Desiderio Amato."

"Yeah? Why is that?" I asked.

"Because I know where she is."

I exited my car and lurched at her. "What did you do to her?" I snapped.

Aleida, with her vampire strength, shoved me away and smirked. "I didn't do anything. I said I know where she is. Do you want me to take you to her or not?"

I forced myself to remain calm and nodded. I only had a few more hours before I would turn, and I needed to get to her before it happened.

"Yes, please."

"All right. Now, give me your keys. I'm driving."

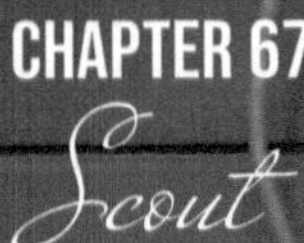

CHAPTER 67

"Are you all right? What's with the sunglasses?" Deanna asked as she came into the back to say hi.

I blinked rapidly but didn't take them off. I couldn't. I had no way to explain how my dark brown eyes were now bright red. I could smell her… blood. I could hear it too. Pulsing and moving through her. My mouth watered, but I quickly swallowed and focused all my energy on talking to her normally.

"I'm just a little hungover, you know." I shrugged.

"You look different. Did you get new makeup?" She leaned in, peering at me.

I leaned away. "No, I mean, maybe. I got a lot of stuff over the summer." I flinched, thinking of Desi.

Our entire story had been one big lie.

But I wasn't going to let it continue, which was exactly why I was here. "I'm actually just waiting for John to come back and talk to me."

"Are you coming back?" She perked up and then frowned an instant later. Her eyes didn't switch over though, revealing that she wasn't as sad as she pretended. "That means that you and that guy broke up."

"I don't really want to talk about it. I just want to get back to where I was." The idea saddened me deeply. Returning to my life before Desi was… depressing.

All I ever did was work. Work, and sleep, and work and sleep. I wasn't happy. I hadn't been happy in a long time. I couldn't have what I wanted, because that life belonged to someone else.

Aleida.

"Woah, what are those?" Deanna pointed to my mouth.

I slammed my mouth shut quickly, which forced me to breathe through my nose. My tongue ran across the new sharp pointed teeth that had sprung up last night. Along with my eyes and the sudden disappearance of all my scars. I didn't know what was happening to me, but I didn't have time to focus on that. I needed a job. I couldn't let myself depend on Desi ever again.

My throat was dry, and the longer I stayed breathing in the scent of Deanna's blood, the more on fire it felt. I spun around and started out of the back. This was a bad idea, returning to the diner. I should have just looked for a new place to work. But who was going to hire someone with red eyes and… fangs?

"I'm going to wait out here," I said, rushing out. I knew if I left that Deanna would come to my house later and try to catch me off guard. I couldn't let that happen. She came by and offered me something to drink and eat. Despite not having eaten since yesterday afternoon, the thought of regular food made me want to vomit. I was just… thirsty.

"Water, please?" I asked. She brought me some, and I drank it quickly, but it did little to quench my thirst. I still wanted… her blood.

"When is John coming in? On the phone, he said he'd be here around nine?" I asked her when she returned with another glass. It was nearly ten.

"Let me go ask. Maybe he called in and I didn't hear about it."

I lowered my head to the table and closed my eyes. I was so confused. One moment Desi and I were fighting about his upcoming wedding; the next I was back at my house, pouring sweat and vomiting blood.

I'd spent all day feverish and sick, and despite not knowing what was going on, my instincts were screaming various things to me. The biggest being, stay away from the sun. So, I waited, showered, and finally came here when night fell. I don't know what had happened, but I was different, and I didn't know what to do.

"Scout!" The familiar voice made my head bolt up and look around. Desi rushed over to me. He grabbed my shoulders and squeezed. "Are you okay?"

I shoved him away. "Of course, I am, why wouldn't I be?" Involuntarily, I inhaled deeply and took in the scent of him. The smell of Desi's pulsing blood hit me like a brick wall. I was stunned, and my new fangs suddenly began to ache. Why did he smell so good?

"Scout, we need to get out of here. There's so much I need to explain to you."

"I don't need to talk to you. I have it all figured out. You lied to me so much. What's stopping you from doing it now?"

"Because you've changed!" he hissed and snatched the sunglasses from my face. The busy diner grew quiet as people stopped talking with their friends and family to stare at us in curiosity. Deanna cleared her throat just as I grabbed them and was sliding them into place.

"Hey guys, uh, John can't make it in today. And if you are going to argue, we can't have that here."

"It's fine, I'm leaving," I said.

"Me too," Desi declared.

"No, I don't think you are." Aleida stormed in, along with three large men. They remained by the door, but she stormed right over to me and shoved me back. I stumbled but didn't fall. I straightened myself and then froze. In the lights, I could see her better, and it was then that I noticed her eyes. They were red too.

Like mine.

"What, is this some weird power play? There's no need to do any of this. He's all yours." I glanced at Desi and shook my head. All the memories of our year together flashed before my eyes in one small moment, causing my eyes to water, and a single tear to fall and slide down my cheek. I sniffled and wiped it away. I looked down at my thumb and shivered.

I was crying blood.

Was I dying? My hands began to shake and I stepped back.

"I'm going home, don't come find me." I looked up one last time at Desi. Despite knowing what he did, and how hard he broke my heart, it still called for him. But I was better than that. I was no one's second choice.

"Everybody on the ground!"

The room erupted in screams and loud smashes of plates and silverware as people scrambled to crouch. I turned slowly, putting my hands up. I looked toward the men that had come in with Aleida. I had a weird feeling about them from the moment they came in. Their blood smelled sour.

"I said, get down!" one of them shouted to me. Something, I couldn't explain what, told me I would be fine. He could shoot me, and I'd survive. But Desi, the human, wouldn't.

The human?

Where did that come from?

"Scout…" Desi's voice was edged with panic. "Aleida, what is going on?"

The vampire men held guns, pointing directly at us.

Vampire.

While it was an absurd concept, somewhere deep in my soul, I knew I was right. All of us except Desi were vampires. Everything was coming together in my mind. My eyes, my fangs, my aversion to the sun. I very much wanted to drink Desi's blood. Of course that's what I was. The men shouted again and I came to. Aleida put her hands up along with us.

"I have no idea," she said slowly. "Bradley, what are you doing?"

"It was a long game, pretending to like you," one of the men said. "But it was worth it. We're going to take down both the Linotti and Amato lines tonight."

"You can't do that!" she screamed. "That's a death sentence. You can't kill us. Bradley, put the gun down."

There were three distinct clicks from each gun and my blood chilled. They were going to kill those two. I couldn't let that happen.

I moved, and that caused them to shoot. The booms were so loud everyone in the diner screamed. I threw myself over Desi, but I wasn't fast enough. He dropped to the ground with a hole in his chest. I felt an explosion of pain as something entered my back, and I collapsed nearby. More shots rang out, and Aleida dropped next to Desi.

No!

No, this couldn't be happening!

Please! I pleaded to a god I wasn't sure existed. If there is someone to listen to me, save Desi. Don't let him die. And then, I heard a voice in my head.

"Care to make a deal?"

"Welcome back, Scout."

I spun around to see a Hispanic man in a suit, standing beside a fireplace. The world around us was dark, pitch black. Just a rug, the fireplace, and two tall, antique-looking chairs. Somewhere off in the distance, creepy music played from a record player. I squinted and stepped forward.

"I know you, but from where?"

"Forget me so quickly? I am the demon Samson. I was called to greet you upon your death as a human. I welcomed you to the vampire world, just last night. That's disappointing that I'm not more memorable." He put his hands behind his back and started to walk toward me.

"We sat down in these very chairs and discussed your life thus far. How you thought it went, what you wished you'd done differently, what you loved. What you'd miss. All the while, your body was up on the earth, changing."

"Into a vampire." I nodded. The memories of him were returning. We had sat and talked. It was terrible, discussing my short, miserable life as a human. I'd been orphaned, then struggled my entire adulthood, only to have my heart broken in my last few minutes of it beating.

He nodded. "Now, you wanted to make a deal. What do you want?"

"Desiderio Amato…" I gulped. "Save him."

"Really? From what exactly?"

"He was shot. I saw him go down."

"Ah, and you were shot too. I see it there." He pointed to my chest.

I spun around and felt for the hole in my shirt. It was there and trickling blood. "I don't care about me. Just save him. I'll do whatever you want. He has my heart."

"I can do that. But everything comes with a price."

"Fine. What do you want?" Time was of the essence. I couldn't let Desi die. "Kill me if you want, just don't let him…" A pool of pain hit my stomach. "Don't let him die."

"Oh, I don't think I'd enjoy that. I'd much rather make a deal. Those always work better for me."

"Just tell me what you want." My thoughts went to a dark place and Samson must have had some power to see them because he shook his head and grimaced at me.

"No, I don't want your body. Disgusting. I'll save him, but in return, I want your memory of him. He will live, but you two will have no knowledge of each other."

"What?" My voice cracked.

"Yes!" His red eyes grew wide with excitement. "You will return to Earth with no memories of this man and vice versa. In fact, I will put you in two separate cities so it will be as if you never met."

"But I don't want that either. Can't you save him and let us have the memories?"

"For a price."

"What do you want, then?"

"Souls. Evil souls. One thousand of them. That should come easy for you, considering your drive to drink now."

"I don't understand."

"I will save the one who has your heart, but you and him will not remember it. If you want your memories back, you need to kill one thousand evil men to send their souls to me. You will remember none of this, except your task. As soon as you get me my souls, you'll get Desiderio Amato back."

"How will I remember?"

Samson drew a line in the air and I gasped as my chest began to rip open. I looked down to see the large gash right where my heart was. Slowly, it began to close back up, leaving a large, ugly scar.

"There. Every time you look at your heart, you'll know something is missing."

"And he lives?" I asked one more time. It was better this way, I decided.

"He lives." He extended his hand for me to shake.

"Deal."

CHAPTER 69

Desi

"Desiderio, you're early."

"Who are you?" I demanded of the man standing by the fire.

"I am Samson, the demon who was supposed to greet you in…" He paused and pushed up the sleeve of his suit. "Thirty minutes. Wow, you were so close."

"What do you mean?" I looked around the room. It wasn't really a room, but a space. Just two chairs, a colorful rug, and the fireplace where he stood.

"You are a vampire, are you not?"

I nodded. "It's my twenty-seventh birthday."

"Ah, but not quite, see, you don't turn until the very moment in which you were born. You are dead, Desiderio. Just a half-hour short of turning."

"What? No, you can't just —" I gulped. "No. I've gotta get back up there. The love of my life is dying. I need to save her. Turn me!"

"Turn you?" He laughed. "I don't think you're in the position to make demands, Desiderio."

"What then?" I threw up my hands. "Am I dead then?"

"Not quite. Close, but…" he paused. "Someone you love is dying. I could save her if you want."

My mouth fell open. I remembered now. I'd been shot. I went down, and she fell down beside me. My brain grew fuzzy. I couldn't see her face in my memories. I couldn't think of her name. But I knew I loved her.

"Please. I need to go back. I can help her."

"You want a second chance at the life you were meant to have, make me a deal."

"A deal?"

He nodded.

I needed to think this through. A deal with a demon wasn't something to just go into lightly.

"I'll do anything to keep her alive."

"Who?"

"Uh—" What was her name? Her face shone beautifully in my head. Lush brown curls, eyes dark as night, and lips so perfectly shaped. Her image was becoming more clear, but still, her name escaped me. I just knew that she was… "My soulmate."

"Your soulmate?" He smirked. "Are you talking about Aleida Linotti?"

I didn't recognize the name, but nodded.

"My soulmate, save her." I repeated. There could only be one person I'd meant. Surely, that would do it. There was something wrong with my brain, and I had a feeling he had something to do with it. He was trying to trick me, but I wouldn't allow that to happen.

"I'll add her to our deal. And in return?"

"Do whatever." I threw my hands up. "Want to punish me for asking? Just fucking do it"!

Samson blinked, and his expression darkened. "I don't like yelling," he growled. "You want to be punished? By all means."

"Now what? Do I go back now?"

"Yes, but you will be forever changed. I'm pushing through your vampirism. You will be given eternal life and all the abilities that come with it, however, you will be marked. Every Bloodborn will know that you are being punished for what you've done. You don't get to disprespect me without paying for it."

"Fine."

"I'm not done." He stormed over to me and grabbed me by the throat. He lifted me in the air and squeezed. "You will also have no memory of the life you're saving. She will never know of you either."

"No!" I screamed through the pain.

He dropped me, and I fell to the ground.

"Do you not accept my deal?"

"No. I can't. Make me another. Make me a vampire like her, save her, and give me the memories."

"If you want your memories back, you can have them after you collect the souls of one thousand evil men."

"One thousand?" I scrambled to stand.

"Ten," he snapped. "Ten thousand! I will save you both, and once I get my souls, you'll get your memories back."

"And until then?"

A wicked grin spread onto his face. "You'll wander the Earth knowing someone is waiting for you, but you'll know nothing else but your task."

He held out his hand.

If I didn't do this, she would die. I'd seen her get shot. I didn't have much time.

"Do I get to say goodbye? Before you take my memories?"

He considered it. "One day."

"Deal." And I shook his hand.

CHAPTER 70

Desi

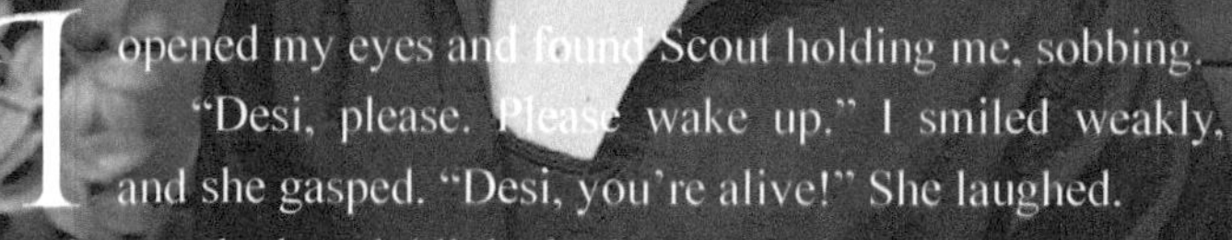

I opened my eyes and found Scout holding me, sobbing. "Desi, please. Please wake up." I smiled weakly, and she gasped. "Desi, you're alive!" She laughed.

I stretched and blinked, then ran my tongue over my teeth.

Fangs.

I looked over at Scout, and her eyes were red like mine must be.

She frowned. "What happened to your eyes?"

"What do you mean?" I laughed. "They look just like yours. We're vampires. Together. We can be together forever now."

"No. Desi, yours aren't red. You used to have blue eyes, the color of a stormy sea. Now, they're bright."

"What? No, that's not right." I stood and looked around. We were still in the diner. People were hiding under tables, crying and screaming. There was so much smoke and sirens and flashing lights.

I took her hand and tugged her forward. "We need to get

out of here. Come with me and I'll explain everything." Together, we ran through the back of the diner and pushed the emergency doors open. I patted my pockets. I didn't have my keys. Why not?

"I'll drive." She saw me struggling. "Let's go."

As we got into her car and took off, I recalled the deal with Samson. I had one day. Twenty-four hours before I lost all the memories of her, and I would be called to give him the souls of ten thousand evil men. I had to make every minute count.

"We're vampires. You know that, right?"

"I'm a vampire," she clarified. "Your eyes aren't red."

I reached for the mirror on the dash and tugged it down. "That can't be—" I stopped short as I got a good look at my face.

"You will be marked. Every Bloodborn will know that you are being punished for what you've done."

My eyes weren't red, like every other Bloodborn. And they weren't blue, like the Bloodsheds either. I had one blue eye, bright like a highlighter marker, and the other one was green, like a clover.

"Oh, fuck me." I sighed and leaned back. "I have fangs, and I feel different. The—" I tried to tell her about the deal I had made with Samson, but my tongue was stuck. I couldn't tell her.

"Well, I am, regardless of my eyes. And I'm going to spend my immortality fixing things between us. I'm sorry about Aleida," I told her, hanging my head.

"Me too." She sniffled. "Desi, I want to take you home, but then I have to go. I—" She stopped short and then frowned.

"What?" I looked up.

"Nothing, I guess. You lied to me the entire time we

dated, and I don't know if I can get over that. But none of it matters because—" She huffed in frustration. "What's your address? I can't believe I dated you for a year and don't even know where you live."

I rattled off the location and she drove us there. We parked in my driveway.

"Will you come in?" I pleaded.

She started to say no but finally relented. "Fine, but—" She tried to speak but then gave up. I helped her out of the car and we went inside.

Instantly, I spun her around and planted my lips on hers. I had less than a full day with her, and I wanted to spend as much of that time as I could inside her.

She kissed me back with matching fervor. The moment she walked out of that door, we'd forget each other.

For a time.

How long could ten thousand take? I grazed my new fangs against her neck. She smelled divine.

"God, you're so fucking sexy with your new eyes and vampire glow. I had no idea you were like me, like my family," I confessed. "That's the only reason I lied."

"To hide what you were?" she asked, pushing back only a little. Despite being angry with me for cheating on her, she wanted me just as much as I wanted her.

"Yes. I thought you'd run."

"I would never have done that, Desi."

"You're running now." I grabbed her thighs and hoisted her up. She wrapped her legs around me and ground her pussy against my groin.

"I have to tell you something. I—" She paused, and I kissed her. I licked her collarbone and began to massage her breasts as I took her to my room. I laid her down on my bed and climbed on top of her. Slowly, I removed her clothes and then mine.

"What's that?" I asked, seeing a large scar in between her breasts. As vampires, all the scars we had from our human life were taken, leaving a perfect body behind. We needed to be as enticing as we could to humans, our prey.

Scout shouldn't have a scar.

She blinked and opened her mouth, but nothing came out. I kissed down the line and trailed to her naked breasts. I took my time, kissing everything, licking everything. Bringing my face to hers, I slid my tongue between her lips and used my fingers to spread her pussy wide and fuck her slowly with them.

"I want to see how many times I can make you come tonight," I whispered as I pushed as hard as I could into her, hooking my fingers, and pressing them on her little button inside her. She arched her back and gasped as I took a nipple into my mouth.

"Desi!" she cried out.

"Yes, say my name, baby. I don't want you to ever forget it. Promise me you won't forget. Promise me," I pleaded. I knew she wouldn't understand, but the more I said it, the more I needed it to be true. As I sat with my face between her legs, lapping at her body, reveling at the noises she made as I ate her pussy, I regretted the deal I had made.

"Promise me you won't forget Journey, or the movies, or the fireballs. Please don't forget all we did together."

I could beg all I wanted. I could fuck her all night and day, but when the twenty-four hours were up, she wouldn't know I existed. And for that, as I finally rolled her on top of me and sank her down onto my cock, I cried. Blood and all.

She cried along with me.

Together, our bodies exploded. We came together, and I

held her tightly afterward. I kissed her forehead. We made love again. Our bodies betrayed us, and we fell asleep, clutching each other tightly. But before I was completely gone, I heard her whisper.

"Desi, I love you so much. Please, remember that, okay?"

CHAPTER 71

Desi

I awoke in my bed, naked.

What happened last night?

I was groggy, but…

I was different. What was going on? Pulling on the pants I found on the floor, I went to my living room and froze. Everything was different. It was… clean. I flicked on the TV and went to the news. What day was it?

My mouth dropped open when the anchor told me it was October 24, 1994.

How?

I closed my eyes and tried to think. The last I remembered was my birthday, yes, but not '94. It was '93. I was twenty-six. How had I lost a year of memories?

How could that be?

I flew to the bathroom and looked in the mirror. I nearly bolted out of my skin. My eyes weren't red, but they weren't blue anymore either. They were bright blue and green. The blue almost glowed.

I opened my mouth and found the fangs, and I began examining my body, looking for my scars from childhood, but they were all gone. I had turned, somehow, but not the way I should have.

I walked around my house aimlessly. I had no idea what was going on, but all my weed was gone and my memory of the last year was shot.

Had I hit my head or something?

Eventually, my throat began to dry. I needed… blood.

Something was itching the back of my brain. I didn't want to be here anymore, in this house. I needed to leave forever. I grabbed my bags and threw everything I could find that felt valuable, which was only my clothes and tarot deck, and then froze at the door.

I couldn't go outside. I had to wait until the night came.

I spent all day trying to piece together everything. My brain felt like it'd been gutted. I couldn't remember large pieces of my past. It was as if something was being purposely blocked. What had gone wrong during my transformation? Night finally fell, and I picked up my bags to go. I wasn't sure how I knew this was the last time I'd be here, but I was sure of it. I stepped out into the darkness and paused.

My car was gone. In its place was a plain black car, far less fun than my Mustang. Again, the itching came from my brain, telling me this was my car. I went to it and found it unlocked, with the keys in the seat. I grabbed them, climbed inside, and turned the car on.

I wasn't sure where I was going, but I knew I wouldn't be returning here.

Ten thousand souls of evil men, Desiderio, and you'll get her back…

I blinked. What was that?

Ten thousand souls? Who? Get who back? Did that mean…

My throat screamed for relief. If I didn't get blood soon,

I'd—A loud rap on my window startled me. Outside my car was an angry-looking man, holding a knife.

"Get out before I slash your tires!" he snapped at me. I stared at him for a moment, the words echoing in the back of my head as my thirst grew louder and louder.

Ten thousand souls of evil men.

I stepped out of the car and grinned.

"What was that?" I asked.

He lunged at me with the knife. "Give me everything on you."

"Or what?" I could smell his blood. It was warm and waiting for me.

"I'll kill you, you idiot!" He thrust his knife out. It stabbed through my gut. It was a sharp pain, but I took it with stride. I snatched his wrist and twisted, breaking the bone. He screamed as I lurched his entire body forward, clamped my mouth down onto his neck, and bit.

Instinct took over. I sucked and drained his body of his rich blood until my thirst was quenched and his heart stopped beating.

When he was dead, I dropped his body to the ground and stepped away. I climbed back into my car. I glanced through the mirror at the body just lying there.

Fuck.

I knew then that I'd never come home. Not just to this house, but to this town. I needed to get as far as I could from this place. I started to pull out of my drive when something caught my eye on the passenger's seat.

It was a cassette tape.

I reached for it, flipping it over. It was a mixed tape, with a woman's handwriting on the case.

Happy Birthday, Desi.

Desi? No one called me that. Ever.

I opened the case, slid the tape into my tape deck, and pushed play. "Lights" from Journey began to play. My brain itched again.

"Is this who I'm looking for?" I asked aloud.

And the voice responded one last time.

Yes.

Well, all right then.

"I can't wait to meet her. I guess it's nine thousand nine hundred and ninety-nine now." I drove, not sure where I was headed. "She has good taste in music."

The End

Afterword

Thank you for reaching the end of Bury Me in Blood. If you enjoyed the book, please consider leaving a review wherever you leave reviews, and if you do so on instagram, tag me in it!

1. Lights, by Journey
2. Boys Don't Cry, by The Cure
3. Drive, by The Cars
4. Weak, by SWV
5. Love will lead you back, by Taylor Dayne
6. Red light special, by TLC
7. Send her my love, by Journey
8. All through the Night, by Cyndi Lauper
9. Linger, by The Cranberries
10. Keep on loving you, by REO Speedwagon
11. Real Love, by Mary J. Blige
12. Don't Stop Believin' by Journey
13. I'll be loving you, by New Kids on the Block
14. Home Sweet Home, by Mötley Crüe
15. Contigo quiero estar, by Selena
16. Someone to Love me for Me, by Lisa Lisa & the Cult Jam
17. Is this love, by Whitesnake
18. Open Arms, by Journey
19. Time after time, by Cyndi Lauper

Acknowledgments

This book has been a full year in the making. As I've mentioned in previous books, during the Little Death series, my dad passed away suddenly, and this book is a product of that grief. However, while I struggled, there were so many people championing for me and this book and for that, I am so, so grateful. Some of those people are, (but aren't limited to) my editor Z. My cover designer and friend, Victoria. Authors Aiden Pierce, Alby Blaze, and Maude Winters. My street team, the whorror babies, and last but certainly not least, Wes and Marie, the models for Desi and Scout.

Desi came first, and through Wes I found Marie, who came on board and has easily been one of the biggest champions for this series. Without all of these people, this book might not have been finished and published, and for that, thank you.

About the Author

After watching Heathers and listening to My Chemical Romance one too many times in her teens, Chicana author, Tylor Paige, was drawn to the darkness where the villains were still villains, but deserved love stories too.

Shifting her focus to Horror Romance, Tylor writes snarky, psycho vampires, troubled but beautiful Goblin Kings, and slashers so sexy you'll be begging your partner to buy a mask.

When she's not writing about women railing the villains, she enjoys watching horror films, sewing, comic books, and overall trolling her readers, one DM at a time. At the time of this update Tylor has now written and published thirteen full length novels.

Oh, and feel free to call her Ty. She prefers it.

Get in touch with me:

- Www.Tylorpaige.com
- https://linktr.ee/Tylorpaige
- Facebook.com/Tylorpaigeauthor
- Instagram: @Tylorpaige
- TikTok: @authortylorpaige
- Join the Coven of Bitchcraft group on Facebook!
- https://www.facebook.com/groups/
  3761909999768893/?ref=share

Also by Tylor Paige

Final Girl Series:

Slash or Pass

Slay Less

Book 3

Book 4

Little Deaths: a Vampire Mafia series

Seven Little Deaths

Lay Your Body Down

Bury Me In Blood- Prequel

Little Taste of Death (FREE VALENTINES SHORT!)

Standalones:

Surrender to Forever- a Goblin King reimagining

Final Girl Featurettes:

Like Father Like Slaughter- a dystopian horror romance novella